Praise for S.C. Stephens

"From page one, this book is impossible to put down."

—Abbi Glines, on *Thoughtless*

"S.C. Stephens at her best!"

—Katy Evans, on *Thoughtful*

"Addicting and heart pounding—you won't be able to put it down until you've devoured every word."

—Christina Lauren, on *Untamed*

UNDER THE NORTHERN LIGHTS

ALSO BY S.C. STEPHENS

Thoughtless Series

Thoughtless (Book 1)
Effortless (Book 2)
Reckless (Book 3)
Thoughtful (Thoughtless alternate POV)
Untamed (Book 4)

Rush Series

Furious Rush (Book 1)
Dangerous Rush (Book 2)
Undeniable Rush (Book 3)

Conversion Series

Conversion (Book 1)
Bloodlines (Book 2)
'Til Death (Book 3)
The Next Generation (Book 4)
The Beast Within (Book 5)
Family Is Forever (Book 6)

Stand-Alone Books

Collision Course
It's All Relative

UNDER THE NORTHERN LIGHTS

S.C. STEPHENS

This is a work of fiction. Names, characters, organizations, places, events, and incidents are either products of the author's imagination or are used fictitiously.

Published by Montlake Romance, Seattle
www.apub.com

ISBN-13: 9781542093545
ISBN-10: 1542093546

Cover design by Caroline Teagle Johnson

Printed in the United States of America

For my "mountain man." Thank you for giving me hope.

Chapter One

Eagerness surged through me as I stared at the bright-yellow Piper Super Cub waiting patiently for me on a bed of crisp white snow. I was dying to get the small plane into the air, feel the rush and freedom that came along with exploring the skies. That wasn't the primary purpose of the trip I was about to take, but it was definitely a perk. There was nothing quite like watching the world from above.

"Are you all set, Mal?"

I looked over at the grizzled man watching me. Nick. He stored my plane for me up here in Alaska. My home was back in Cedar Creek, Idaho, but that was too far of a trip for a bush plane like this, so Nick kept it secure for me, kept it ready for my annual trip into the wilderness. "Yep. The plane's all gassed up; supplies are all loaded. I'm just going to do my preflight check—then I'll be on my way."

Nick nodded like he wasn't expecting a problem with the plane. He usually took it out for a spin or two before I arrived, so he knew its condition even better than I did. Safety was high on his list of priorities. Mine too. I fully planned on coming back alive, and with the remote spot I was headed to, that meant being prepared. For anything. As my grandfather used to say, "Live each day expecting the worst possible thing to happen, and you just might get to see the next day." Considering what I did for a living, I took those words to heart.

My love, my passion, my reason for being, was to photograph the world's finest creatures in their natural environments—the more untouched by man, the better. I got a rush from capturing pristine landscapes that had remained unchanged by civilization for centuries and photographing wild animals that, until me, had probably never laid eyes on a human being. It was exciting and invigorating, and it filled me with purpose. It was also sometimes extremely frustrating. Truly wild animals weren't exactly camera friendly. The herbivores were skittish, more likely to run than pose, and carnivores . . . well, it was challenging to take an award-winning photo when you knew you were being stalked. I loved the challenge, though, and the environment—and even the isolation, if only for a few weeks out of the year.

Taking a slow walk around my small plane, I checked for any imperfections that could lead to a disaster in the air. When I was satisfied that the wings were fine, I moved around to the front of the plane. It had already been winterized, skis replacing the tires, and I thoroughly inspected them for any sign of damage. Skis were more reliable for landing on snow, but they didn't have brakes, and they took quite a beating whenever the plane touched down. Being able to land safely was of utmost importance anywhere, but it was even more so for me, since I wasn't landing anywhere near civilization. If my plane broke in any major way, I was stuck, possibly for months. And I was only bringing supplies for a few weeks. I wasn't worried, though. *Precaution* was practically my middle name—and this trip was important to me, worth the risk.

Everything looked good with the skis, so I moved on to the engine. It seemed to be in working order, so I was good to go. Finally! After reaching into the cockpit, I primed the engine, cracked the throttle, then spun the propeller. It caught just as I expected it to, and the engine roared to life. Yes . . . time to leave. I couldn't wait!

Looking back at Nick, I waved a goodbye. "See you in a few weeks," I told him, the joy in my voice uncontainable.

He laughed at my enthusiasm, then shook his head. "See ya, Mallory. Have a safe flight."

Excitement pounding through my veins, I climbed into the cockpit and put on my headset. Nick's runway was in his backyard, and his giant log cabin behind me had a thick plume of smoke coming from the chimney. *Warmth.* That was something I was going to crave over the next few weeks, since the northern Alaska Range wasn't exactly a tropical beach, but one thing I never skimped on was insulating clothes, blankets, bedrolls, and the best boots money could buy. I was going to be as comfortable as possible while I was roughing it.

My plane sped down the runway, the skis making it a bumpy ride until I smoothly lifted into the air. A huge smile was on my face as I soared above the treetops. Takeoff was my favorite part of flying. Feeling that pull, the force pushing against your stomach in reminder that humans weren't meant to be in the air . . . it was a little addictive. Grinning as I sailed higher into the sky, I glanced back at my cargo. Somewhere back there, safely nestled next to my survival pack, was my professional-grade Nikon camera. My pride and joy and the sole purpose of making this potentially dangerous trek into one of the remotest places in America. I was almost giddy to discover what surprises my camera and I would uncover this year. This job was so unpredictable—I could find nothing, or I could capture the photo that would become the epitome of my career. I loved the mystery of it all. The unknown called to me.

Once I was at my plane's cruising altitude, I headed south, toward the range I'd been frequenting for the last ten years. My favorite spot to land was about a three-hour flight from Two Rivers and about one hundred miles south of the Arctic Circle. It wasn't on the way to anything, and I'd never once seen another plane or person while there. It was isolated heaven. It was also bear country, and the grizzlies were plentiful. As were the wolves. That was why I had a rifle strapped to the outside of the plane, and I never went anywhere without it. While I lived for photographing animals doing what animals did, I had no intention of becoming their dinner.

There were so many creatures I wanted to encounter on this trip. The bears should be out, gathering food for hibernation. I'd come across a gigantic male last year, and I'd absolutely love a repeat encounter with him—from a safe distance, of course. Seeing some wolves would be amazing. Alaskan gray wolves were some of the smartest creatures out there. They hunted in packs that could take down a moose. Dangerous, yes, but so incredibly beautiful. Lynx were on my list too. Plus eagles, owls, martens . . . there was so much I was eager to see.

I'd gotten interested in photography in high school when I'd gone to an art exhibit with my mom and had seen some of the thrilling shots captured by professionals. My mind had spun with the possibilities. In what other line of work could you spend ample amounts of time outdoors, go all around the world, and see extraordinary things that most people never got to see? It had seemed like the perfect career for me. My parents had thought otherwise. They just hadn't been able to see how photographing animals could sustain me financially. And of course, they'd worried about my safety. Accepting that your child was going to be alone in the middle of nowhere all the time was difficult for a protective parent. They wanted me to stay home and stay safe.

There had been countless arguments with my parents over the years, especially in the beginning, before I'd started earning money from my photos. I'd been living with them back then, and not a day had gone by without one of them telling me that I should give up my improbable dream and get a real job, a paying job, a less adventurous job. They'd been over the moon when I'd finally relented to my incessant boyfriend, Shawn, and agreed to marry him. My parents adored Shawn and thought he would be a stabilizing influence on me. I thought they'd secretly been hoping he would convince me to stay home and give them tons of grandbabies. But it hadn't worked out that way, and marrying Shawn had been a huge mistake, probably the biggest mistake I'd ever made. The two of us had always been better at being friends, and even as I'd said "I do," I'd known Shawn wasn't the right one for me. He was too much like my parents and spent too much time telling me everything that I couldn't and shouldn't do. Within a year, Shawn and I had divorced. My parents had been crushed. Shawn too.

But none of them had understood and accepted the vision I had of my life and that nothing short of achieving my goal would make me truly happy. And it had taken a lot of hard work, time, and determination, but I'd done it. I'd managed to make a name for myself, and I'd eventually found a way to make a small but steady income doing what I loved, on my own terms. I'd been my own boss ever since graduating high school more than a dozen years ago, and even though Shawn and my family hadn't entirely approved of my risky passion, I wouldn't have it any other way. I had to live life *my* way and not within the confines of someone else's expectations. I hoped someday they could appreciate that and forgive me for not compromising.

A heavy splatter landing on my windshield distracted me from my reminiscing, and when I looked up at the sky, my chest tightened with dread. Clouds were billowing across my projected path, and they were getting darker and more ominous by the second. Damn it. The weather report had been telling me all week that my path would be clear; this wasn't supposed to happen. But the unpredictability of Alaska's weather was about the only thing you *could* be certain of up here. You had to adapt to survive, and I was pretty good at adapting.

But getting caught in a sleet storm was one of the most dangerous things that could happen in a small plane like mine. Like most bush planes, my Cub didn't have any navigational instrumentation. All I could rely on were my eyes—I *had* to be able to see the ground at all times—and low, dark clouds releasing a thick rain-snow mix meant no visibility. And no visibility meant I could easily crash into something . . .

like a mountain. Ice buildup was also a problem. If too much formed on the wings, I'd be too heavy—I'd go down. I needed clear air, so I had no choice but to land and wait for the storm to pass.

God, I hated having to make emergency landings in unexpected places. So much could go wrong . . . but even more could go wrong if I stayed airborne. Trying not to worry, I started studying the ground, looking for a place suitable for landing—it needed to be a long enough stretch that I could slow to a stop without running into something. Panic started creeping up my spine as I studied the earth. I wasn't seeing anything even remotely close to an open space—everything beneath me was dense forest. But having gone this way several times before, I knew there was a wide-open meadow in a low valley, just on the other side of the first pass. I had no choice but to brave the storm . . . and pray that I could see well enough to pick my way through the mountains.

Heart racing, I lifted a small golden cross hanging around my neck, brought it to my lips, and said a quick prayer. *Help me see—help me find the path.* I let out a slow, calming breath once my prayer had been whispered and concentrated on my training, my years of experience, and my knowledge of the land. This wasn't my first scary moment in a plane, and it probably wouldn't be my last. *Hopefully* it wouldn't be my last. No, I couldn't think that way. I had to stay positive, had to stay focused. I could do this. I'd done it before.

The ceiling was getting lower and lower as more clouds moved in, and that meant I'd have to hug the bottom of the pass while making sure I still had room to maneuver. One wrong move, and I'd be a permanent part of the countryside. Shit. I'd had to do this once or twice before, and it always made me feel ice cold inside, almost numb with terror. I hated this . . . but it was my only option—I needed to get to the meadow on the other side of this pass.

My heart thudded against my rib cage as I dipped toward the earth, and my hands started trembling. As I inched lower, I visualized clear air, a pristine runway, a perfect landing—anything to keep calm. It was hard to do while my windshield was being pelted with heavy raindrops; I needed to be on the ground—*now*—before it was too late.

The clouds were still lowering, the mountains seemingly rushing up to meet them, cutting off my view of the gap between the giant peaks. Keeping as low as safely possible, I searched for a way through the pass . . . a pass that I was rapidly, inexorably approaching. And then, a split-second clearing of the clouds showed me a sliver of blue sky. A hole! The clouds quickly hid it again, but it had been there . . . I was sure of it.

I kept my eyes glued to the spot where I'd seen the patch of blue sky; I didn't even blink for fear of losing my path. My stomach felt like jelly, and my heart was thundering so hard that it was almost louder than the rain pounding against my plane. Knowing I was taking a huge risk, I crossed all my fingers and toes and flew into the gray taffy that was blocking my view. *Please let this be a hole and not a mountainside.* As the clouds enveloped me in a blanket of haze, my body tensed in anticipation. This was it . . . all or nothing.

Fear tried to seize control of my limbs, tried to jerk the plane left or right, up or down. It took a tremendous amount of willpower to fight the instinct, to resist the urge to move. Sweat formed on my brow as I concentrated . . . as I prayed. When the fog didn't clear right away, I started to panic; this was how planes hit mountains. My entire body started vibrating, wanting to flee, but I didn't alter my trajectory. This was the last course I'd known to be true. I had to stay on target.

My breath came out in frantic bursts. "Please, please, please," I murmured over and over. "Clear up . . . show me the way." And just like that, the ceiling lifted, and I saw the mountains piercing the sky on either side of me. I'd made it through the pass. Relief instantly washed over me. "Thank you. Oh my God, thank you . . ."

Maybe to show me that I wasn't entirely out of the woods yet, the weather made a turn for the worse, and heavy, icy sleet pellets started pummeling me. I'd made it between the mountains, but I still needed to land. Spotting the clearing off to my left, I started banking the plane toward it. And that was when the unthinkable happened . . . the engine stalled.

"Shit, shit, shit!" I'd never had the engine stall on me before. Horror flashed through me, paralyzing me. *What do I do?* Jesus, I had no one to ask, no way to call for help, and my mind was completely blank—I couldn't remember anything my instructor had taught me. It was just . . . gone.

The plane was unnaturally silent with the engine off. All I could hear was the sound of my fierce breath and the sleet assaulting me. Panicking was the absolute worst thing I could do right now, so, closing my eyes, I tried to refocus. All I needed to do was restart the engine and find a place to land. No problem. *I can do this.*

Blowing out a long, slow breath, I opened my eyes and tried restarting the engine. Nothing. I tried again and again and again. Still nothing. Shit. My plane was gliding, but with no real way to gain altitude, it was only a matter of time before I ran into the ground.

No, no, no . . . this could *not* be happening. I'd made it through—it was supposed to be smooth sailing from here! I didn't want to die. I wanted to see my home again; wanted to see my sister, Patricia; wanted to let her know how much I loved her, even though she was a know-it-all pain in the ass. I wanted to see my parents again, wanted to help them out with their diner, like I did every summer. I wanted to see my dogs again, spoil them rotten like I did whenever I came back from a long trip. I even wanted to see Shawn again. I wanted my life. I loved my life. I did *not* want to die in the woods, alone.

But I was getting lower and lower, the ground was coming closer and closer, and the damn engine still wouldn't restart. The tops of the trees started scratching the underside of my plane like claws, trying to tear me from the sky. "Oh God . . . please start, please start, please, please, please . . ." Begging had worked before; maybe it would again.

But my plane sank even lower into the tree canopy. The steering column started vibrating in my hands as branches smacked the fuselage. Gritting my teeth, I tried in vain to pull up, to glide as long as possible. Landing like this was . . . unthinkable. This couldn't happen. I had to do something. I had to fix this. *Shit, how do I fix this?*

A large bang and a snapping sound vibrated through the plane, tossing me forward. The landing skis . . . the treetops had torn them off. Somehow having that safety net gone made everything startlingly real and even more terrifying. My heart hammered in my chest, my palms were slick with sweat, and I was breathing so fast I felt light headed. Oh my God . . . this was really happening. I was going down, I was crashing, and the odds of me living through it were . . . impossible.

"Mom . . . Dad . . . Patricia . . . I'm so sorry."

Tears poured down my cheeks as my family flashed through my mind. I'd done this so many times . . . I looked forward to this trip every year. I never thought . . . I never imagined. *This can't really be the way I die. I have so much life left . . . please don't let this be the end . . .*

Branches began smacking against my windshield with whipping cracks that reverberated through my bones. The deeper I went into the trees, the more violent the blows became. Metal groaned; then something snapped with a sideways jolt that made my head hit the window in an explosion of pain. My vision faded in and out as realization struck me—the wings . . . one of them, or maybe both of them, had broken off. It wouldn't be long now until I was torn to pieces like the rest of the plane. I couldn't stop the screams of terror that left my lips, but the chaos of sound around me was so deafening—like standing in the jet wash of a commercial airplane—that I couldn't hear them.

Then the nose of the plane touched the earth. I hit the steering column hard, and every cell inside my body seared with pain. I couldn't inhale. I couldn't exhale. Gasping for breath that wasn't coming made stars explode in my vision, erasing the flash of green, white, and brown rocketing up and over the windshield. Glass splintered, metal whined, and objects in the cabin flew in every direction as momentum caused the plane's body to shift sideways, toppling, turning, and twisting. I smelled gas; I tasted blood; I felt agonizing pain . . . everywhere. And then, mercifully, my entire world went black.

Chapter Two

Sound was the first thing that came back to me. And then surprise. Was I alive? How was I alive? I shouldn't have survived that. Something was dripping nearby, a steady drop . . . drop . . . drop that was slowly bringing me back to awareness. Awareness brought sharp, burning agony, and I instantly wished for the unconsciousness to return. Every muscle in my body felt ripped in two; every bone felt snapped in pieces. There wasn't a single inch of me that wasn't radiating with pain, and I hadn't even moved yet. I was terrified to move.

But I couldn't stay in this destroyed airplane forever. I carefully opened my eyes, and whiteness blinded me as my vision spun and pulsed. It made me nauseated, and it was difficult to wait it out without throwing up. My sight finally cleared. I was slumped over the broken steering column, and fractured glass from the windshield was everywhere. Sleet from the storm was splashing all around me, chilling me to the bone. It echoed off the remaining portions of the plane; there wasn't much of it left in one piece.

A thick branch was sticking through the windshield like a sword. Seeing it sent a strange surge of relief and panic through me—a foot to the right, and the branch would have impaled me. I tried lifting my head, and the world swirled again like I'd put it in a blender. Resisting the urge to lie back down, I tried to sit upright. My chest was on fire.

Every inhale was agony, every exhale torture. I wished there was a way to breathe without using my lungs. Tears stung my eyes as I endured the pain and looked around.

The cockpit of my small plane was absolutely decimated. The body of it too. There was a gaping hole in the side of the plane where my door used to be, and what was left of my cargo was spilling out of it. My insides felt similarly torn apart. Scared of what I might find, I gingerly checked my chest and torso for blood. Every inch of me was tender to the touch, and there was a ragged cut over my eye, dripping blood down my face, but I didn't feel any other open wounds. Of course, my legs were half-buried under the dash. I'd have to move to get them out, and I was really scared to do that.

Mentally preparing myself, I tried scooting out of my seat. A shock wave of pain radiated from my left leg, and a cry of agony escaped me. Inhaling and exhaling stuttered breaths, I tried looking through gaps in the wreckage to examine my leg. I couldn't see much from my angle at first; then I shifted enough to see the problem, and my stomach clenched with disgust and fear. Sometime during the tumbling and tossing of the fuselage, a branch had punctured a hole through the thin metal. It had also gone into my thigh; my pants and the part of the branch still visible were coated in thick red blood. Jesus. Bile rose up my throat, and my stomach twisted so hard I knew I was going to throw up—no holding it back this time. Leaning to the side, I let it out. Oh my God, how was I going to get out of this metal death trap with a tree branch through my leg? And if I did manage to get out, how the hell was I going to find shelter before it got dark? How could I build a fire? Patch up my thigh? Find my pack holding all my food? Melt snow for water? Keep the hungry animals at bay? How the hell was I going to *survive*? Did I really live through all of that just to die out here? Was life really that unfair?

I began to sob as the reality of my situation struck me like lightning. Even though it felt like my chest was cracking open, I couldn't stop crying. It would have been better if I'd died in the wreckage. This . . . this was cruel.

But no . . . I wasn't dead yet, and I had too much to live for to give up. My protective, loving family—they would never forgive themselves for reluctantly letting me pursue my dream if I died out here. They would forever be weighted with guilt, wishing they had tried harder to stop me. All of my friends back home, including Shawn—even though our marriage had failed, we had been close since the first grade, and he would always be important to me. My three adorable pug pups—Frodo, Pippin, and Samwise. My sister was looking after them while I was gone, but they were *depending* on me to come home. And my gratifying career, which was just starting to become something I was truly proud of . . .

No, as long as I was still breathing, I wasn't going to give up. I was *alive*, and that meant I still had a chance. And a chance, even a slim one, was better than nothing. I just had to be strong and remember that pain was fleeting.

Fortifying my stomach, I looked at my leg again. I had no idea how deep the branch was buried—or if it had nicked an artery. Pulling it out could cause as much damage as leaving it in. But I couldn't stay here, so I didn't really have a choice. I timidly touched my leg. Avoiding where the branch had pierced the skin, I felt the other side of my thigh. My pants were in one piece, and I couldn't feel any protrusions, so I didn't think the branch had gone all the way through—thank God. If I used enough force, I should be able to yank my body off the half-inch-thick stick. Shit, it was going to hurt so much. Could I do this? Yes, I had to.

Wiping my bloody, tear-stained cheeks, I prepared myself for an inevitable burst of pain. "You can do this, Mal. Count of three, and it will be over. Nothing to it." Letting out a long, slow breath, I started counting. "One . . . two . . . three."

Right on the count of three, before I could freeze up and change my mind, I pushed against the wrecked dash, tossing all my body weight to the right, away from the steering column, away from the branch spearing my leg. As momentum carried me all the way outside, through the smashed-open hole that used to be a door, a tidal wave of agony ripped through my body. I'd never felt anything so paralyzing, and I screamed at the top of my lungs before finally, thankfully passing out. The last thing I heard before darkness covered me again was the ominous howl of a wolf.

When I came to, I wasn't sure where I was. Blissfully delirious, I thought I was back at home in the mountains of Idaho, making snow angels with my sister. It was too cold, though, and my entire body was shaking with the frigidness of the earth below me. Then I remembered the plane, the crash, the mangled heap of metal, the branch piercing my thigh. The tears resurfaced as the pain and desolation consumed me. God, why couldn't my delusion be real? I'd give anything to be moments away from a hot fire and warm cocoa. Free from pain, free from misery, free from despair.

But I wasn't home, I wasn't free, and the longer I remained lying on the ground, freezing and bleeding, the closer to death I crept. And I couldn't give in to death. Life was a gift, one I cherished, and I was going to fight to keep it. Through sheer strength of will, I managed to sit up on my elbows. My thick insulated pants were torn and stained, ruined, and a pool of dark blood was collecting on the snow. The sight made me nauseated again, but I needed to staunch the flow before I lost too much blood; I already felt dizzy, like I might pass out at any moment, and if I did, I might not wake up again. Firmly placing my palm against the wound, I pressed down. Pain flared under my touch, threatening to consume me with agony.

Just that little bit hurt so much, and it was only a temporary fix. I needed to do something more, make something tighter to truly keep the blood loss at bay. That was just one of the many things I had to do. Exhaustion weakened my spirit as my to-do list overwhelmed me. Everything on the list felt like it was a top priority. Heat was essential. My fingers were already stiff, hard to move. If I didn't get them warmed up soon, I might lose them. Fear made me reach into my pocket with my free hand. There were two survival items I always kept on me—a Swiss Army knife and a lighter. Feeling them still there lessened my panic. Thank God, I could get warm. I could smell gas, though. I would have to get away from the plane before I started a fire. I would also need wood—dry wood. Shit. Where was I going to find wood dry enough to burn in this?

Worry made me look around. The sleet had turned to snow, and a thin layer was already covering me and the plane—freezing us both. Finding my survival pack was a must—hopefully it was nearby and not hundreds of feet away, where the plane had first started ripping apart. My pack had everything I'd need to stay alive . . . for a few weeks at least. The fear started returning, and I tried not to think that far in the future. I had to keep focused on what I could do *now*. Now was all that mattered. And if I could find my pack, then I stood a much better chance of surviving the night.

That was when I remembered hearing the wolf. And where there was one, there were always more. I had to get my gun from the side of the plane so I could defend myself if they decided to come closer; the strangeness of the wreckage should hold them off for a while, but the smell of blood would eventually draw them in. Grizzlies too. They could smell blood for miles, and at this time of year, they were desperate for food. Oh God . . . I couldn't stomach the thought of being eaten by the animals I loved. I prayed my gun was still attached to the plane.

Panic began to knock on my soul, darkening and frightening the frail hope inside me. I tried to push it back, tried to convince myself that I could do everything I needed to do—that all of this was going to be fine—but it was so hard. I wanted to crawl into a ball and sob, cry, curse the world. But none of that would help me live, and I wanted to live more than anything. I loved my life.

So I needed to fix my leg. That was step one.

Breathing made my chest burn, and I knew it wasn't just the chill in the Arctic air that was hurting me. I'd probably cracked a rib—several of them, by the feel of things. There might be internal bleeding too. My vomit had been clear, and I took that as a good sign, but still, I wouldn't know until it was too late. As much as that thought sent icy terror through me, I knew it was out of my hands. All I could do was worry about taking care of the outside of me. Finding my cross necklace intact and still around my neck, I placed my chilled fingers upon it and strengthened myself for the task at hand. *You can do this, Mal. You have to.*

Looking around, I tried to find something nearby that I could use to bind my leg. The wing covers were dangling from the hole in the plane, billowing in the breeze. I could cut the straps off and use them to tightly wrap my thigh—that should keep the blood loss at a minimum. I hoped.

Having a plan in mind made me feel a little better, mentally at least. My body was in an endless cycle of pain. I made myself sit all the way up. It was agony to move, but what concerned me even more was how much I was shaking. Was I cold? Or in shock? Or had I lost too much blood? Cold I could fix. The other two . . . there wasn't much I could do about either of them, and that fear shook the mild hope-fueled peace I'd found, leaving me torn between terror and confidence. I had to keep going. Stopping wasn't an option.

After every part of me was clear from the crash, I began the process of shifting over so I could grab the fluttering covers. Every inch was a battle, pain ebbing and flowing in a cycle that made me cry—I just wanted it to end. I didn't give up, though, and eventually, I won. Grabbing the canvas, I yanked it over to me. Snow was still lightly burying the earth, and each short breath escaping me was a puff of steam.

The cold made everything ten times as difficult. I could barely move my fingers. God, I hoped it wasn't too late for them. I couldn't remove them myself . . . I just couldn't. Even thinking about it made my stomach rise and my throat tighten.

Ignoring that fear, I grabbed my knife and started sawing the straps off the cover. It felt sacrilegious to destroy them, but I wouldn't need them for what they were intended for anymore. Several straps in hand now, I set to work on wrapping them around my thigh, creating a makeshift tourniquet. Just getting the strap underneath my leg was difficult, but cinching it tight was pure torture—like I was sticking my finger in the wound and wiggling it around. My stomach clenched more than once, and my eyesight narrowed to pinpricks. But somehow, I managed to pull through without throwing up or blacking out.

Leg firmly bound now, I tried to stand. Even with most of my weight on my good leg, it was almost impossible to get up. I managed only by using holes in the metal fuselage to pull myself up. Fighting back tears, fighting through the pain, I gingerly tested how much weight my injury could handle. Not much. Just shifting my weight over made me feel like I was going to topple to the ground. I couldn't possibly do all of this on one leg. Banging the side of the plane in frustration, I felt the edge of my sanity slipping. I couldn't do this. I just wanted to lie down . . . just for a minute. Rest . . .

But no . . . I couldn't crack, couldn't give in. I was still alive, and that was something. That was everything. I'd rest when I was done. When I was safe.

Praying for strength and luck, I looked over to the section of the plane where my rifle had been resting. Miraculously, it was still attached. Relief made a small, weary laugh escape me. Thank God, something was going my way. Dragging my bad leg, I shuffled over to the weapon. It was hard to remove the gun with numb fingers, but I finally managed to slide it free of its metal holster. I slipped the strap across my chest so

I could hold it without my hands. Just having a way to defend myself renewed my spirits. I was getting there. I could finish this.

Finding my pack was my next priority. Hoping beyond hope that it would magically be at my feet, I searched the ground. Damn it, nothing. I looked around the crash site, scouring for clues and resisting the urge to scream in frustration. My injured leg was starting to throb, and all I wanted to do was sit down. I needed a fire. I needed to rest. I needed that damn pack!

While I couldn't find my bag anywhere, I did find a tall, sturdy branch with a *Y* at the top that I could use as a makeshift crutch until I found something better. Jerking it free from the plane, I tucked it under my shoulder and prayed it was as solid as it looked. A rush of relief surged through me when it held. I could move. It was still agony, with each step sending a searing jolt through my body, but at least it was possible now.

With halting movements, I shuffled to the back of the plane to try and find some sign of my black survival bag. There was a trail of debris and damage from where my little plane had crashed through the woods. Dear God . . . it seemed to go on for miles. How the hell had I survived that? Speckled throughout the debris were bits and pieces of my gear and most of my food supply. The bins holding my things had burst apart during the crash, and everything was scattered now. Despair crashed over me as I stared at the wreckage. There was too much; I was too weak . . . I couldn't possibly search the entire path of the crash. And if the bag had landed in a tree, been dragged off by an animal, or had broken apart like everything else . . .

That bag had been my plan B. There was no plan C.

Panic took a firm grasp on me. *What do I do? How do I survive now?* Exhaustion poured into me, sapping my spirit. Lying down in the snow suddenly sounded like the best idea in the world. Why not? Without that pack, I wouldn't last long.

Some willful part of me was screaming to rebel against the idea growing larger and larger in my head, but I was rigid with cold and worn thin with exhaustion, and every inch of me was radiating with bursts of pain that siphoned my fading strength. I just wanted something to feel better, even if it was superficial, even if, in the end, it wouldn't help me.

I was doing it in my mind, picking a spot to rest. Maybe under the tail of the plane so I wouldn't get snowed on too much. And that was when I spotted something out of place to my left. I'd thought it was a rock at first glance, but it was too dark, too black. Black . . . like my bag. Renewed hope suddenly obliterated my momentary grief, and I shifted toward my survival bag. Toward life.

Getting there seemed to take an eternity, but seeing that the bag was resting near some tall intact trees—shelter—filled me with determination. Once I was there, it was the last place I'd have to go for a while. That knowledge gave me a burst of adrenaline. *Just a little farther, and I can stop—I can rest.*

Tears of relief and joy coursed down my cheeks as I pulled my bag free from the snow. The durable material was still in one piece. Inside the bag was an easy-to-set-up one-man tent, a below-zero blanket, emergency food, and a pot to boil water. There was also a first aid kit and pain relievers. I knew whatever I had with me wouldn't be strong enough to take away all of the pain I had, but it would be better than nothing. The bag was hope, and I clung to it with everything left inside me.

There were loose small branches and twigs under the safety of the trees. I gathered them together into a pile, then got to work igniting them. With my shaking fingers, it took longer than I wanted, and my joy shifted to frustration. I couldn't give up, though—not with physical relief in my grasp—and eventually the dry wood caught, and a small fire started growing into a larger one. The immediate heat was an instant mood elevator, and I was smiling so hard that my cheeks hurt. There was nothing like warmth when you were chilled to the bone. And as an added bonus, the flames would help keep away any predators who might have discovered me. The fire didn't ensure my survival, but it was a much-needed step along the way, and I finally began to believe I could do this.

I suddenly wanted to sit in front of the fire, but I needed to finish first—when I was finally able to rest, I wouldn't want to get up again. Setting down my crutch, I carefully pulled the tent out of the bag and popped it open. Then I grabbed the insulating blanket and wrapped it around myself. After pulling out my meal for the night—beef jerky and dehydrated fruit—I finally and thankfully sat down on a log near the fire. It was so heavenly a sob of joy escaped me. Thank God . . . I made it.

Adding sticks to the blaze, I reveled in the heat as it soothed my aching body. Breathing wasn't any easier, and my leg radiated with pain, but I felt more at peace. I'd made it through my checklist, accomplished everything I'd needed to do to survive. For today. Tomorrow, the list would start again. And again. And again. Until finally, I somehow managed to get out of here. But that was far down the line and not worth stressing about at the moment. For now, I was simply overjoyed to be alive, and I was going to revel in that feeling.

Setting my pot on the edge of the fire, I filled it with snow. I'd give anything for some wine right about now or some whiskey, but water would have to do. When it was ready, I set the pot in the snow to cool the water down. Then I drank my fill. It wouldn't seem like you could get dehydrated in severe cold, but you could, just the same as in the desert. Once I was satiated, I melted more snow and washed my face as best as I could. Sharp stings—especially above my eye—reminded me just how scraped up I was. After my face was clean, I loosened the straps around my leg. Grabbing a flashlight from my bag, I tried to get a good look at my injury. It was hard to see around my pants, so I found some scissors and made a larger hole. The wound looked nasty, but it didn't appear to be bleeding heavily anymore—just oozing. I was grateful for that. Digging through my small first aid kit, I grabbed antibacterial ointment and some gauze pads. I cleaned up the wound as best I could, then rewrapped my thigh. Even though I left the straps looser than before, pain still washed through me in waves when I cinched it. But still, in as much agony as I was in, I knew I was blessed; I shouldn't have survived that crash.

As I sat there enjoying the heat of the fire, the sun sank past the horizon, and darkness settled around me. The temperature would truly start to plummet now. Just as I had that thought, an icy wind whipped through my little camp, slightly lifting an edge of my tent. The sky had cleared somewhat since the crash, but if another storm was on the way, waiting it out inside my shelter was the safest place to be. I poured the remaining water on the fire, then grabbed my bag and crawled inside my tiny tent. It was tight with both me and the bag inside, but I didn't have a bear-proof container handy—all the ones I'd brought with me had been destroyed. And besides, I wasn't about to let the bag out of my sight after everything I'd gone through to find it.

The wind picked up, howling just as ominously as the wolf I'd heard earlier. The sides of my tent rattled in the gusts, shaking so hard it was like someone was outside, playing a practical joke on me. But this was no joke. I was safe, though, and relatively warm. I could move all my fingers and all my toes, although I tried not to move the ones on my injured leg. All things considered, I was very lucky. Counting my blessings, however small they might be, I closed my eyes and let the day's exhaustion overtake me.

That was when I heard something alarming in the breeze. A huffing, grunting sound. A sniffing nose, searching the ground for food. A large nose, belonging to a large beast. A grizzly. A deep snort somewhere off to my left confirmed my suspicions. There was a bear somewhere in the woods, somewhere close by, probably going through all the food that had exploded from my belongings during the crash. I put my hand on the rifle that I'd also brought into the tent with me, and then I reclosed my eyes. Even though I was shaking with fear, I knew there was nothing I could do about a curious, hungry bear, except pray that it would be satisfied with the food I'd left scattered and would leave me alone.

Please don't let me live through a plane crash only to be mauled by a bear . . .

Chapter Three

I awoke early the next morning when the sun was barely gracing the sky. How I'd managed to sleep at all was beyond me. Pure exhaustion, probably. The bear had sniffed and snorted its way around my campsite, but for reasons unknown, it had left me alone.

My body hurt ten times more than it had yesterday. I knew that was both a blessing and a curse. Aching muscles and cracked ribs would heal, given enough time, but the pain had to get worse before it could get better. The only thing that truly concerned me was my leg. My pants were stained and splotched with blood, and I was sure I should probably have stitches to close the gaping wound. I didn't have those kinds of supplies with me, though . . . and I wasn't sure I could sew my own skin even if I did. Just the thought made bile rise up my throat. I'd just have to trust that the wound would close completely on its own and hopefully wouldn't get infected in the process. Aside from the antibacterial ointment, I didn't have anything on me that would help with an infection.

While that was a fear that filled my stomach with icy dread, I had to ignore it. There was nothing I could do about it, and there were too many other things that needed to be done. I needed to gather wood for fires and find a way to keep it dry—staying warm was essential. I'd need to add to my food stores if I was going to make it here long term, and considering I couldn't blindly walk home, I'd say I was going to be here for a while. The search for food might have to wait until my leg healed somewhat, but considering that the grizzly had probably devoured every piece of nutrition that wasn't in my bag, I knew I'd have to go out while injured. And like everything else, that would make hunting a thousand times harder. I hated what I was going to have to endure soon—what I was enduring *now*—but it was what I had to do to survive. Giving up wasn't an option.

But first, wood and maybe a more substantial shelter . . . something a little more bear proof. Unwrapping myself from my blanket, I began the process of sitting up. And it *was* a process—everything was. Breathing was still hard to do, and I wished I had something to wrap tightly around my chest. Any form of support would be a comfort. Letting out short, unsatisfying huffs, I unzipped my bag to find breakfast—dried meat and protein bars. I figured I had about a couple days' worth of "real" food in there, and then I'd be on to the emergency freeze-dried food.

I'd planned ahead when I'd prepared my plane, but the crash and the bear had changed all that. I'd have to supplement my stash with wild meat—fish, deer, rabbits. Life here was abundant, if you knew where to look. Of course, this wasn't my normal stopping area, and I had no idea what the geography was like, where the lakes and rivers were. Fear and doubt started crowding the edges of my brain, fighting for dominance, but letting those emotions take over would only hurt me, and I was hurting enough.

Shoving them aside, I focused on what I knew. I was good at tracking, and I understood animal instinct. I was positive I could set some traps and find some food. After foraging for wood and fortifying my shelter, of course. God, I had so much to do, and I was so weak, so tired . . . in so much pain. But I had people waiting for me . . . I had to keep going. *Just keep going.*

Gnawing on my breakfast, I tried redirecting my darkening thoughts by thinking about what I would have been doing right now if I'd made it through the storm and my plane had landed normally. I'd be eating the same food and staying in the same shelter, but I'd have full use of my body, and I'd be excited about the day's possibilities. I'd be looking for tracks, preparing my camera. Oh God, my camera. It could be anywhere in the woods—finding it would take a miracle. Not that it really mattered if I did happen to stumble across it . . . my camera was most likely broken, if not completely shattered. A surge of grief struck me like a physical blow, and tears swelled in my eyes and rolled down my cheeks. On the list of things that I'd lost, my camera seemed trivial, but a part of my soul was wrapped in that glass and plastic, and it killed me to know it was gone. Wiping my cheeks dry, I reminded myself that objects could be replaced. My life couldn't be.

If I hadn't crashed, I'd be snapping my favorite animals, capturing photos that would sustain me for months, if not longer. Foxes, hares, moose, bears, wolves: I'd be eager to see them. But now . . . a lot of those creatures I hoped to *never* see while I was here. Everything was different now that my life was on the line, and that made me want to weep. The very animals I'd come here to see might be what destroyed me.

If I hadn't lost my plane, I'd be returning to Idaho in a few weeks. That was the hardest what-if to think about, and my eyes stung with tears again as home floated through my mind. My dogs would cover me with sloppy kisses. Mom would hug me like she'd been sure she'd never see me again. Then she would tell me I shouldn't go out into the wilderness alone, and I should stay and work at the diner with her full time. But right after that she would give me a small, relenting smile and ask to see my pictures. Dad would agree with Mom's every word about me staying home; then he'd contradict himself by excitedly telling me every fact he knew about all the animals I'd photographed. Dad's passion had fueled my own—I'd learned more about the natural world from listening to him than from *National Geographic*. Patricia would listen intently to all my stories, then start psychoanalyzing why I'd chosen such a dangerous, antisocial career. Shawn would hover, not-so-subtly watching over me, making sure I was truly okay. Then he would tell me we'd made a huge mistake and beg me to take him back. But I wouldn't, because I knew we were only ever meant to be friends.

That was what should have been in my future, but now . . . the odds of me getting back to that life were so slim I might as well have been planning a trip to the moon. I was never leaving these woods. I would never see my loved ones again, and they would never really know what had become of me. They'd miss me; they'd mourn me . . . for ages. And in their hearts, they would believe that they'd been right—that I should have shelved my dream and lived a life of safety and certainty. That wasn't what I wanted . . . but neither was this.

Despair started settling over me like a wet blanket, dragging me down deeper and faster than I could resist. Despondency cut off the light, the oxygen—the love—until all I felt was cold, alone, and in pain. I was going to die here. The wolves would feast until my bones were the only remaining trace of me.

As if to punctuate my point, a lone wolf howled in the distance. Anger shot up my spine, obliterating the chill and easing the depression. No, I wasn't ready to stop fighting. I'd never stop fighting, not until the last breath escaped my lips. So long as I was alive, there was still hope.

After my energizing meal, I felt a little better, less prone to mood swings. It never ceased to amaze me how having something in my stomach, even if it was only dried fruits and a handful of nuts, could lift my spirit. Securing my pack, I strapped the gun across my back and opened my tent. The cold struck me as hard as a fist, reminding me just how well my deceptively simple shelter retained heat. Struggling to get to a standing position, I twisted around and sealed the tent. After a quick bathroom break, I made a fire with the last of my dry wood. That was a problem I'd have to fix right away. Fire was my lifeline, my preservation against the chill ceaselessly trying to encapsulate me.

Sitting on a fallen log beside the fire, I propped my aching leg on a nearby rock. While I warmed up, I examined my thigh again. The gauze pad was bloody, so I carefully replaced it with one in my pocket. The wound was still wet, still seeping blood. That was bad. It shouldn't still be bleeding. Anxiety began to crawl up my spine as I wondered how I could seal the skin, promote faster healing. I had nothing for stitches . . . so cauterize the wound? God . . . could I do that? Stick a flaming-hot piece of wood into my body? Willingly? No . . . it could wait. I'd figure that out tomorrow, if I had to. Maybe it would be fine soon.

When the fire died away, I grabbed my makeshift crutch and prepared myself to gather more wood. Warmth was the greatest thing I could do for myself right now—and it was far less stressful to think about. Walking was a struggle, though, and I was breathing heavily after just a couple of paces. My lungs felt on fire from the exertion, but I didn't give up. I couldn't. I needed heat. Trudging past the plane wreckage reminded me of the crash, and painful memories flashed through my brain. Averting my eyes from the warped metal, I saw the evidence of last night's predator. Wrappers, Tupperware, and tinfoil packets that used to hold food were everywhere, and it was clear every morsel had indeed been picked clean by the bear. All I had left was stuffed in my emergency bag. Damn it . . . I'd secretly been hoping *something* would be left, and it was crushing to learn that wasn't the case.

Since I was firmly holding on to the crutch with one hand, I had only one arm to carry back wood. It was inefficient and frustrating, but it was all I could do. Close to camp, I found a pine tree that had thick branches. The bottom branches were so low that they were partially buried in the snow covering the ground. Wearing my warmest gloves, I removed a section of snow and pulled the branches up. Near the base of the tree was a clear, dry spot that was now my woodshed. Good. I didn't think I had the strength to build one.

It took all morning and a good chunk of the afternoon to fill the space beneath the tree with wood. When I was done for the day, I was disappointed. It had taken far too long, and I hadn't gathered nearly as much as I'd wanted to gather. But days were short here, and I only had an hour or two of light left . . . and I was utterly exhausted. Every time I moved, bolts of agony radiated through my leg and chest. Everything hurt so much that I was almost getting immune to the pain. Almost. I wanted to rest—more than anything—but I needed to strengthen my shelter first. That was too important to set aside, even for a day.

Taking a second to rest, I mentally prepared myself for the task. I'd need to cut some thick branches, then tie them together in an A-frame. Then I'd need to cut some boughs off the pine tree, making pseudo-shingles for the sides. Simple, yet at the moment, exceedingly difficult. More than my brain or body could handle. I had no choice but to press on, though. Even still, I stared at my shelter for a solid ten minutes before I gathered enough willpower to get started.

Since everything took so long for me to do, I cut only half of the large branches I needed before darkness fell over me. Cursing my weary body, I called it quits and grabbed some logs so I could make another fire. I was trying to get the still-damp wood to light when I noticed something that froze my heart. A pair of eyes reflecting light from the moon. I'd only seen it for an instant, but it had been long enough to know what it was—trouble. Ice flooded my veins. My heart started beating harder, and my breaths grew faster, making my bruised chest ache.

"Get out of here!" I yelled, again trying my damnedest to light the fire. Some predators were scared off by loud noises they didn't understand. Some. Not all. Staying near a blazing fire was my best bet, but I needed flames first.

A low growl in the night raised the hairs on the back of my neck. It sounded like a dog, which instantly made my blood go cold. Oh my God . . . no . . . wolves. Wolves were among the most intelligent hunters in these woods. They had speed, strength, and the numbers to make them a near-impossible foe, and as I recalled the flash of eyes I'd seen in the darkness, something my father had told me once popped into my mind: *It's not the wolf you see that you should worry about. It's the other ten you don't see that are the problem.*

Fear made my fingers shake, made flicking the lighter even more difficult. The wolves were probably surrounding me right now. They could smell my blood, sense my nervousness. To them, I must seem like easy, injured prey, certainly a lot easier to take down than a five-hundred-pound moose—and they didn't have much trouble with those. I wasn't exactly defenseless, though. I had a weapon, and in a minute, I'd have a fire. Sudden indecision made me pause. *Shit. Do I continue struggling with the fire, or do I unsling my rifle and blast a couple of warning shots at them?*

That was when I saw three of them slinking their way out of the tree line. Their teeth were bared, hackles raised, and a menacing growl was escaping their lips. They were clearly telling me, *Don't do anything stupid.* I wasn't about to meekly let them eat me, though.

Heart in my throat, adrenaline rushing through me like a river, I fumbled for my gun. Like I'd signaled a race to start, the three wolves surged forward. Oh God . . . I heard sounds behind me and knew more of them were closing in that way. I could almost hear a countdown to my death beginning. *Five. Four. Three . . .*

Yanking the rifle off my body, I swung it around, chambered a bullet, and fired. Something yipped in pain, but I couldn't tell which dark creature I'd hit. I hadn't been prepared for the recoil, and I lost my balance. Putting too much weight on my bad leg, I felt my knee buckle, and I started falling backward. I immediately tried to correct myself, but the log I'd been using as a chair was in my path, and I landed hard on the rough bark. My ankle caught underneath the wood, and I felt something wrench before it pulled free. Pain made me cry out, but I was still falling. I slid off the log, and my back hit the snowy ground. I could hear the huffing, puffing sound of animals running my way, could feel a ripping pain in my thigh as the wound protested the violent jerking. Gun still clutched in my fingers, I chambered another bullet, raised it over my head, and fired blindly.

Another wolf cried out in pain, but the rest of them weren't stopping. Fur and teeth crashed into me. I blocked as best I could, but my strength was ebbing, and eventually the snarling, snapping ferocity would overwhelm me . . . especially once the wolf's help arrived. I yelled, screamed, fought, but in my head, I was again saying goodbye to everyone I'd left behind. *God, please . . . not like this.*

The animal was going for my neck—going for the kill. Its teeth were getting so close that I could feel its hot breath on my skin. Jesus. Would I still be alive when it started devouring me? Just the thought made me want to throw up. But if I did, I would die, so I fortified my stomach and kept fighting with everything inside me.

Somehow, I pushed the beast away long enough to grab my rifle. It wasn't made for close combat like this, but it was the most effective weapon I had within reach. I loaded the gun again and pulled the trigger in almost one movement. The creature I'd been fighting had been lunging for my throat when the bullet exploded through its chest. It fell in a heap just to my right; then two more beasts took its place.

Even while I fought for my life, raising my gun like a shield, I felt like sobbing. It wasn't supposed to be like this. Then more blasts rang out through the night, and the animals trying to kill me yelped in pain. One fell over and didn't get back up. The other one limped off as quickly as it could. More shots echoed in the night, and the growls around me subsided into silence.

My brain couldn't comprehend what had just happened. Had a bear learned to use a gun? Because right now, that was the only thing that made sense. I tried to sit up, to look around, but I didn't have the energy; I fell back to the ground with a grunt. And that was when a man dropped to his knees at my side.

"Are you hurt? Did they get you?" The voice was gruff and blunt, with an edge of annoyance.

I was alone in these woods. Was I hallucinating? Had I died? "Who are you?" I choked out.

"Are you hurt?" he repeated, definitely annoyed now.

Slinging his gun over his shoulder, he reached into his jacket and pulled out a flashlight. Flicking it on, he ran it over my body. My vision was hazy like I'd been drinking all day, and the sudden brightness wasn't helping anything. I tried to focus on his face, but all I was seeing was a frost-covered beard and a pair of startlingly blue eyes. "No," I whispered.

The ice-blue eyes narrowed as they locked on mine. "Your pants are torn and bloody, and there is a barely healed cut above your eye. Want to try that again?"

Annoyed myself now, I shook my head. "The wolves didn't do that. I was . . . in a plane crash."

His expression softened as he looked me over. "Oh . . . I see." Pursing his lips, he looked around my makeshift campsite with his flashlight. "I can get you to my cabin, but it's going to take a while, especially if you can't walk well." He returned his eyes to me. "We'll stay here tonight, head out in the morning."

Either the pain was catching up to me, or the adrenaline was wearing off and leaving stupor in its place. He had a cabin here? "Who are you?" I asked again, baffled that I was in the middle of nowhere, talking to another human being. Who apparently lived here.

"Name's Michael. Michael Bradley." He stuck his hand out, and I gingerly took it.

"I'm . . . Mallory Reynolds."

He gave me a soft smile, full of compassion. "It's nice to meet you, Mallory."

Our greeting was so oddly normal . . . but none of this was normal. I'd narrowly survived my plane going down; then I'd somehow managed to set up my shelter and make a fire, escaping freezing to death and bleeding to death; and now . . . now I'd barely made it through being something's dinner. It was too much to take, and the last several minutes tumbled through my mind in an endless, terror-filled loop. I started shaking.

"I think you . . . I think you just . . . saved my life."

I wasn't alone in the woods. I wasn't about to be eaten by wolves. I wasn't going to die. Relief and lingering fear washed over me in waves, overwhelming me. Needing human contact, I reached out for him, drawing him into me. He smelled like pine and campfires and fresh snow. He smelled like life, and it was the best scent in the entire world. I had help now; things would be easier. I started sobbing as that realization struck me. I was going to be okay. "Thank you, thank you . . ."

He made an awkward-sounding soothing noise as he rubbed my back. "It's okay. You're okay—everything is okay," he murmured, sounding conflicted.

When I finally calmed down, embarrassment flooded through me. "I'm sorry," I said, letting go of my fierce grip on him. "I just . . . I thought for sure . . ."

"It's all right . . . I understand," he said slowly. Clearing his throat, he indicated the pile of wood that I hadn't been able to ignite in time. "Let's get you warm."

Chapter Four

My savior—Michael—had the fire going in no time. He helped me get up, then helped me move to the other side of the log so I could sit down. My leg hurt worse than ever. I could tell the wound was bleeding again, and now, to make matters worse, my ankle was throbbing. As I hissed in a strained breath, Michael propped my leg up on a rock. Removing my boot, he checked my ankle. I whimpered when he touched the tender spot.

Looking up at me, he frowned. "It's pretty swollen. I think you sprained it. Ideally, you should stay off it for a few days."

A small laugh escaped me. Right. Like that was possible out here. Michael seemed to understand my reaction, and he gave me a sympathetic smile. "Can I check that?" he asked, pointing at my bloodstained pants.

I gave him a weak nod. "During the wreck, a branch . . . stuck in me. The cut is pretty deep. It was sort of healed, but I think it reopened when I fell."

Michael undid the straps, then flipped on his flashlight again. The gauze pad was soaked through, and when he gently pulled it off, I could see that I was right: it was flowing pretty well again. My stomach rose at seeing it, and my vision swam. Michael's flashlight shifted to my face. "Hey, hang in there. It's going to be okay. I can fix this."

I wasn't sure how he was going to do that in the middle of nowhere, but his assurance was comforting. Slipping a pack off his back, he started rummaging through it. Moments later he had the one thing I hadn't brought with me—needle and thread. I started hyperventilating as I looked at it. "No, no . . . just slap a bandage on it. It will close."

He gave me a sad smile. "It will close faster this way." I begged him with my eyes, but he shook his head. "I'm sorry, but I need to do this. And I know how much it hurts." He patted his side. "I've done it to myself."

Panic made me shake my head. "It's not sanitary. I'll get infected."

He grabbed a small pot hanging off his pack, then filled it with snow. Putting the needle on the snow, he put the pot in the fire. "It will be sterile enough soon," he said.

My heart sank as I watched the snow begin to melt. "Okay," I whispered. "I have some rubber gloves in my first aid kit." I indicated my tent with my head, and Michael swung his eyes in that direction.

Nodding, he returned the gauze pad and had me hold it in place while he went to retrieve the rest of what he needed to fix me. When he returned with my kit, he pulled out the scissors and cut my pants open even wider. I couldn't believe I was about to have surgery in the middle of the woods. This wasn't something I'd ever pictured happening out here. Maybe I should have.

After the water had boiled for a while, Michael poured it out, put on the gloves, and retrieved the needle. Handing me the flashlight, he said, "I'm sorry you're going through this, but I need light, so . . . hold it steady."

Somehow, I nodded at him. Oh God . . . I couldn't do this. Just a few moments later, the needle was sliding through my skin, and I *was* doing it. My hand shook, and I had to bite my cheek to stop from crying out. The pain came in waves, retreating and exploding over and over. My stomach rose into my throat, threatening to spill out again. I swallowed it back as I felt warm tears slip down my cheeks, and I prayed over and over for the pain to be gone soon.

Michael murmured encouragement the entire time he worked on me, and the sound was oddly soothing. Once he was finished, sitting back on his heels to examine his work, I blew out a staggering breath. "Oh my God . . . I don't ever . . . want to do that again."

"Hopefully you won't have to," Michael said, smiling as he covered the stitches with ointment, then put a fresh gauze pad over it. He loosely replaced the straps, then looked up at my face. "Anywhere else hurt?" He brought the flashlight up to the cut above my eye.

I immediately help up my hand. "It's fine. No more stitches."

His smiled widened. "I think a bandage will do." He tended that wound with a simple butterfly bandage, then looked me over again. "Anything else? I wouldn't want to waste these," he said, lifting his gloves.

I shook my head. "Just my ribs, but I don't have anything for that in my pack."

He frowned. "I don't either . . . but I've got plenty of wrap at my cabin. That will help." I nodded, relieved that the painful inspection was over for now. "Rest up," Michael said, pulling off the gloves. "I'll take care of the bodies."

I was so distracted by the fact that he had a cabin out here that I wasn't sure what he meant by bodies. Seeing my confusion, he pointed at the wolves that we'd been forced to kill. I instantly felt bad that we'd had to take the lives of such beautiful creatures, but we really hadn't had a choice; it had truly been life or death.

While Michael disposed of the wolves, I scooted as close to the fire as I could. There was a deep frown on his face when he returned to the fire and sat a little way from me.

"What's wrong?" I asked. *And who the hell are you? What are you doing out here in the middle of nowhere? How did you manage to save me, right in the nick of time? How did you know exactly how to patch me up?*

Politeness stopped me from bombarding him with those questions, but they were at the forefront of my mind. Feeling like I was right smack in the middle of a miracle, I fingered my necklace.

His thick, frozen beard began to melt as he sat within range of the heat, and fat drops trickled down the strands to land on his heavy jacket. "I'd normally skin the wolves, take the meat and the pelts. I hate being wasteful, but just getting you back to my cabin is going to be a challenge. I hadn't expected to find . . . survivors." His frown deepened after he said that, and he looked guilty, like he'd done something wrong.

"You knew about the plane?" I asked, wondering why he looked that way. What could he have done about a plane crashing?

Nodding, he started pulling apart a thin twig. "I wasn't entirely sure it was a plane, but I heard the crash, saw the smoke, and made an assumption. It was either a plane or a UFO. Either way, I thought I might find some supplies I could use," he added with a shrug.

A small laugh escaped me at his UFO comment, but it instantly faded. "It was my plane . . . the engine stalled on me. Couldn't get it restarted."

"Oh," he said quietly. "That must have been terrifying." His eyes drifted up to the sky to where the stars were so bright they were like LEDs stuck in the darkness. I studied him while he was distracted with his inner thoughts. Dressed for warmth, his head was covered by a hearty hat with Sherpa earmuffs that hung down off the sides. Even though I couldn't see it, I had to assume his hair was the same dark color as his beard. He was a little shaggy and unkempt, but even still, he was quite attractive. If I had to guess his age, I'd say he was in his mid- to late thirties, too young to be living in seclusion. What was he doing out here?

"Yeah, it was . . . all of this has been," I answered. His gaze drifted back to mine; his eyes were laced with pain. Why did he look that way? Not comfortable enough to ask him that, I instead asked, "How far is your cabin?" No matter how far it was, with how battered my body felt, it would be too far for me to walk there. Unless he wanted to carry me. Not that I'd let him.

Sticking the twig into his mouth, he looked off to my right and pointed. "It's about a day's walk from here." Looking back at me, his eyes shifted to my leg. "I set off this morning, stopping once to eat. I was moving pretty briskly, though. Getting *you* back there is going to take longer than that."

"Yeah . . . ," I said, glancing down at my leg.

Michael was studying me when I looked back at him. "We'll make it there, Mallory. The hard part is over with."

His words settled inside me, as warm as the fire, and I truly believed he was right. While I was sure it wouldn't be smooth sailing from here on out, the worst of the storm had passed us by.

Michael had his own one-person tent, so we weren't going to have to share my ridiculously small space. He set his up next to mine, the drab olive green a stark contrast to the brilliant-white ground. Settling into our makeshift beds, we attempted to get some sleep. The events of today kept running through my mind, making relaxing difficult. I loved animals, did everything in my power to show people how beautiful and fascinating they were, and today, I'd almost been killed by one. I knew it wasn't the wolves' fault—instinct was instinct—but I couldn't help but feel a little betrayed. That unreasonable emotion would pass with time, though, I was sure.

I heard Michael beside me start to snore, and I momentarily cursed the ease with which he'd shut off the day. Of course, his hadn't been quite as traumatic as mine. Putting a hand on my necklace, I squeezed my eyes shut and prayed for the image of yellow teeth and frosty breath to be eradicated from my memory. *You made it. Let it go . . . let it go.*

The sound of a zipper opening woke me up. I felt like I'd just fallen asleep, but by the grayness in my tent, I could tell the sun was beginning to rise. Gingerly, I started sitting up. Everything was even more sore than yesterday; I'd really been hoping that I'd already climbed that crest so I could begin a speedy downhill trek to recovery. No such luck.

My ankle hurt so badly I had to bite my lip to stop from crying out. A groan escaped me anyway.

"Mallory? You all right?" Michael's voice was just outside my tent; he sounded genuinely concerned.

"Yeah, I'm fine." It was more of a stretch than an outright lie, but admitting I was in bad shape wouldn't help either of us.

Several minutes later, when I could hear the snapping crackle of a hungry fire, I unzipped my tent. The shocking cold once again slapped me in the face, but the true challenge was trying to get out of the microscopic tent. Michael was frowning as he watched me emerge from my cocoon into the frigid outdoors, and I could almost see his mental gears turning, trying to solve the problem of my limited mobility. As I hobbled to get my crutch, he finally said, "I'm going to check out the plane, see if there isn't anything that can be salvaged. You should rest. Relax in front of the fire. It's going to be a long day."

I couldn't help but agree with that—just going to the bathroom was a challenge—so I shuffled to my sitting log after he took off in the direction of my mangled plane. From my vantage point, I could see the wreckage, and curious, I watched Michael pick his way through it. He pulled out sheets of metal, parts from the dash, a cushion from a seat. He seemed most interested in the engine area, though. I had no idea why. Scraps from the engine weren't going to help us get back to his cabin any faster.

After an eternity of watching him, my eyes started to feel heavy, and I let them close without a fight; I was already exhausted, and I hadn't even done anything yet. I could hear Michael hacking away at something, but I was too tired to open my eyes and see what he was working on. What felt like seconds later, he was tapping me on the shoulder. Startled awake, I looked up at him.

"We should go," he said, his eyes scanning the forest. "We need to cover as much ground as we can while the sun is out."

I nodded, then started to stand. Michael helped, putting a hand under my arm to steady me. I'd need to pack up my tent and shove everything into my survival bag before we could go. Hopefully that wouldn't take too long. Sunlight was a precious commodity here. But as I looked over to where I'd left everything set up, I could see that Michael had already packed everything, even his stuff. How long had I been out?

"Thank you," I murmured, indicating my pack.

Scratching his beard, Michael nodded. "You looked like you were dozing pretty good. Didn't want to disturb you."

Since I hadn't slept well the night before, I was grateful for the nap. "Did you find anything useful from my plane?"

He sighed like he was disappointed. "Not what I was hoping for . . . but I found something that might help our current situation."

He pointed over at something, and my eyes shifted to follow. I had no idea what he'd been hoping to find, but when I saw what he'd indicated, a burst of awe and surprise went through me. He'd crafted a travois out of wood, twine, and metal from the plane—I wouldn't have to wobble in pain all the way to his cabin. He was quite resourceful. I supposed he had to be, living alone in the wilderness.

Even more grateful now, I hopped over to the sled. "I feel bad that you have to drag this all the way home."

His expression completely serious, he said, "It's self-preservation, really. The faster I can get you back to the cabin, the safer we'll both be. You're kind of a mess, and wolves aren't the only thing in this forest."

The practicality of his sentence made me swallow a thick knot of tension. We weren't out of the woods yet, figuratively speaking. Feeling useless and moronic, I sat down on the slim sled. Michael handed me my pack, and I clutched it to my chest. He frowned as he looked me over. "I'm sorry, but this is going to be really bumpy for you."

Right. The Alaska Range wasn't exactly flat and easy to traverse. There were going to be a lot of rocks, trees, brush, hidden dips, and abundant snowdrifts. All that jarring was going to do a number on my body. "It's all right. I can take it." I had to.

Michael had attached a sort of harness to the front of the travois so he could keep his hands free while pulling me. His rifle was loosely hanging around his neck so he could grab it easily if he needed to. Mine was attached to my pack, secured but still available at a moment's notice. With the rope holding my sled firmly around his chest, Michael started pulling. The sled jerked forward, and a sharp pain ripped through my ankle, my thigh, my chest . . . my entire body. A small cry escaped me, and Michael instantly stopped.

"You okay?" he asked, looking back at me.

Gritting my teeth, I nodded. "Just keep going." If he stopped every time I was in pain, we'd never get to his cabin.

Preparing myself for a day and a half of incessant discomfort, I kept my jaw as tight as possible. *Please help me get through this.*

I said that small prayer at least every five minutes until we finally stopped for the night. Hauling a bulky sled over this rough terrain was slow going, and there had been several small breaks along the way. It wasn't until Michael set about making a fire that I finally let myself truly relax. It was over. For now.

"Are we close?" I asked, hoping against hope that he would tell me his place was right around the next corner.

He was breathing heavier when he answered me; the journey had been hard on him, too, for entirely different reasons. "No. We didn't even make it halfway."

I felt tears prick my eyes but didn't let them fall. Crying about our situation wouldn't make it any easier. Tossing the pack off of me, I began shifting myself so I could stand up. Michael suddenly looked concerned. "What are you doing?"

"I'm helping," I answered.

"You should be resting." He pointed at the sled almost like someone would point at the ground to get their dog to sit.

Lifting an eyebrow, I gave him as wry an expression as I could. "I managed to wrap my leg, collect firewood, and put up my shelter before you came along. I'm not completely incapacitated."

"You also almost got eaten by wolves," he countered.

I looked around for my crutch before realizing that we hadn't packed it. "I think I did pretty well, considering. And besides, you worked hard today—you were sweating. You should let me help build the fire so you can start drying your clothes. They're probably semi-frozen, and they *definitely* will be when the sun goes down."

He frowned but didn't argue with me, and I reveled in my momentary victory. Balancing on one leg, I bent over and started collecting twigs and small branches that hopefully would be dry enough to burn. When I'd recovered all I could, I started hopping toward a tree; there might be some gems hiding beneath the lowest branches.

Michael sighed, and when I looked back at him, he was shaking his head at my stubbornness, but he remained silent. Smart man.

It was exhausting to collect firewood while only putting weight on one leg. I refused to give up, though. Not even when Michael sighed for the millionth time and muttered under his breath that I was being ridiculous. After the shelters were up and the fire was roaring, Michael found us some logs to sit on. I collapsed onto mine with a groan, and he cocked an eyebrow at me.

Ignoring the pointed look on his face—a look that clearly said, *Maybe you should have listened to me, huh?*—I took off my thick protective gloves and held my hands up to the fire. The heat was heaven. Michael sat beside me again, his eyes glued to the flames like they contained all of life's mysteries.

"Drying off?" I asked, indicating his zipped-open jacket.

He gave me a stiff nod, his eyes still on the flames. I really wanted to know what had him so entranced, but it felt wrong to ask. Intrusive.

And he was the reason I was still alive. The last thing I wanted to do was be a prying nuisance.

As questions blazed through my mind about this mysterious mountain man, the sharp crack of a branch breaking disrupted the stillness of the crackling fire. Michael was on his feet in an instant, picking up his gun from the ground where he'd set it and pointing it toward the sound. My heart raced as I started envisioning the wolf encounter that had almost ended my life. Was the pack following us? Hell bent on exacting revenge for the lives we'd taken? I knew animals didn't think that way, but even so, it seemed probable to me.

The sun was still low in the sky, but it was pretty dark deeper in the woods, hard to see what might be lurking. Just as I was about to ask Michael to fire a warning shot into the air, a dark-brown shape stepped into view between a couple of nearby trees. My throat tightened in fear and anticipation before I could stop it; the creature was massive, but it wasn't a wolf or a bear. No, it was a moose. An animal that was typically friendly, as long as we didn't provoke it or it wasn't mating season; a male during the rut could be extremely aggressive.

A long, relieved exhale escaped me as Michael lowered his gun. "Damn," he muttered. "I wish we'd run into him closer to home. Moose meat is tasty, and there's a lot of it." He looked back at me with a small grin on his face.

As he sat back down, I watched the majestic mountain of a mammal as it lumbered past before turning to head deeper into the woods. "I wish I had my camera," I said, my voice wistful.

Michael looked over at me with a strange expression on his face like I'd just said the oddest thing ever. And I supposed it was odd to someone who saw these creatures all the time. "I'm a photographer. It's what I do for a living, the reason I'm out here."

His face turned speculative; then his gaze drifted over to my tent, where my pack and my gun were resting. "You didn't strike me as the . . . photographing type."

Feeling defensive, I told him, "Just because I prefer animals to be alive and well in their natural environments doesn't mean I won't do whatever I have to, to survive."

His lips curved into a bigger smile. "Maybe we're not so different then."

Looking around the quickly darkening expanse of wilderness around us, I asked him, "How long have you been out here? In the middle of nowhere?"

He scratched his beard, thinking. "Four . . . no, five years. I don't know. I'm not really keeping track."

Five years in isolation . . . what would that do to a person? "And . . . besides me . . . do you ever see people?"

There was amusement in his eyes as he studied me. "Are you asking me if you're the first woman I've seen in five years?"

His pale eyes drifted down my body then, and an unexpected flash of interest washed through me. Whoa . . . no. It might have been a while, but I wasn't so hard up that an attractive face would undo me. Was *he* that hard up, though? I might be walking out of the frying pan and into the fire. "That wasn't precisely what I was asking . . . but yeah, am I?"

He studied me a moment longer, then laughed. "There are some things I need that the forest can't provide. I go into town once or twice a year, and on occasion, I do run into women."

That got my attention. "You go to town? How? Do you have a plane?"

With a small laugh, he nodded and said, "I sure as hell don't want to walk to Fairbanks every year."

No, walking that far for supplies would be dangerous and impractical. Of course he'd fly, just like a lot of the people in Alaska who lived far from cities did. Just like I had done. Oh my God . . . if Michael had a plane at his cabin, that meant . . . I could go home.

Chapter Five

It took two more days to finally reach Michael's cabin. Good thing, because I was beginning to believe it didn't exist and we were going to wander the woods forever. When it came into view, I thought it was the most beautiful thing I'd ever seen; it looked like heaven, like salvation.

There were three buildings on the homestead, all of them made from logs cut from the surrounding forest. There was the main cabin, where Michael obviously lived; a shedlike shack that was probably some sort of workshop; and an outhouse, complete with a cutout half moon on the door. Everything had been made by hand—had to be, way out here—but it was all well made with tight, level seams and perfectly symmetrical windows. Even though I just wanted to be inside, out of the cold, I took a moment to appreciate Michael's craftsmanship.

With a grunt, Michael dropped the sled in front of the cabin. His breath was heavier as he rubbed his chest, and a flash of guilt went through me. He'd carried me so far, and without a word of complaint. "Thank you so much for getting me here," I said, struggling to stand without putting too much pressure on my ankle; it still ached.

Michael looked over at me with a small frown on his face. "We should get you inside, check out your stitches, wrap your ribs."

He'd been cleaning the wound on my thigh, changing the gauze pad each night, but he had told me more than once that he wanted to thoroughly examine the injury. I wanted that, too, and heat, but first, I really wanted to see what I'd been hoping to see—my way home. "Where's your plane?" I asked.

Walking over to me, eyes on my bloody pants, Michael motioned in the direction of the outhouse. "About a half mile away, in a clearing where I like to land."

Excitement and relief flooded through me. A plane. He could take me to Fairbanks. I could have my leg checked out at a hospital, and then I could hop on a jet and get back to Idaho. "Can we leave tomorrow?" *Can I go home?*

Dashing my spirits, Michael shook his head. "Plane's broken. I ordered a part, and they're supposed to deliver it when it comes in, but that won't be until spring, at the earliest." He paused to frown. "I'd been hoping to find the part I needed on your plane, just in case my supplier doesn't pull through, but no luck—everything was too damaged." He gave me an odd look, one full of both sympathy and trepidation. "I'm sorry, but I think you're going to be here awhile."

Like a tin can being compressed by a steamroller, I felt all my hope slowly being crushed. "Spring? I can't stay here until spring. I have people waiting for me. They'll think I'm dead."

His face was firm but sympathetic. "I'm sorry there isn't another way. But your family thinking you're dead is better than you actually being dead. They'll get over it once they see you again."

I knew he was right, but still, my eyes watered at hearing the news. Spring. It sounded like an eternity from now. What would my family do when they knew for a fact I was missing? Mourn me or search for me? As much as I wanted to be found, I didn't want them to start a search and rescue party. With the weather turning soon, it could lead to another crash and more lost souls, and I didn't want the weight of that possibility on my shoulders.

As my mood sank, I grew weary. I accidentally put too much weight on my injured ankle and started to stumble as a burst of pain hit me.

Michael's arms were around me an instant later, holding me up. I flung my arms around his neck, and our eyes locked. His were the palest shade of blue I'd ever seen. It gave them such depth, like I could see all the way into his soul. His grip was firm, solid, and steady, and a sense of peace and protection swept over me. I wanted to go home, wanted to see my family and my dogs, but if I had to stay here for months, at least I felt safe with him.

Michael made a hard swallow as he studied my face. I couldn't imagine that I looked all that great right now, with healing cuts all over my face and my long brown hair in a snarled tangle, but he seemed affected as he stared, and that made an odd warmth go through me. But then, like he'd been stung, he flinched, relaxed his grip, and averted his eyes. "We should get you inside, off your ankle."

The moment between us passed, and I eagerly nodded. Even though I'd been lying down for a couple of days, getting off my feet sounded wonderful.

Michael helped me inside the cabin, and I was struck by how comfortable it was. It was clear he'd built every piece of furniture, and even though the cabin wasn't huge, every item inside it was useful and practical. Everything belonged. A slab of wood attached to a wall formed a bed; bear-proof containers below it held supplies. A couple of chunky chairs surrounded a square table, and a huge bookcase filled one wall. There was even a hard, benchlike couch that looked long enough to lie down on. Michael directed me that way, and I sat on the unforgiving surface. He had me shift sideways so I could put my legs up, and then he started undoing the straps around my thigh.

Once all the straps were free, Michael examined my pants, then looked up at my face. "You should take these off now so I can get a good look. I'll make a fire . . . so you won't be cold."

As I thought of being half-naked in front of a stranger, a flush of embarrassment went through me. I quickly pushed it back, though.

Modesty was a luxury I couldn't afford at the moment. "I'll need help . . . at the bottom."

He glanced at my leg again, where my pants narrowed at the ankle, then nodded. Before getting up to make a fire, he took off my boots and set them beside the couch. I started wriggling my toes, then stopped when a shooting pain went up my ankle. God, I hoped it was just a sprain.

As flames began to slowly come to life in the airtight stove nestled in a corner, I unzipped my pants and carefully started sliding them down my body. The chill of the not-yet-heated room hit me instantly, pebbling my skin. Every movement hurt a little, but shifting my body so I could slide my pants down my hips and over my injured thigh was the worst. Once I pushed them as far as I could go, I called for help.

"Michael, a hand?"

He looked my way and froze. His eyes were glued to my hips, and I was again reminded that he lived most of his life in isolation. I pulled my jacket down as far as I could, and his eyes snapped to my face. "Of course," he murmured, seemingly embarrassed. At least we were both uncomfortable with this.

Removing his hat, he ran his fingers back through his hair—it was long and scraggly and just as dark as his beard. "The fire's going . . . it will warm up soon."

A shiver ran through me, a physical reminder of the chill I'd momentarily forgotten. Michael walked over to the couch. Tenderly, he placed his hands on my shins. Even though I knew I was about to be in pain, his touch was surprisingly comforting. "This might hurt a little," he said.

I gritted my teeth in anticipation. "I know." Lying down flat, I pressed all my weight into my good leg and lifted the bad one.

Michael waited a moment, then gently pulled off my pant leg. In my head, it was going to hurt as badly as when I'd sprained it, but much to my relief, it wasn't as horrible as I'd imagined it would be. Once the pant leg was off, I let out a low, even breath.

"Good," Michael murmured. "One more, and we're done with this part." My other one required me to put more weight on my bad leg, but I found that if I moved onto my hip—while being careful to avoid the wound in my thigh—it was tolerable.

Once my pants were off, I sighed a prayer of thanks. Michael heard and gave me a quizzical look, but he didn't say anything about it. "I'm going to heat some water, clean this up so I can see how it's healing. Then we'll take a look at your ribs. In the meantime, I've got a little something for the pain."

I raised an eyebrow in question, and he smiled as he moved over to a long counter with deep shelves beneath it. Bending over, he started gathering supplies he'd need—a first aid kit he kept in a Rubbermaid tub, a thick gray blanket, and a bottle of whiskey. I had to assume that was what he'd meant for the pain.

A small laugh escaped me, but I snatched up the bottle when he lowered it to me. I'd been in pain for far too long; a small reprieve was just what I needed. Sitting up, I pulled the cork out of the bottle. Michael draped the blanket over my good leg, giving me some warmth while keeping my injured leg exposed. I was hesitant to look at my injury again and took a swig of the golden liquid instead. It burned, but I knew that burn meant eventual numbness, so I embraced it and took another one.

"Easy," Michael told me, heading over to the stove. "You don't want to make yourself sick." Grabbing a pot, he filled it with water from a five-gallon bucket in the corner and set it on the stove to warm.

Once the water was started, Michael opened the first aid kit. The amount of supplies he had in the tub was impressive. Living out here full time, he had to be prepared for everything.

"So how do you know how to do all this? Stitch people up, wrap ribs? Did you train as a survivalist before coming out here?" I asked, pointing at the bin. He had things in there that definitely weren't standard issue in a kit, including what looked like a scalpel and a small hand saw; I did *not* want to know what he might use those for.

Michael searched through the tub until he found a bag full of elastic bandages. "No, I'm a doctor. Or I was, before I came out here."

Surprise washed through me. "A doctor? Why . . . ?" Why would a doctor be out here alone in the woods?

He smiled as he stood to go check on the water. "Why did I become a doctor? I liked helping people." His voice grew quiet, and his eyes grew sad. Turning his back to me, he grabbed the pot of warm water, removing it from the stove.

Why he'd become a doctor hadn't really been my question, but his expression evaporated my original curiosity. Why would the thought of helping people make him look so full of . . . despair? And if he liked helping people, why was he living in isolation? All of those questions felt too rude to ask right now, so I stayed quiet.

Michael walked back over with the water, then flashed me an embarrassed smile like he was grateful I hadn't pried. Dipping a cloth into the pot, he started washing my skin. It was uncomfortable, especially around the stitches, but manageable.

I took another small sip of the whiskey, then pushed the cork back on and set the bottle down. A numb warmth was already beginning to envelop me, and Michael was right—I didn't want to overdo it and get sick. I knew from experience that vomiting with cracked ribs sucked.

Michael smiled when he was satisfied with how my stitches looked; I took that as a good sign. "Everything is okay?" I asked.

He nodded. "As far as I can tell, the branch didn't nick an artery. Your muscles will take time to heal, but the stitched skin is doing nicely. You'll just need to continue taking it easy, and that will be a lot simpler now that we're here."

Now that he was done with my thigh, his professional eye moved down to my ankle. He jostled and twisted it in a way that made me cringe. "You can stop that anytime," I snapped.

"Still sore then?" he said, letting go.

"Yeah."

"But you can move it on your own?"

"Yes, I just don't want to."

"Humor me," he said with a small smile.

I let out a groan worthy of a sullen teenager but did what he asked. It hurt less when I moved it, but it still didn't feel good. I had full mobility, though, so it probably wasn't broken.

"Good," Michael said. He carefully removed my sock; I bit my lip the entire time. Once my foot was free, he grabbed a wrap and began working it around my ankle. "This will help with support," he said, and I had to admit that when he was finished, it did feel better.

Once he was satisfied with my ankle, he smiled up at me. "Let's patch up your ribs, and then you should be good to go." His eyes stopped on my chest, and he awkwardly said, "I'll need you to . . . take that . . . off."

I crossed an arm over my chest. "Why do I have to be naked?"

A nervous laugh escaped him. "Just . . . your jacket."

Embarrassment washed through me. Of course he'd need my heavy jacket off to wrap my ribs. God, I was an idiot. Carefully unzipping the jacket, I slipped it off my shoulders and dropped it to the ground. I had multiple layers on underneath the jacket—a thin tank top and a long-sleeved Henley. I left both of them on as I lay down on the board beneath me, and then I slowly pulled them up as high as they would go. That would have to be good enough. Attractive doctor or not, I wasn't about to strip any further in front of a man who'd only had sporadic access to the opposite sex for years.

Michael was still staring at my chest. I was almost offended, until I realized he wasn't looking at my body—he was enraptured with the cross hanging around my neck. Again, he looked grieved. I wrapped my fingers around the necklace, and his eyes snapped to mine. He gave me a brief smile like he hadn't been staring. Then he reached into his bag for another roll of bandages.

Curious, I asked him, "Do you go to church? Or . . . did you, before you came out here?"

He frowned and studiously began unwrapping the tan, clingy fabric. "Once upon a time. I don't buy into all that anymore, though."

Sadness swelled in me. I knew a lot of people who had either never believed or who had stopped believing, and most of the time, it was grief that had caused the break. "I'm sorry."

His eyes flashed to mine; they were guarded now. "For what?"

"For whatever made you turn away." He averted his eyes, and unmistakable pain flashed over his face. It made me want to hug him and tell him everything was going to be okay, like he had with me earlier. "It's never too late to change your mind," I offered. "God loves finding lost sheep."

The pain was instantly replaced with anger. "I'm not lost. I don't want to be found—by him or anyone."

Anger was also a common response from people. And it, too, usually masked pain. "That's too bad," I said, trying to keep my voice light.

The airiness in my tone seemed to do the trick, and his anger faded. "That's debatable," he muttered, rolling his eyes.

"Most things are," I said with a smile. He rolled his eyes again and reached over to begin wrapping the bandage around me. I grabbed his hand, stopping him. "Even still, I'm sorry you lost your faith, Michael."

He opened his mouth, and for a moment, he looked like he wanted to start arguing again. But then the spark in his eyes faded, and he sighed. "Let's just get you patched up, okay?"

I nodded, then relaxed on the hard bench and let him get back to work. It was none of my business anyway.

Chapter Six

I was stiff and sore when I woke up the next morning. Michael had politely offered me his bed when we'd turned in for the night, but I hadn't felt right taking it, so I'd declined and slept on the hard bench-couch instead. It hadn't taken me long to realize it wasn't the most comfortable place to sleep, even using some of Michael's extra blankets for padding. But being in the cabin felt like a four-star hotel after my one-man tent, so I wasn't about to complain. As I carefully stretched, it was a relief to feel that my injuries were somewhat less painful than yesterday; my body was starting to repair itself.

The cabin was gray with the soft light filtering in through the front windows, and I could see Michael sitting on a kitchen chair, pulling on a boot. There was a fire crackling behind him, filling the room with a pleasant warmth. A cast-iron pan was resting on top of the stove, and something inside it was sizzling and crackling; the smell wafting from it made my stomach growl. It had been a while since I'd had more than dried meat and protein bars.

Noticing that I was awake, Michael walked over to me once his boots were on. "How are you feeling?"

I tried flexing my wrapped ankle but stopped when a slight spasm of pain went through me. "Better . . . but still not great."

He nodded, not too surprised. "Keep your leg up—try to stay off it."

His advice was good, and I knew that, but I hated the idea of just lying there while he did all the work. I'd gone on enough extended camping trips to know how much there was to do every day. The look he was giving me broached no objections, though. Sitting up, I smiled and told him, "Okay, Doc."

He immediately frowned. "Don't call me that. It's not who I am anymore." Like he knew he was being a bit rude, his expression softened, and he added, "Please, just call me Michael."

"Okay . . . Michael," I amended.

His smile was swift but appreciative. Nodding back at the fire, he said, "Breakfast is just about done. You almost slept through it."

"Yeah," I mumbled, nibbling on my lip. "Guess I was a little tired."

"Understandable—you went through a lot yesterday." His gaze drifted to the floor, and he almost looked guilty. "I'm sorry you were out there so long on your own. I really didn't think . . . I took an oath once to do no harm, yet I didn't come running the second I heard that plane go down. I assumed no one survived, and in doing so, I almost made my assumption a reality."

Knowing he was being too hard on himself, I started to stand so I could walk over to him. He instantly pointed at the couch, and I stayed put. I pursed my lips in protest for a second, but then I said what I'd been going to say. "You're not search and rescue. You weren't obligated to come check out the wreck. I'm just grateful you showed up at all."

His face instantly filled with remorse. "I only went because I needed a part for my plane. I wasn't . . ." He sighed as his voice trailed off.

I tried to think what I would do in his situation—isolated, out in the middle of nowhere. Would I have taken the time and energy to check out a lost cause? Yes. But I hadn't been through . . . whatever it was that Michael had been through. "It's okay if you're hesitant to help people. But when the chips were down, and it really mattered, you came through. You could have let the wolves kill me, but you saved my life."

He stared at me a moment, clearly in thought, and then he pointed at my necklace. "You think that distinction matters to the big guy? Think he's fine with me not wanting to help people?"

I shrugged. "I can't exactly answer for him. But . . . I know he'd forgive you. And if he can forgive you, maybe *you* should forgive you."

His eyes remained locked on mine for a moment longer; then he rolled them. "This is going to be a long winter," he mumbled. Then he turned back to breakfast.

When the meat was done sizzling, he pulled out a couple of plastic plates and loaded us up with what turned out to be little sausage patties. Then he made pancakes. God, I could get used to this. We were silent as we ate—him at the table, me on my bed—and I took the opportunity to look around. There were books on the bookshelf and animal trophies on the walls, but not much else in the way of decoration. No photos, no obvious mementos, nothing to clear up the mystery of who Michael had been before he'd decided to hide away in the woods. Maybe he was a wanted man, and that was why he lived so far from people. I didn't feel like I was in danger with him—he *had* saved my life, after all—but maybe there was darkness inside him that I hadn't seen yet. And considering the fact that I was trapped with him for the next several months, that was a chilling thought.

"So . . . where are you from?" I asked, trying to dislodge the image of the ax-wielding murderer that had just popped into my head.

Michael indicated the cabin with his fork. "Here. I thought that was obvious."

Now it was me who rolled my eyes. "I meant before here. Where did you live five years ago?"

He studied his plate as he pushed around a piece of pancake. "New York City."

His answer couldn't have surprised me more. New York was the exact opposite of where we were now—a concrete wilderness instead of a forested one. I'd kind of assumed he'd come from a place similar to this one, like maybe he'd chosen to live out here because this was what he was used to. "Oh . . . what made you come out here?"

He gave me a dismissive shrug. "I like the quiet." He looked up at me then like he was warning me to drop it.

With a swallow, I went back to my meal. "This is good . . . thank you."

"You're welcome," he murmured, relief clear in his voice.

I really wanted to ask him more about his previous life, but since he didn't seem to want to talk about it, I figured he probably wouldn't give me a straight answer. Most likely, I'd upset him if I pressed. And since there was a microscopic chance that he might be a serial killer, upsetting him seemed like a bad idea. Taking his not-so-subtle hint, I quietly finished my meal.

Michael cleaned up afterward, doing the dishes in a metal basin on the floor. I felt completely useless doing nothing but lying there while he worked, but I stayed where he'd asked me to stay. When he was done, he wiped his hands on his pants, then turned to face me. "I've got a bunch of stuff to do—collect water, wood, and most importantly, hunt. I hadn't planned on having two mouths to feed this winter, so I need to get some more meat put away. There's an outhouse on the side of the property, but if you can't make it, there's a bucket under the couch."

I lifted an eyebrow at that. I was *not* about to pee in a bucket that he would later dump for me. I wasn't a ninety-year-old woman in a nursing home. "I'll make it."

Not very successfully, he tried to hide a smile. Seeing it warmed something inside me, and I instantly knew that my swift, irrational fear of him being a murderer was completely off base. He wasn't an evil man, wasn't a criminal hiding from the law. He was just someone who'd come out here to be alone . . . for some reason.

After Michael left, I quickly grew bored. Lying still with nothing to do except stare at the log seams was enough to drive a person crazy. After a too-long trip to the outhouse, I rummaged through his books to help pass the time. He mostly had westerns. Not my favorite, but I was desperate for entertainment. Lying back down, I propped my leg up on a pile of blankets and got to reading.

I was halfway through a book about a group of reformed outlaws trying to save a town from a gang of thugs when Michael finally returned. He smiled when he saw me reading one of his books, and I was again struck with how soothing his grin was. "How was work?" I jokingly asked, setting the book down.

A brief laugh escaped him. "Good and bad."

"Oh, how so?" I asked, amused that he was playing along.

Scratching his beard of frost, he said, "Good because I shot a moose. Bad because I had to cut it up and drag the pieces back to camp. Then I had to prep it, store it . . . I'm a mess. I think it's a bath night. But on the bright side, we're having moose steaks for dinner."

That was when I noticed that his clothes and hands were stained red. Having hunted with my father before, I knew what a mess dissecting a meal was. It was easy to sympathize with wanting to feel clean after an ordeal like that. And man, a bath sounded amazing. I'd combed out my hair as best I could with my fingers, but it was greasy and dirty. Me too. But I had to wonder . . . how did one bathe in a cabin with no running water? And where exactly could he bathe here? I'd only ever taken a bath in a bathtub, and I didn't see one of those in the cabin. "And how does that work exactly?" I asked.

He pointed at the large basin he'd used as a sink this morning. "I heat up water, one pot at a time, until that's full. It takes a while, but it's just about the best thing on earth. Totally worth it." His grin suddenly turned massive, and my breath caught in my throat; he had such an amazing smile. His face still bright, he indicated my leg. "Once your stitches are healed enough to be removed, I can make one for you."

His smile infectious, I grinned too. "I'd love that. I feel disgusting."

He laughed at my comment. "I've seen worse," he said, then he winked at me. Immediately afterward, his smile fell, like he'd just realized what he'd done and felt weird about it. Before I could react, he grabbed a pot and headed to the corner of the room, where a few five-gallon buckets with lids were waiting. Water. Removing the lid from one of the buckets, he filled the pot, then returned to the stove and set the pot on the top.

While the water was warming, he dragged the large metal basin closer to the stove. My face felt flushed, and I wasn't sure if it was because of his mild flirting earlier . . . or because I'd suddenly realized that he was going to take a bath right in front of me. "Are you going to do that . . . here?"

A bit of his humor returned as he looked over at me. "You want me to freeze to death outside? It's easier and safer to do it in here. And so long as I don't dump the basin, it won't make too much of a mess."

Yep. He was going to strip and bathe in the middle of the room . . . with me watching him. "Do you have a curtain or anything?"

Clearly trying to keep a straight face, he shook his head. "No. I'll just have to trust you not to look."

Right. I could do that. I was a responsible, thoughtful, considerate, mature adult. And besides, if the tables were turned, he'd probably do the same for me. Because if he didn't, I'd toss him out into the snow.

I tried to return to my book as he began filling the tub with pots of steaming water, but it was getting darker outside, and the words were getting harder to make out. Michael lit a few candles for us, but the flickering light didn't help my eyes much. It just made everything in the room intimate, romantic, which didn't help the situation at all. Book now lying in my lap, my eyes were firmly glued on Michael when he put the final pot of near-boiling water into the basin.

He smirked at me as he set the empty pot down. "I'm gonna strip now, so you might want to look somewhere else."

It was hard to be respectful when curiosity was pounding on the door, but I forced myself to avert my eyes. I could do this. No problem. I heard rustling sounds as Michael removed his clothes and then a dull thump as he dropped the thick, heavy material onto the floor. My mind started picturing what I couldn't see—a sculpted chest lightly speckled with dark hair; hard, flat abs; biceps to die for . . .

It had been a while since I'd been in a room with a naked man. Just the thought of being engulfed in his masculinity was enough to start bringing dormant parts of my body back to life. This was *not* good. It was so difficult to resist sneaking a peek that I had to slap my hands over my eyes, especially when I heard the sound of water splashing against the sides of the tub. I pictured his lean, hard body slipping into the soothing heat, imagined the droplets clinging to his skin. Shock went through me when I realized my heart was beating faster. Why was this affecting me so much?

I tried focusing on something else—anything else—but right at that point, Michael let out a satisfied sound that was way too erotic for my mind's current state of revved-up hyperawareness. Shifting my body so my legs dangled over the side of the couch, touching the ground, I prepared to stand up. My eyes drifted to Michael as I moved. Fully in the tub now, the bulk of him was hidden. His head was lying back on the rim while his arms rested along the sides; his biceps were just as spectacular as I'd imagined.

Lifting his head, he frowned; his pale eyes seemed amused, though. "What are you doing?" he asked. The humor instantly shifted to caution, like he thought I might try to join him in that tiny tub, and he wasn't entirely thrilled about the idea. Given my brief fantasy about him, the mild rejection kind of stung.

"Need to pee," I muttered, standing.

Michael's hand shifted to point at something on the table. "Take a flashlight. And a pistol. You never know what might be waiting in the dark." Immediately after he said it, he put his hands on the side of the basin and shifted his weight like he was going to get up. "Maybe I should go with you."

Shielding my eyes, I told him, "I'm fine. I can handle peeing in the woods without an escort." What I couldn't handle was him standing in the tub, showing me all the delicious things I'd pictured. Jesus, what had I been saying earlier about being mature?

When I peeked over at Michael, I saw him relaxing back into the basin. A relieved sigh escaped me. Thank you, God. If he'd stepped out of the tub, I wouldn't have been able to stop myself from openly staring, and both of us would have been mortified. Possibly me more than him.

Michael had cut me a new stick to use as a crutch. He'd set it by the couch before leaving for the day so getting up and around—if I'd absolutely needed to—would be easier. Grabbing it from its resting place, I hobbled over to the table to pick up the flashlight.

I was on my way to get the pistol hanging on a holster attached to the wall when Michael's voice broke the silence. "Damn it . . ." When I looked back at him, he cringed. "I don't suppose you could do me a favor before you go?"

He was still mostly hidden from view, but now that I was in front of him, I could see the defined muscles of his chest. It was distracting, to say the least. "What?" I asked, annoyed at myself that I couldn't be in the same room with a naked man without having steamy thoughts about him.

Face still remorseful, he pointed to the long counter with shelves beneath it. "I forgot the soap. It's in one of those bins."

My hand tightened around the flashlight. I'd have to get really close to give it to him. Unless I just tossed it. A resigned sigh escaped me. No, I would be an adult and hand it to him. This was already awkward enough; no need to make it worse. Tossing on a smile that felt tight to me, I said, "Sure," and set about looking for the soap.

"And a washcloth," he added.

Gritting my teeth, I told him, "No problem," then shuffled over to the bins. With his help, I found everything quickly enough. Eyes downcast, I hobbled over to him. When I got close enough, I extended my hand in what I thought was his direction; even though resisting the temptation was torture, I still wasn't looking his way.

I felt his wet, warm fingers close over mine, and my eyes ignored my instructions and snapped to his. "Thank you," he quietly said as he pulled the cloth and soap from my grasp. His eyes were so captivating that even though I knew I'd only need to look down a few inches to see . . . everything . . . I couldn't. I was ensnared.

"You're welcome," I whispered. Then I spun on my heel and quickly limped away before I lost all control. And for once, the frigid air of the outdoors was welcome on my heated skin.

Chapter Seven

A couple of days after the bath incident, my ankle was finally strong enough to support my weight. I still had to be careful so I didn't accidentally reinjure it, but walking around on two legs instead of hobbling around on one was such a blessing.

It also gave me the opportunity to help out more. Something Michael objected to at first. "I've been handling doing everything around here for years. You should keep resting."

Crossing my arms over my chest, I told him, "No, I've rested enough. Now I need to start helping. You said it yourself that you hadn't planned on feeding two people this winter. You have more important things to do than collect water and chop firewood."

He looked like he wanted to keep arguing with me, but he knew as well as I did that I was right. I was needed outside helping, not inside slowly going stir crazy. "Okay, fine. I need to start setting traps anyway."

"Traps?" I asked, inclining my head.

He ran a hand through his thick beard as he nodded. "Yeah, I need cash for the supplies I buy a couple times a year. Selling fur and leather is about the only thing I can do to make money around here. I can't exactly open a pizza place."

"Or a doctor's office," I said with a smile.

His grin slipped at the mention of the word *doctor*, so I quickly changed the subject. "Anything I should know? Any words of wisdom?"

He walked over to me and handed me my rifle. "Keep this on you at all times. The bears might still be foraging for winter. They can be on you before you know it."

That was smart advice, one I followed when I went out to take photographs. Man, I would be almost halfway through my trip right now if my plane hadn't gone down. But now . . .

Michael was studying my face as I slung the rifle over my shoulder. "You okay? Your expression changed."

Knowing that his expression changed all the time and he rarely explained himself made me feel a little stubborn. I pushed the feeling away, though, and opened up to him. Maybe he would do the same if I set a good example. Or if he felt closer to me—and nothing had a way of binding people together like sharing pain. "I just . . . the thought of being out here for so long . . ." I stopped to sigh. "I just really miss my family."

His face grew contemplative. "I understand. This kind of life . . . isn't for everyone."

And why is it for you? I wanted to ask. Before I could, Michael said, "Do you have siblings? A brother or sister?"

I nodded as I thought of Patricia. "Yeah, one sister. She's a shrink, so she thinks it's perfectly acceptable to analyze people without their permission." Chewing on my lip, I wondered if that was what I was doing with him. It was mainly in my head, though. I hadn't pried when it was clear he hadn't wanted me to.

Michael's lip curved up in a small smile. "That explains a lot," he said.

Knowing I'd been as respectful as possible—even though I was swarming with questions—made me want to smack him. I refrained, but it took a lot of willpower.

"Are your parents still with you?" he asked as a follow-up.

Thinking of them made me smile. "Yeah, they run a diner in town. Have since I was a kid. I used to go there after school every day to help my mom. We'd make cookies and pies, and she'd let me pour coffee for the regulars. It was a fun way to grow up."

Michael's smile was warm at hearing my story. "What about you?" I asked. "Fond memories? Brothers? Sisters?"

His entire demeanor changed, hardened. I thought he'd ignore me or change the subject, but he surprised me by answering. "One parent . . . my father. He's still back in New York, as far as I know. Haven't spoken to him since I moved out here."

He sniffed and started gathering the supplies he'd need for the day. "Oh . . ." I said, carefully watching him. He seemed like a coil wound too tight. "You weren't close?"

Pausing in what he was doing, he quietly said, "We were once . . ." Clearing his throat, he shook his head. "But that was a long time ago. Things changed."

"What changed?" I timidly asked. So much for not being as intrusive as my sister.

Michael looked back at me. "When you get to the river, test the ice before you go on it. If the shelf breaks and you're swept under, you're never coming back up."

Knowing a dismissal when I heard one, I nodded. "Okay." I hoped he knew that I wasn't just telling him I understood his directions by my one-word answer. I also meant I understood his pain and his desire to keep it to himself.

After he was finished collecting his things, Michael headed to his shop to collect his traps. Since he didn't have a horse, dogsled, or snowmobile, he had to hold everything he took with him. I really thought that once he fixed his plane, he should invest in some sort of local transportation. It would help him so much with his everyday life. Mine, too, while I was out here.

Since I didn't feel overly confident on my feet yet, I took only one five-gallon bucket with me to collect water. I figured we'd need at least two each day, so I'd be making trips. Awesome. Every trudging step I took, I wished for a horse. Anything to help traverse the snow. Since Michael took this path every day, there was a trail cut into the snowbanks, but whenever more snow fell—like now—the trail was partially buried, easily hiding rocks, roots, branches. A hundred things that could trip me up, injuring me again.

When I finally got to the river, I let out a low whistle. It wasn't some small stream running through the backwoods. No, this was a massive highway of water, only partially frozen over. The edges, where the river was quieter, were the first to succumb to the ice. To gather the good stuff, I'd have to walk over that ice until I got to an open area. Then I had to dip the bucket in without also dunking myself. Because Michael was right. If I fell in and the current got me, finding a hole and dragging myself out of it before I ran out of air—or became hypothermic—would be an almost impossible task.

Collecting water wasn't new to me, but I'd never done it quite like this before. Usually, I'd just fill my small pot with snow and boil it. But Michael needed water for drinking, washing dishes, cleaning animals . . . bathing. He was here for the long haul, so everything was on a much bigger scale. Melting snow in the quantities he needed just wasn't feasible. As dangerous as an icy river could be, it was the best option.

I found a large branch along the bank that I could use to test the ice, and then I started making my way across. Every step caused a strange creaking sound somewhere along the shelf. It made my heart race, but the stick I was jabbing into the slick surface was being met by firm resistance, so I kept going. It was fine. I was safe.

Getting to the edge of the ice was the truly scary part. The light snowflakes falling through the air floated into the exposed areas and disappeared instantly, swallowed by the swiftly flowing river. That could be me, if I wasn't careful. I thoroughly tested the area to find where the firm parts stopped and the frail parts began. When I had a clear grasp of the breaking point, I got down on my knees and extended the bucket into the water. The frigid stream of liquid life quickly filled the bucket. Pulling it out, I set it on the ice bank, on a spot that I prayed was firm enough to support the weight. I stared at it for a solid ten seconds before I moved; if the ice cracked, I wanted it to crack around the bucket, and not around me. But the ice was holding, and everything looked good.

Carefully, I got to my feet, reached down, and picked up the bucket. That was when something small and furry darted across the ice in front of me. Startled, I backed up a step and dropped the bucket. The heavy container struck the ice with the force of a hammer, and I heard distinct cracking noises all the way around me. The bucket began tipping, the momentum of the sloshing water pulling it over. Then the ice broke around it, and it disappeared into the rushing water. Damn it!

My anger was short lived, though, as fear instantly took its place. The break wasn't stopping where the bucket had landed—it was racing toward me like a snake zipping along the desert. I backed up so fast I tripped over my own feet and stumbled to the ground. Only it wasn't ground—it was still ice. I was at least a half dozen feet from the safety of the shoreline. Like a thing possessed, the crack was still coming toward me. I wanted to yell at it, scream at it to leave me alone, but it wasn't an animal that could be reasoned with or intimidated. Nature was going to do what it wanted to do. You either adapted, or you died.

That morbid thought in mind, I started scrambling backward on my hands and feet like a crab. The ice disappeared into the water just seconds after I passed a spot. If it caught me, if it broke around me, I'd be swept away. And all because a stupid marten had surprised me. I needed to be more careful than that.

Finally, I felt something hard against my gloved hand, something stable—actual earth, not frozen water. I hoisted my body onto the bank, right as the last of the ice gave way. My boots dropped into the icy river, but I was able to pull them out with no real damage done. Lying back on the bank, I pulled in painful pants as I tried to calm down. That had been so close. Everything here was so close, like every corner held something even more dangerous than the last. Could I really make it all winter in these conditions? What choice did I have?

My chest ached, and my thigh burned, but I made myself get up. I still needed to fetch water. Just because I'd failed didn't mean I could choose not to do the task. That was one unfortunate thing about survival. Giving up wasn't an option.

Half the day was eaten up by the time I had two full five-gallon buckets back at camp, luckily with no more near-death instances and no more missing buckets. Sadly, I'd have to tell Michael I'd lost one. There was no resting once the water was collected, though. No, there were still chores that had to be done before the daylight faded completely; firewood didn't chop itself. After grabbing a quick meal of my final bit of jerky and my last protein bar, I grabbed an ax and got to work on the pile of rounds that Michael hadn't had a chance to split yet.

I was only a few swings in when I instantly regretted offering to help today. I'd forgotten how labor intensive splitting wood was. Each swing was torture on my already-tired body—my chest burned, my ribs ached, my thigh throbbed, my ankle felt wobbly, and my arms felt like Jell-O. I couldn't quit, though. Besides the fact that it needed to be done, I'd told Michael I would do it, and even if my stitches burst, I was going to follow through. At least this was less dangerous than collecting water.

Once I had enough cut pieces that I felt okay stopping for the day, I started stacking the wood in Michael's handmade lean-to off the side of his shop. My breaths were fast, and I was dripping with sweat—sweat that was starting to freeze to my skin. The way my body was shivering, I was sure it wasn't just fatigue that was getting to me. Grabbing as large an armful of wood as I could, I made my way back into the cabin to warm up.

I put away the wood, then quickly made a fire, stoking it until the cabin was nice and toasty. Once it was warm enough inside, I took off my jacket and my long-sleeved outer shirt so they could dry. I'd have to wash my clothes soon. I'd have to wash *me* soon. Everything was coated in grime and filth. Disgusting.

After setting a large pot of water on the stove to boil, I debated what to do next. Even though every part of me ached, I was reluctant to sit down; I might not stand again. I could start dinner—that would be helpful. Although I had no idea when Michael would be back from his hunting and trapping expedition. It could be minutes, could be hours, and I had no reliable way to keep his meal warm. It would be best to just wait for him. So what could I do to pass the time?

Sighing, I looked around the cabin. I could grab another western. The one I'd finished hadn't been so bad. Walking over to his bookcase, I started studying the spines for something that looked interesting. While Michael had quite a few titles to choose from, at this pace, I'd blow through them all long before we could leave. Not finding anything I wanted to read at the moment, I started looking through his shelves instead. Most of his bins held supplies, practical items that were essential for survival. Aside from the books, there wasn't much in the cabin that gave any hints about Michael's personality. It was frustrating. Feeling rather intrusive, I looked through bin after bin after bin, but still, nothing of interest. No mementos, no journals, no photo albums documenting a previous life. Nothing. It was like he hadn't existed before he came out here. I wouldn't even have suspected he'd once been a doctor if he hadn't told me.

Just when I was about to give up on my passive-aggressive snooping, I found something in the very bottom of a bin containing warmer-weather clothes. It was a photograph of a woman, stapled to a Ziploc bag holding a pair of rings. Wedding rings. My eyes widened in surprise as I stared at the woman in the photo. She was very beautiful with a warm, welcoming smile; dark hair; and eyes that were the same pale shade as his. I'd almost think she was Michael's sister if it weren't for the rings. She was obviously his wife. Why wasn't she here with him? Messy divorce? I'd gotten lucky with mine; Shawn had been pretty reasonable about everything, but I knew that wasn't the typical experience. Was that why Michael was hiding out here? Still in love with his ex? The one who got away . . .

I could hear rustling outside, boots stomping on the ground to loosen the snow on them, and knew Michael had finally returned. Shoving the photograph into the bottom of the bin, I closed the lid and slid it back into place on the shelf. Humiliation and embarrassment rushed through me. I shouldn't have been searching through his personal belongings; it wasn't any of my business. Spying on the man who'd saved my life was no way to thank him. But that photo had ignited my curiosity, and it was killing me now. Was that woman his wife—had she driven him to live out here? Did she know he was out here all alone, isolating himself from everyone? Would she return for him one day?

I hoped so. Michael seemed like a nice-enough guy; he didn't deserve to have to spend his entire life alone. Even if that was what he thought he wanted, I was sure it wasn't. Loneliness was crushing; that was why isolation was used to torture people. And no one *wanted* to be tortured. No one.

Chapter Eight

All through dinner I wanted to ask Michael about the photo and the rings. I had to stop myself from doing it about a hundred times. There was just no good way to explain how I'd found them other than saying, *I was totally spying on you while you were gone*. All I'd get from him was irritation or anger if I mentioned that. I might even spend a night out in the cold. Well, maybe not, but I was sure he wouldn't be happy.

"How did your chores go?" he asked as he cut up his moose steak. "Any problems?" By the way he raised an eyebrow at me, I felt like he had cameras stashed in the woods and he'd somehow witnessed my near debacle.

Feigning nonchalance, I shrugged and shook my head. "Nope, no troubles. Everything was fine. Easy peasy."

He stopped chewing at that, and I knew I'd gone a little too far with my casual answer. I wasn't about to admit how hard it had been, though; I'd tell him about losing the bucket later. Trying to move along the moment, I grabbed my glass of water and asked him, "Any problems on your end?"

With a smile that stirred something deep inside me, he shook his head. "Nope. Easy peasy."

His remark made me grin. Michael's humor was elusive at times, but when it seeped out, it lit up the whole room. I again wanted to ask him about the photo, but I was still blocked by the unlawful way I'd obtained it. As I chewed on my dinner, I tried to think of vaguer ways I could ask the same question.

"My ex-husband, Shawn, was a hunter. He brought back an elk once. Wasn't near as tasty as this." I gave Michael an appreciative smile, and he smiled back. Knowing I'd opened the door, I continued to walk right on through it. "Shawn and I were only married a year. Turned out being married didn't suit us. We were much better as friends." Although Shawn tended to forget that. Clearing my throat, I quickly asked Michael, "What about you? Ever been . . . married?" I wanted to cringe after the question left my lips. To me, it seemed so obvious why I was asking. It didn't seem possible that Michael wouldn't know what I'd done, what I'd found.

He chewed on his steak silently, his eyes glued on his plate. Just when I thought he was simply going to ignore me, he swallowed his food and quietly said, "Once. But that was a while ago."

"Oh . . . what happened? Didn't suit you either?" I added a laugh to try to lighten the mood; the cabin suddenly felt stifling.

Michael's eyes slowly lifted to mine. His expression was blank, but then he smiled. "Yeah, something like that." Pushing away his plate, he stood up. "I should check your stitches. It might be time for them to come out."

I sighed as he walked my way. Having stitches removed sounded just as bad as having them put in. "Is this going to hurt?" I asked.

He worked his bottom lip before answering me. "It's going to be . . . uncomfortable, but it shouldn't hurt too badly."

Too badly. Great. While he grabbed a flashlight, I pondered his answer to my marriage question. I wasn't an expert on human psychology like my sister, but it hadn't seemed like an honest response to me. It was deflection, a safe way to avoid opening up to a complete and total stranger. At least he'd admitted to being married. That was something, and I felt fractionally closer to him as he knelt beside my chair.

Wishing I had his bottle of whiskey in hand, I watched him undo the threadwork from when he'd sewn up my pants. "I could have just taken them off," I murmured.

He looked up at me with a half smile on his face. "It will give me a chance to practice my stitching again when I sew them back up. You'd be surprised at how little I get a chance to practice out here."

With a shrug, I said, "If you came back to the city, you could practice all you wanted."

Even as I said it, I knew I shouldn't have. His expression immediately hardened, although his eyes flashed with pain. "Going back isn't in the cards for me."

I wanted to know why, but I felt like I'd probed him enough today. Sticking the end of his flashlight into his mouth, he opened the hole in my pant leg wide enough to check out my healing wound. His lips curled into a smile around the light, a promising sign. Popping it out of his mouth, he looked up at me. "They look good. Let's pull them out."

My heart immediately started pounding. "What's this *let's* stuff? I'm fine if they stay in forever."

Michael stood up with a laugh. "You won't be when the skin grows over them and they get infected. I don't have dissolving thread, so what goes in must come out."

I sighed again as I watched him get the supplies he needed. Mainly gloves, a pair of scissors, and a gauze pad. For blood. Awesome. When he came back to my leg, he handed me the flashlight. "Do me the honor?" he asked, his voice playful.

Who knew he only needed surgery to turn his mood around. Made me wonder why he'd stopped being a doctor, why he'd stopped wanting to help people. As he propped my leg up on a chair, I held the light over the area. I wanted to close my eyes as he leaned in, but I had to focus the spotlight for him. Right before he touched the scissors to my leg, he glanced up at me. "You'll be fine, Mallory. Just breathe."

Doing what he said, I inhaled deeply. The cool metal touched my leg, and I flinched. It didn't hurt as he cut the thread—it just felt odd—but then he started pulling the threads out. The tugging was uncomfortable but tolerable, just like he'd said it would be, but occasionally the thread would stick on something. That downright sucked. I hissed in breath after breath, trying to endure the discomfort. When he tugged on a particularly stubborn one that clearly wanted to be a part of me forever, I let out a nasty curse.

Michael's eyes flashed to my cross necklace, an amused smile on his face. "Shouldn't you not do that?" he asked. "Given your faith and all."

My fingers were holding the flashlight so tight my knuckles were white. "If I were perfect, I wouldn't need God's help, would I?" I said through clenched teeth.

"Yeah, I suppose that's true," he murmured, his face suddenly thoughtful.

He was quiet as he finished tormenting me. Just when I couldn't take another second, when I was about to push him away and make a run for it, he sat back on his heels. "All done."

Letting out a relieved breath, I looked down at my wound. The skin was puckered, irritated, and slightly smeared with blood, but it was holding together without the stitches. Considering that the stitches hadn't been done in a hospital, the healing wound looked really good. "Wow, that looks great. Thank you," I told him, my smile full of appreciation.

Michael's gaze was locked on my lips; then he turned away before sheepishly glancing at my eyes. "It was nothing," he said, starting to stand. I grabbed his hand to stop him from leaving. His fingers were rough from years of hard work but surprisingly warm and comforting too.

"No, it was huge. I probably wouldn't have survived without you, so . . . thank you. For everything."

I held his hand and his gaze until he acknowledged my gratitude. With an uncomfortable nod, he finally said, "You're welcome," and I let his hand drop. I instantly missed the connection.

Michael cleared his throat and ran his fingers through his shaggy hair. He indicted my leg. "I can put a bandage on that, unless . . . you want to take that bath now?"

The air was thick with some kind of tension—awkwardness, nervousness, embarrassment, attraction—I honestly wasn't sure. Maybe it was a mixture of all of it. The thought of undressing in this emotionally charged environment made my skin pebble with anxiety, but . . . a bath. I'd give just about anything to feel clean again. "A bath, please . . . that sounds like heaven."

He smiled, then nodded. "It really is."

He held gazes with me again, his small grin making my chest tighten. Then he blinked and turned around to start preparing the water. My heart was beating harder than it should have been, and the feeling of tension in the air didn't die once we weren't looking at each other. It was like an electric charge was zinging around the room, building in power instead of diminishing. If I mentioned it, maybe it would dissipate without exploding; things had a way of self-correcting when exposed to the light. But I wasn't sure if I wanted the feeling to end, and I definitely didn't want the embarrassment that would come from talking about it, so I stayed quiet while Michael boiled pot after pot of water.

When the basin was full of steaming liquid, Michael indicated the door. "I'll step outside. Holler if you need me."

I hated the thought that I was chasing him away, but I appreciated the privacy he was offering. "What are you going to do out there?" I asked.

He shrugged, looking uncomfortable. "I don't know . . . chop some wood for tomorrow."

A frown curved my lips. "I already chopped some." And I planned on chopping more in the morning. He had his tasks, and I had mine, and maybe we'd only been doing it for one day, but I thought it was working. Why was he changing it up? I thought I'd done well, all things considered, but maybe he disagreed?

Michael sighed like he knew he was stepping on my toes. "I'm not trying to steal your chore. I just—I need something . . . physical to do."

His eyes flashed down my body, and I suddenly understood. I had to assume it had been a while since Michael had been with a woman, and now one was about to be naked in his cabin—*I* was about to be naked in his cabin—and the thought of that was making him antsy; he needed to blow off some steam with backbreaking labor. My reaction to him taking a bath had been similar. As soon as I could, I'd run out of the cabin just as swiftly as my injured leg had allowed. I was affecting him just like he'd affected me. That thought made me surprisingly warm all over; my cheeks felt like glowing coals.

I stared at his shoes, just in case he could tell I was flushed. Then I peeked up at him. "Before you go . . . do you have a razor I could borrow?"

His expression morphed into one of confusion and intrigue. "A razor? Why do you . . . ?" His gaze drifted to my leg, still propped on the chair. Setting it on the ground, I slowly stood up.

I shrugged as I faced him. "I know it's silly and frivolous, it's just . . . everything in my life right now is so different. I want to hold on to some small shred of normalcy. I want to feel like I'm still me . . . like I'm still a woman."

Homesickness swelled in me, making my voice warble and my vision hazy. I'd never felt this out of sorts on any of my trips before. But then again, before now, I'd always had the option of going home whenever I wanted. I'd never been stuck in a survivalist situation with a stranger before. And while Michael was attractive, sometimes alluringly mysterious, and exceedingly generous and gracious . . . he wasn't family. He wasn't home.

I was staring at the floor, but I could hear Michael's footsteps as he approached me. In my fragile state, I was hyperaware of his nearness. The woodsy scent of pine on him, the way his breaths were smooth and even, the way his hand started lifting to me before dropping to his side. I wasn't sure just what I wanted from him, but I suddenly didn't want him to leave just yet.

His voice was soft when he finally spoke. "It's not silly or frivolous." I looked up to see him smiling warmly at me. "You didn't ask for this life—not like I did. And while you've made the best of everything that's been thrown at you, I don't blame you for wanting a little piece of comfort. Why do you think I have the whiskey?" he added with a wink.

That familiar look of unease washed over him, but it quickly morphed into a regular, untroubled smile. "I'll get you a razor and some soap, but you get to wash all the tiny hairs out of the tub when you're done."

He pointed at me with a playfully stern finger, and I laughed at the look of mock indignation on his face. "Deal."

We stared at each other for a second then, and I was struck by an overwhelming urge to hug him; I even almost took a step toward him, but somehow, I knew that if I did, he would get uncomfortable and turn to leave, and I just wasn't ready for the connection to end.

Eventually, though, I had to break the silence. "Thank you, Michael."

Clearing his throat, he averted his eyes. "You thanked me already . . . but you're welcome." Looking back at me, he indicated the tub. "The water doesn't stay warm for long—you should get in. I'll get your stuff."

Then he was gone, moving around the cabin, gathering supplies. He left them at the edge of the tub, then disappeared into the darkness of the night. The cabin felt colder without him in it, and a weary sigh escaped me. It was so odd to be holed up with a stranger, but . . . it had its moments too.

Shaking my head at the peculiarity of my life, I peeled off my clothes and then carefully stepped into the tub. And just as I'd predicted, it was heaven.

Chapter Nine

As time went on, Michael and I settled into a nice routine. He stayed busy shoring up our food supply, while I chopped an impressive amount of wood. My body was getting stronger every day. Actually, aside from my ribs, I felt pretty good. My ankle was fine, and my thigh didn't even ache anymore. I almost felt normal, and it was wonderful to feel that way.

Things with Michael were getting better too. We were getting more and more comfortable around each other, not that that stopped the awkward, tense moments. We were just able to bounce back from them more quickly. Although bath nights were still strange for both of us.

It had been almost two weeks since the crash, a fact I still found hard to process sometimes. I should be packing up to go home, but instead, I was hunkering down for the winter with a man I barely knew. Getting through the homesickness was an hour-by-hour task at times. But there was a light at the end of the tunnel—Michael would eventually fix his plane, and I would eventually be able to get in it and go back to my pets, my friends, and my family. I just had to be patient, something that was difficult when there were few mental distractions during the day and even fewer distractions at night; home seemed to be on my mind twenty-four seven.

"You seem quieter than usual. Everything all right?" Michael asked. He was on his knees beside the metal basin we used as a sink and a tub, cleaning up our dishes from dinner. Whenever I saw the tub now, I pictured him in it, arms on the sides, head resting against the back. It was an image that stirred something inside me and made me incredibly uncomfortable, all at the same time.

"Yeah," I said. I was doing my part to clean up for the night by sweeping a floor that didn't seem to get any cleaner, no matter how many times I brushed it with the broom. "Just thinking about winter . . . about being here." Not wanting him to feel offended by that in any way, I quickly added, "Does it get bad? Lots of snow?"

He paused in his cleaning to study me. "It can. The snow can come down so hard sometimes I can't even go outside. I had to dig my way out once." He said it with a smile, like it was funny. Being trapped, nearly buried alive by snow, didn't sound humorous to me. Maybe realizing he was freaking me out, he raised his hands. "I'm sure it won't be that bad this year. It was a pretty mild fall."

I knew from experience that using the previous season as a reference wasn't a reliable way to forecast the weather, but I appreciated the attempt to reassure me. "What do you do when you can't . . . do anything?"

Michael scratched his scraggly beard, and I wondered if he'd let me cut it; it was long past out of control. "I read a lot. Play games—chess, cribbage, checkers . . . poker." A short laugh escaped him. "To be perfectly honest, I'm kind of looking forward to snow days this winter. It's going to be a lot more fun playing games against someone else for a change, although I should warn you, I can be a sore loser."

His comment made me smile; my sister had once accused me of being petulant after she won the fifth straight game of Chutes and Ladders. To this day, I swear she cheated. "So can I," I told him. "This should be interesting."

Michael was smiling as he went back to cleaning dishes. As I aimlessly swept the floor, I found that a part of me was almost eager for those lazy winter days when there was nothing to do because nothing could be done. But just as the anticipation swept through me, a sobering thought cooled me. My arrival had jacked up Michael's plan for the winter, and he'd gotten a late start in making the proper adjustments. Would he be able to do enough before the heavy storms hit?

"Do you think we'll have enough food?" I asked, biting my lip. He'd be fine here if it weren't for me crashing his party. I hated the thought of him starving to death because he'd saved my life. Of course, I wasn't excited over the idea of *me* starving to death either. I wanted both of us to come out of this in one piece—happy and healthy.

Drying a clean dish, Michael threw on a carefree smile. A very calculated carefree smile. "Hunting has been good to me lately, so as long as that keeps up before the weather turns, we'll be fine."

Even though he was trying to disguise it as good news, he was basically telling me "maybe." I tried to take solace in the fact that Michael had been living here for a while now, so he knew what it took to survive. He knew how to hunt and where to hunt—plus he had an almost superhuman amount of drive and willpower. He wouldn't stop until we had what we needed. We would get through the next few months. We would be fine.

Months . . . a quarter of a year. It sounded so long when clumped together in a block of time like that. It made me think of everything I'd be missing. Winter meant the holidays—Thanksgiving, Christmas, New Year's. It was a time when you were supposed to be home, wrapped in blankets, sipping hot chocolate, and chatting with loved ones. But now . . . everyone would be worried, sad, and scared. There would be a hole in the family get-togethers this year, a hole that no amount of turkey could fill.

Thinking of my family mourning me made me tear up. Would Mom still bake? Would Dad still complain about the price of Christmas trees? And what about my dogs? Patricia had cats, so they couldn't live with her. When it became clear that I wasn't coming home, would someone take them in? So they weren't alone *all* the time? And what about my home? My mortgage? My mail? My bills? What about . . . life? Would my family take care of everything I'd left . . . unfinished?

Not wanting to worry or cry, I slapped on a smile and asked Michael, "I don't suppose you have any turkeys or hams in your stores? Something we could carve for Christmas?" Saying the holiday out loud made a surprising wash of sadness sweep over me, almost pulling away my forced grin.

Michael seemed to sense I was barely holding it together and looked truly apologetic. "Sorry, no . . . plenty of deer, though. And a couple rabbits. And scores of potatoes." He grinned like that was great news. And it was. It might not be stuffing and pumpkin pie, but it was better than death.

"I guess that will have to do," I said, my smile finally feeling genuine.

While my expression brightened, Michael's suddenly fell. "I'm so sorry you have to miss the holidays with your family this year." He gave me a weak half smile. "At least you'll get to be with them next year."

That was surprisingly comforting, but yet sad too. I'd be going back home, but Michael would be here alone. That didn't seem right. Holidays were meant to be spent with people, not alone. "Yeah, unless I come back to visit you," I told him, only half joking.

He gave me an odd look, like he wasn't sure if I was serious or not, and for a second, I wasn't sure if I was kidding. Maybe I could come see him for the holidays next year, just so he wasn't by himself. But no . . . it wasn't feasible to fly out here during the thick of winter. I'd crash again or worse. Holiday visits . . . just weren't possible. And besides, my plane was a pile of scrap metal. I wouldn't be flying anytime soon.

A strange expression crossed Michael's face. He was smiling, but there wasn't any joy in it. "Yeah . . . sure," he said, and I knew he was well aware that it would never actually happen. He would be alone next Christmas; there was no getting around that.

I was just about to tell him that maybe I could visit during the summer instead, in a couple years when I had a plane again, but before I could speak, we both heard a loud clatter outside. Michael instantly snapped to his feet, his face intently focused as he listened for further sounds of trouble; he had no human neighbors to speak of, so things were generally silent here.

Fearful curiosity was killing me, and I was dying to ask him if he knew what was out there, but I didn't want to disrupt his concentration. And it turned out I didn't need to ask. Seconds later, I heard the deep, resonant, unmistakable growl of a bear. Shit.

Michael turned my way, his expression serious. "Stay here."

He grabbed his high-powered hunting rifle, and my heart started thudding. Was he nuts? If there was a hungry bear out there, we should be barricading the cabin, not going out into the wilderness. "What do you think you're doing?"

Lips twisted in a frown, he told me, "All our food is out there, our meat. If I let the bear destroy it, we'll have nothing to get us through the winter."

I knew he was right, but still, I was terrified. "Okay . . . I'll help." Setting down the broom, I grabbed my gun and checked it for bullets. It wasn't as powerful a rifle as Michael's, but it might hurt the bear enough that it would change its mind about gorging on our food stash. Or it might just piss it off.

Studying my gun, Michael shook his head. "No, stay in here—guard the cabin."

His answer made me frown. "The bulk of the food isn't in here. There's nothing to guard."

His eyes softened then. "Yes . . . there is something to guard."

My cheeks heated when I realized he meant me. "Be careful," I whispered.

"Always am," he stated; then he darted out the door.

Racing to the window, I peered outside, searching in vain for some sign of Michael or the bear. The moonlight wasn't strong enough to illuminate much, and even though only candles were lit in the cabin, it was enough to wreck my night vision; I couldn't see a damn thing out there. My nerves spiked, and my heart started racing. I felt like I was out there in the woods, possibly about to get mauled, and following Michael's orders and staying put grew harder and harder with every second.

I strained my ears, listening for the bear since I couldn't see it. Sounds of lumbering steps crashing through brush met my ear. Then I heard the dreadful sound of sharp claws raking down wood. With no electricity, freezers weren't an option here. Michael stored his food the old-fashioned way, either drying it into jerky or curing it with salt. The prepared food was kept in his enclosed workshop, and while Michael had bear proofed the shop as much as possible, hungry bears were tenacious. With food being so close to its reach, the grizzly might not stop until it had ripped the door to shreds.

Knowing where the bear was outside calmed my nerves somewhat. I fingered my rifle, debating whether running out there would help Michael or hurt both of us. It was dark, and if Michael thought I was inside, he could shoot me just as easily as the bear. And verbally warning him would get the bear's attention—attention I'd rather not have. No, it would be best to stay put and let Michael handle it. But still . . . that was hard to do.

I heard Michael shout then, yelling at the bear to leave. A gunshot rang through the night, startling small nocturnal animals and rattling the windowpanes. Another one followed shortly after, and fear trickled down my spine. Was that a warning shot? Or was the bear attacking?

Michael wasn't shouting anymore, and the night was still, silent. Oh God, no . . . The ball of dread in my belly was too great to ignore, and I nearly tripped in my haste to get to the door. "Michael!" I screeched into the night as I flung the door wide.

A dark shape was suddenly right in front of me, and as I stared in shock, a gaping mouth of thick, sharp teeth opened, and a powerful roar pushed me back a step. I'd never been so close to a bear before, and my legs felt like water. I couldn't move them, couldn't move anything. My mind was trying to avoid the here and now by drifting off to happier times with my family, my friends. Death was once again staring me in the face, but even still, the part of me that was cognizant of the present was awed and amazed by the ferocious beauty of the beast before me. There was a reason these creatures ruled the forest.

The bear rose up on its hind legs, visually warning me that it was bigger, stronger, and most likely hungrier. My eyes flashed to the various weapons it could use in an instant to end me—talonlike claws, ice pick–like teeth, or just its massive weight. All I had was a gun.

Thinking of my own weapon jostled me from my state of panic. Raising the barrel, I chambered a bullet and yelled at the bear to back off. It seemed a poor tactic at this point, but I didn't really want to kill the animal. If I could scare it into submission, I'd take that as a win.

The bear, however, was unimpressed by my shouting. Landing heavily on its front feet, it began lumbering toward me. Damn it, I was going to have to shoot. And hope my gun did more than anger it. With shaking fingers, I lined up my shot. "Please go away," I murmured, putting light pressure on the trigger.

Like it heard me, the bear suddenly looked to its left. It growled again and took a step back, away from the cabin. I heard Michael's voice, and then a gunshot rang out in the night. The bear roared again, then seemed to realize it was outmatched. It turned and ran, its winter bulk vibrating with each thundering step.

I was still shaking as Michael stepped into view. Disengaging the gun, I dropped it on the ground and flew over to him. Before I knew it, my arms were around his neck, and I was pulling his firm body into mine. Thank God he was okay. Thank God *I* was okay.

"Oh my God, Michael," I murmured into his shoulder, inhaling his woodsy scent. "That was terrifying. I thought for sure . . ."

Once I fully comprehended that I was squeezing the life out of him, I froze, every limb rigid with tension. I wasn't sure if Michael would push me away or not, but then he surprised me by wrapping an arm around my waist and pulling me into him just as hard as I was holding him, maybe harder. As we held each other, the anxiety and fear started easing, and I was flooded with warmth; I'd never felt more at peace.

Michael broke the connection by stepping back so he could look at me. "I told you to stay in the cabin," he scolded.

"I did!" To prove my point, I indicated my gun, still in the cabin where I'd dropped it. It wasn't my fault the bear had tried to enter.

Michael pursed his lips. "You scared me half to death," he said, his voice tight with an emotion that hadn't been there the first time he'd saved my life.

"I did?" I whispered, a little mystified by how much things had changed in such a short amount of time. Did I matter to him now?

His eyes flitted over my face before shifting to the ground. "Of course," he muttered. "I'm trying to keep you alive . . . to get you back to your family . . ."

For the first time ever, the thought of going home saddened me a little. Or maybe it was the look on Michael's face. His fear had stemmed from more than just his desire to keep me living: I was sure of it. He liked having me around. He liked the comfort, the companionship, the help around the cabin. No matter how hard he tried to convince me—and himself—Michael didn't really want to be alone. I was positive of that. And a part of me . . . liked being here too. I enjoyed spending time with Michael, and I enjoyed helping him. I liked how he made me feel—like we were equals, teammates . . . partners. I felt . . . free with him.

"Michael," I said, my voice feeling weak. "I was worried about you too. I thought for sure when you stopped yelling that the bear had . . ."

Swallowing, I couldn't speak my dire assumption or my relief that it hadn't been true. I felt like I was drowning in the feelings that were swelling between us.

Clearing his throat like he was suffering from his own emotional rollercoaster, Michael indicated the cabin. "Well, we're both okay, so we should go back inside." I nodded, and Michael sighed. "That bear might come back, though, so we'll have to stay sharp until it hibernates."

I really hated the thought of having to go through this night after night. Hopefully, we'd startled the bear enough that it would search for goods elsewhere; otherwise I might have an aneurism before winter hit.

Chapter Ten

The next several nights, I was a nervous wreck. I kept hearing things that weren't there—crashing in the woods, growling in the night air. Whenever I went outside, I felt like I was being hunted; it was not a comforting feeling.

"You don't need to be worried, Mallory; the bear won't act out of spite or hatred. That's just one of many reasons why animals are better than people." He grinned at me after he said that, like his words were comforting, but the official start of winter was still a few weeks off, so we weren't in the clear yet. Maybe seeing that I still wasn't cheered by the news, Michael shrugged and added, "It will either make another attempt on the food, or it won't. Stressing about it won't solve anything."

I knew he was right, and I knew we had a lot of work to do before winter struck full force, so I tried to push the fear from my mind and focus on the task at hand. "Okay, so remind me again what we're doing way out here? Besides being potential bear bait, of course."

He rolled his eyes at my comment, and I felt my worry lifting at seeing his humor. "We're felling trees for firewood."

Now I rolled my eyes. "I understand that, but why are we doing it way out here?" We'd walked at least a mile to get to this spot, and considering we didn't have transportation, we'd have to walk the wood all the way back to camp. "Your place is surrounded by trees. Why not just chop up one of those?"

Michael stopped and stared at me with a contemplative expression. "That's my yard," he finally said. "I want it to look nice."

My jaw dropped; then a laugh escaped me. "I can't believe you're worried about aesthetics when you don't have any neighbors."

He lifted his chin, his pale eyes defiant. "I have myself . . . and I have you."

That made me pause. *He has me?*

A flush of color brightened Michael's cheeks, and he immediately averted his eyes. "You know what I mean," he muttered.

Something warm and pleasant flooded through me as I watched him walk over to a clump of trees and begin to inspect them. I might only be visiting Michael for a short time, but he was already claiming me. I loved that he was, but it filled me with a foreboding sense of sadness too. All of this was temporary. Then Michael would be alone again. And in a way, I would be too.

As Michael began to swing his ax into the far side of one of the trees, biting deep into the wood, I thought of all the things I did for him now that he would have to do himself once I was gone. "Have you ever thought of a chainsaw?" I asked him. "Or a snowmobile? Four-wheeler? Bobcat? Something to help make your life a little easier?"

He paused in his work to look over at me. "Of course. But I spent all my money getting out here. All that stuff is a luxury I can't afford right now. It's on my wish list, though." Chuckling to himself, he began swinging at the tree again. It was going to take us a couple of days to get all the wood back to the cabin. Maybe longer. He should seriously consider making his wish list more than a wish. But if there wasn't money, then there wasn't money. There wasn't much he could do about not having enough.

It began to lightly snow while Michael was working, and I half-heartedly watched the lazy flakes as they drifted to the ground. Just a couple of days short of three weeks . . . that was how long I'd been stuck here. It seemed both longer and shorter; time had a funny way of fluctuating around Michael. Nick would just be beginning to worry about me, since I hadn't returned to his place with the plane. He'd wait a few more days, and then he'd inform my parents that I hadn't come back. Then everyone would start worrying.

Everyone would be in a panic . . . just in time for Christmas. God . . . Christmas. Like most families, it was a huge event for us. Since we all lived in the same small town, we saw each other frequently during the holidays. Mom would have us over for dinner at least two to three times a week. Patricia and I would go shopping for everyone together. Shawn would swing by with a jug of spiked eggnog. Patricia and I would help Mom and Dad find the perfect tree for their house; even though we'd hadn't lived with them in a while, it was one tradition we both hadn't been able to give up. We even helped them decorate their house. Of course, that was because Mom bribed us with sugar cookies.

Mom was a pro when it came to decorating cookies. She had a glass case in the diner where she would display all of her works of art, and customers would stand around, admiring her confections. Patricia and I hadn't quite developed Mom's decorating skills yet, but we were getting there. I made a damn cute Christmas tree.

Thoughts of trees and cookies made my mind spin with memories. I could nearly smell the pine and cinnamon, nutmeg and vanilla. The holidays always smelled so good. And tasted so good. And felt so good. It killed me to know I was going to miss it.

A sharp crack resounded through the woods as the huge tree Michael was chopping began to disconnect from its roots. A low groaning sound emanated from the base, and then the top of the tree began rushing to the earth. Branches snapped off as they smacked against other trees nearby. Michael stepped back, ax held loosely in his hands. His breath, frosty in the cold, was heavier after the exertion of chopping the tree. There was a small smile on his lips, though; he loved this stuff.

Michael's grin widened as he looked back at me. "That should keep you busy for a few weeks."

His comment reminded me of my earlier thought. "A couple weeks . . . Christmas."

Expression softening, Michael walked over to me. "Right . . . I almost forgot." After a short sigh, he shook his head. "It will get easier once the day passes. I promise."

The light snow collected in his beard, dusting his lips as he spoke. It was clear by the look on his face that he understood what I was going through, and it made me wonder if this time of year made him miss his family too. Michael didn't seem too close to his dad anymore, but sometimes the holidays had a way of bypassing rifts and reconnecting people.

"Have you ever thought of going back to New York and visiting your dad? Just for the worst part of winter," I quickly added so he wouldn't think I was suggesting moving home.

Michael immediately shook his head. "No, I haven't." I waited for him to expand on that, but of course, he didn't. I opened my mouth to ask him why he hadn't considered it, and he lifted a hand to stop me. "I'd rather not talk about my dad and why I do or don't want to see him, okay?"

I let out a heavy sigh. "Fine. I just thought with the holidays approaching, you might want to open up about some of the stuff that's clearly eating at you. But if you'd rather keep it all bottled in, ready to explode at a moment's notice, then fine. Who am I to tell you how to live?"

Michael's pale eyes widened at my outburst, and I was immediately hit by a wave of embarrassment. I usually tried hard to hold my tongue, to not pry or push in areas where he didn't want me to. Thoughts of the upcoming celebrations were clearly making me fail. "I'm sorry—that was uncalled for. It's just . . . Christmas has always been a very special time of year for me. Not being home with my family, my friends, my dogs . . . it's really hard, but that doesn't mean I should take it out on you. So . . . I'm sorry if that sounded bitchy."

A small smile returned to his lips. "I've survived worse, but thank you for apologizing."

Wanting to change the subject, I grabbed the ax that was slung across my back. "Guess we should start working on cutting this monstrosity down to size." The scope of work before us made a weary exhale escape me. "I can tell you right now, though, the second I get back home, I'm ordering you some decent equipment. You need a freaking chainsaw. Maybe two or three."

Michael laughed, then shook his head. "I can't let you do that, Mallory . . . but it's a nice thought, so thank you."

I stopped and stared at him. "You saved my life. The very least I can do is make yours a touch easier."

He stared at me a moment, his eyes soft with warmth and compassion. "You already have," he whispered.

The look on his face . . . the sweetness and sincerity in his voice . . . my heart started beating harder, and a warmth as pleasant as a sunny spring day began to radiate inside me. God, that was so . . . sweet.

Michael's demeanor changed the second the words left his mouth. Eyes downcast, he started searching the snow-covered forest floor like he'd lost something in it. "We should get started," he murmured. "Getting this back to camp will take a while."

It took a lot of time to cut the log into manageable circles and even more time to load the circles onto our makeshift sled and pull them home. Four solid days, to be exact. But once we were done, it was clear we would have enough wood to last quite some time, possibly a couple of months. Of course, it still needed to be split and stacked so it could dry.

Michael resumed his trapping while I resumed my water gathering and wood splitting. Now that I was mostly healed—my ankle was back to normal, the scar on my thigh was a beautiful pink color, and my ribs were no longer wrapped—my strenuous daily chores were much easier. I was a heck of a lot stronger, too, and I could generally split a log in one swipe now . . . instead of my previous three. It gave me a surprising amount of satisfaction to see the physical results of my labor. I might suffer from homesickness on occasion out here, but I was also in the best shape of my life; my pants were even starting to get a little loose. There was something to be said for living an extremely simple life. I was still buying Michael a chainsaw, though.

My conversation with him rang through my ears while I worked. *You saved my life. The very least I can do is make yours a touch easier.*

You already have.

You already have . . . Whenever I found myself getting down about the upcoming holiday season, those three words gave me a tremendous amount of lift. There was power in that short, sweet sentiment, power derived from the mysterious, reclusive man who had said them. Michael was self-sufficient, didn't need or want anybody. But in one simple phrase, he'd cracked open a door for me, a window inside himself. And he was clearly uncomfortable with that fact. It had taken him a solid twenty-four hours to look me in the eyes again. He wanted to remain a fortress, cold, hard, able to weather any storm. And that made me wonder . . . once I was gone, would those internal cracks weaken him? Or would he simply plaster over them and move on? Either solution made me sad. He'd done so much for me; I didn't want him scarred in any way because of me.

Exhausted, I loaded up the last stack of split wood and put away the ax. I'd just had a bath the other night, but maybe I could take one again. I felt like a cesspool of dirt and sweat. At the very least, I would need to wash my clothes. That could be done in cold water, though, so it wasn't quite as much of a hassle. It just meant I'd need to collect even more water tomorrow; the cycle of responsibility never ended out here.

Trudging up to the cabin, I stomped my boots to get them clean of snow and wood chips. The scent of freshly cut wood was so strong on me that I still smelled it when I stepped inside the cabin. Definitely a bath night.

Michael was already home, a rarity when he was checking his traps. I smiled at seeing him here, then frowned. "Hey, I know I just had a bath, but I really need another one, so you're going to have to occupy yourself outside. Hopefully our curious bear friend doesn't get you . . . I'd feel really bad about that."

I expected him to scoff at my never-ending bear phobia, but he didn't stop grinning. He looked like a man with a secret, and I was instantly on guard. "Why are you . . . ?"

He stepped to the side, and I instantly knew why he was wearing a Cheshirelike smile. The scent of wood I'd been smelling wasn't coming from me. Tucked in a corner of the room was a four-foot-tall evergreen tree stuffed in one of our five-gallon buckets. It was barren of any type of decorations, but it was clearly meant to be a Christmas tree.

"Oh my God . . . you . . . ?" My hands flew to my mouth, and my eyes instantly started watering.

Michael's smile softened, and his eyes began to shimmer. "I know you're far from home, far from your holidays . . . but I thought since you had to be here . . . with me . . . then maybe we could have our own holiday." He glanced back at the tree and frowned. "We'll just have to be more creative about it."

The tears were dripping down my cheeks now. "Oh my God, this is amazing! Thank you, Michael. Thank you so much." I felt like I was about to start sobbing. Christmas was my favorite holiday, and I really thought I'd have to give it up this year. It hadn't occurred to me that I could have all the same festivities here, with Michael. "This is perfect . . . just perfect."

Needing to seal the thank-you with a hug, I took a step toward him. Like he could sense my intentions, Michael turned and grabbed a towel. He handed it to me, both doing me a favor and subtly deflecting my approach. Knowing he wanted space, I took the towel and thanked him again.

He frowned, but it was a playful grimace. "You keep saying thank you . . . I'm going to have to ban those words soon. But you're welcome. I just . . . I want this to be as easy on you as possible."

His comment echoed the sentiment behind the phrase that had been swirling in my mind all day. I wanted to make his life easier, and he wanted the same for me. It was the basic building blocks of friendship that we were creating, and I cherished the fact that we were forming them. With every day that passed, bonds were being strengthened. Michael was quickly becoming much more than just my savior and my salvation, and I was sure the same could be said of me to him.

Running an awkward hand through his hair, Michael indicated our tub basin. "Want me to get the water started for your bath?"

I smiled as I wiped my tears. "I'd love that, Michael. Thank you." He gave me a warning look, since I'd used his banned words, and I laughed. Seeing my humor made him relax, and he laughed, too, before moving to the stove to grab the pot. Yes, bonds were definitely forming. Things were definitely changing.

Chapter Eleven

A few days later, I was standing at the window, astonished by what I was seeing. Winter had hit full force, and the landscape was muted by a white curtain of huge, fluffy snowflakes floating to the ground. On the bright side, that damn nosy bear was most likely sleeping now, but the entire yard was covered with a blanket so thick that I couldn't make out any of the paths we took for our daily chores. I could barely see the shed holding our precious stores of food. If it kept up like this for too much longer, the snow would cover the window, and I wouldn't be able to see anything; as it was, the snow line was only a foot or so beneath the glass. I was instantly grateful that Michael had installed heavy-duty storm windows when he'd built this cabin. They did a good job of retaining the heat and keeping out the cold.

"Guess you were right about snow days. We can't go out in this." If we tried, we could easily become blinded by the never-ending sheet of white. Then we'd get lost and probably never make it back to the safety of the cabin.

Michael idly looked out the window with me. "Yeah. These storms can get pretty bad, but they usually don't last very long. Two to three days on average. Five or six at the most."

Five or six? That sounded like an eternity to me. Especially considering all our food was out there. "What about the meat?" I asked, curious how we would retrieve it.

"I've got a system," he said with a smile. "We can get back and forth to the shed and the outhouse."

Turning around to face him, I raised an eyebrow. "How?"

Still smiling, he walked over to the door and opened it; the chill smacked me in the face as I stepped beside him. Michael pointed to a couple of metal rings embedded in the thick logs of the cabin, near the front door. I'd never noticed them before, probably because nothing had been attached to them before. But now, one had a bright-yellow cord tightly tied to it, the other had a bright-pink cord. Both were easy to see against the backdrop of white snow, and they hovered above the ground at around shoulder height. The yellow cord stretched off toward the direction of the shed; the pink one led to the outhouse.

Michael kicked a bucket. It was full of carabiners attached together by foot-long ropes. "Snap one end on to you, the other end to the cord. Snap it back on when you're coming back. It makes it almost impossible to get lost."

"Clever," I said, impressed with his ingenuity.

He gave me a soft smile. "Yeah . . . unless the snow or the cold snaps the cord or a creature gnaws it in half or the cords somehow become untied or the metal rings pull free from the walls . . . then you're pretty much screwed."

I suddenly felt less impressed as he pointed out every potential flaw in his system. "Good to know."

Lightly laughing, he shut the front door. "It hasn't happened yet, so I wouldn't worry too much. Just don't feel overly confident and forget to use it. That is the most likely reason that it will fail."

Nodding, I took that to heart. Even if it was bright and sunny outside, I'd religiously use his safety measure. The last thing I wanted was to get lost and freeze to death. Or create a situation where Michael had to come looking for me, and *he* got lost and froze to death. I couldn't handle that happening. Our lives were tied together now, and we each had to be cautious and careful of the other. And that meant not doing anything stupid.

After a full day of doing nothing but watching the snow fall, boredom began to set in. Unfortunately, I'd already decorated the small tree Michael had brought in for me. There wasn't a lot to adorn it with out in the forest, but I'd gathered a handful of pinecones and tucked them throughout the branches. I'd also collected numerous small twigs and had spent several evenings twisting the sticks into shapes . . . most of them haphazard circles. It wasn't the most elaborate tree in the world, but I loved it. All the more so because Michael had gone out of his way to get it for me. It was the epitome of everything Christmas stood for.

No longer having the tree as a boredom buster, I turned to Michael, who was sitting on his bed reading a book. "Want to play one of those games you mentioned?"

Closing the book and setting it on his lap, he smiled at me. "Cabin fever set in already?"

A small laugh escaped me as I nodded. "I'm just used to doing something, I guess." Pursing my lips, I added, "Doing chores didn't entirely take my mind off things . . . but it helped. Not having anything to do just reminds me of all the things—" Snapping my mouth shut, I stopped talking. If I kept complaining about how much I missed home, he was going to start taking it personally.

He only smiled at me, though, like he completely understood that I wasn't in my preferred situation and he wasn't offended by the fact that I'd rather be somewhere else. Although I wasn't 100 percent sure that was how I felt anymore. It wasn't that I didn't want to be here . . . with him . . . it was just that I also wanted to be home. There were people in pain right now because of me, and that was a hard fact to live with. If I could somehow let my family know I was okay and would be home when the weather got better, then this little excursion with Michael might not be so bad. Downright pleasant even.

"What do you want to play?" he asked, standing up.

As he headed to the bins under his workbench, I tried to think of something that might stop my mind from spinning. "How about crib? It's been forever since I've played. I'm not even entirely sure I remember the rules."

He nodded, then adjusted what bin he was going for. "Crib it is then."

It took me a while to get reacquainted with the game; I hadn't played in over fifteen years, back when I was a teenager. But considering we had nothing to do for the bulk of the day but play, after a couple of afternoons of snowed-in conditions, I was damn near an expert.

"I win. Again."

Michael frowned at my statement. "You really shouldn't brag. It's not becoming."

He gave me a one-sided grin after his statement that was both alluring and mischievous; there had been a lot of smiles over the past forty-eight hours of captivity as we both became more and more comfortable with each other. Our stares were longer, and we always seemed to be brushing against each other. Michael's nearness, combined with the inability to leave the cabin for an extended amount of time, was slowly driving me crazy. I just couldn't tell if it was a bad kind of crazy, or a really, really good one.

Reaching out, I touched his arm as I laughed. "And you shouldn't be making moonshine in your backyard, but you do. It's darn good too." We'd dug into his stash early this morning and had been sipping on it all day. It helped ease the boredom, but it was also dissolving all the awkward inhibitions between us. Again, I didn't know if that was a good or bad thing. Playfully pushing my cup toward him, I grinned and said, "Fill 'er up."

Michael let out a beleaguered sigh as he moved to stand up. It was clearly fake, though. He was having a good time, same as me. As his arm pulled away from me, his hand flipped over so our fingers touched. The connection, however small, sent a zing of electricity up my spine. What would it be like to have those fingers touching me everywhere? It was a thought I tried to never have, but my resistance was crumbling the longer we stayed in our cramped quarters.

I bit my lip as I watched Michael saunter over to the long counter to grab the large mason jar holding his homemade moonshine. I could tell from the ease of his steps that he was feeling the effects of the alcohol; we should both probably stop soon, before we regretted it.

Walking back to the table, Michael flashed a grin at me before pouring the clear liquid into my cup; most of it made it inside. He moved on to his cup, refilling it just as full as mine; then he returned the jar to the counter. My heart started beating harder as I stared at him returning to me. His eyes were locked on me, too, and a blazing heat passed back and forth between us, over and over in an escalating rhythm.

When he sat back down, his chair was much closer to mine than it had been; he even had to move his drink closer to himself. My skin pebbled at the thought of sticking my hand out and placing it on his thigh. Would he let me? Or would he instantly back away? I wasn't sure, so I stayed where I was. It was torture.

Rolling his head my way, he put on a playful frown. "Ready for another win?" he asked.

"Always," I answered, angling my body closer to him; our heads were almost touching now. His nearness and his comment made a carefree smile erupt on my face. He was right about my winning streak—I was on a rampage. But even still, I'd yet to see any signs of true irritation from him. For someone who claimed to be a sore loser, he'd handled my multiple wins exceedingly well . . . almost too well.

I frowned as I twisted to face him; his eyes slipped down my body before returning to my face, and a warmth deeper than the moonshine filled me. I had a legitimate concern, though. "You're not letting me win, are you?"

Michael smiled as he leaned toward me. "Really? I was just about to ask you if you were cheating," he stated. "How do you keep getting such great cards? It's a little suspicious, if you ask me." His lips curled into a frown, and the effect tantalized me. God, with so much tension swirling around us, if we stayed cooped up for much longer . . . who knew what could happen. And that, I knew, would be bad.

Trying to be discreet, I minutely pulled away. His comment made me smile, though. He'd also wondered if maybe things were being rigged. Sometimes our minds were closely synced. Too closely synced. "Today is just my lucky day, I guess. If only I'd been so lucky a month ago . . ." A brief swell of sadness stole my smile. It had been over a month now . . . everyone must know by now that something had gone wrong. They were worrying about me, right at this moment. And with this weather, they couldn't search for me. Not until spring.

Michael slightly pulled away, too, and I felt some of that wondrous tension dissolving as my mood sank. He studied me while he shuffled the cards for another round. Then, as he began to deal them, he softly said, "I think you were lucky a month ago too. I saw the wreckage, Mallory—you shouldn't have survived that." He pursed his lips, then nodded to my cross and said, "Someone was looking out for you."

It was clearly difficult and uncomfortable for him to say that. He had a . . . jaded view of faith. It made his words even more moving and profound; it gave them weight that I couldn't ignore, and while I'd thought several times that I was blessed, his simple comment truly sent the message home. For whatever reason, I was meant to crash and meant to live. It was a humbling, powerful, encouraging thought, one that made me feel closer to God. And closer to Michael. "You're right," I quietly responded.

Since I meant he was right on both counts—that I'd been sent down and saved by forces I couldn't even begin to understand—I didn't clarify my answer. I knew enough about Michael to know he wouldn't want to talk about the spiritual implications. He looked even more uncomfortable as he absorbed my answer, and he took a long swig of his moonshine.

The mood between us had changed again, and I hated that it had; I'd been enjoying the flirty tension, and I thought Michael had been too. Wanting to bring some of that back, I picked up my stack of cards and playfully bumped his shoulder with mine. "I think the real question is . . . are you ready to lose?"

My teasing comment combined with physically connecting with him seemed to work. He tossed a grin my way. "I'm due for a win. It's in the cards."

He flicked his hand for emphasis, and a throaty laugh escaped me. "We'll see about that."

A half hour later, with my peg just two spots behind his, he crossed the finish line. "Yes!" he exclaimed, beaming like he'd just won the lottery. Guess he actually did have a competitive streak.

So did I. I shoved his shoulder away from me, making him laugh. And somehow, when he righted himself, he was even closer than before. Our shoulders were touching now, and I sank into his side with a contented sigh, resting my head on his shoulder. Maybe being housebound wasn't so bad. I felt like I could stay here like this for eternity.

Michael stiffened as our bodies collided, but then he relaxed into it. While I rested against him, inhaling the manly scent of nature on him that I loved, he began idly shuffling the cards again. A comfortable silence settled between us. It was a blanket of contentment that I wanted to wrap around me every day, for surely nothing could keep me as warm as this feeling. Then I twisted so I could peer up at his face, and as his pale eyes flicked down to take me in, the contentment shifted into something else entirely.

While the delicious tension reignited, Michael's gaze darted between the table and my face. He played with the cards, not really shuffling them, just moving them around. After nibbling on his lip for a second, he quietly said my name. "Mallory . . . I . . . I'm probably going to regret saying this . . . but it's . . . it's been nice . . . having you here. I think I might . . . I think I might miss this . . . when you're gone."

His voice was laced with pain by the end of his statement, and my heart squeezed for him. By the way he isolated himself, by the way he was reluctant to reach out to people, by the way he seemed almost disconnected from society, I knew his admission of missing me was huge. Possibly life changing. I mean, he'd been alone and content with being alone for five years, and here he was saying he'd be sad when I left. I couldn't comprehend how hard that was for him to say. And as his eyes shifted to lock on to my face, I saw the struggle in his eyes . . . the regret, the embarrassment, and . . . the hope. The hope that maybe I'd feel the same way about him. He was reaching out for human contact. For me. I suddenly felt like the stove had kicked into overdrive and the room was blazing with heat.

"I . . . I think I . . ." *I think I might miss you too.*

Before I could properly string together the words, Michael quickly stood up. His chair screeched against the floor in his haste, and I lost balance as the support of his body was yanked away. "I shouldn't have said that, Mallory. I'm sorry. I was out of line." He ran a hand through his hair and turned around, looking for an escape. There wasn't one, though. That was the problem.

The thought of him feeling bad for voicing his loneliness broke my heart. I hurried to my feet as well. Rushing to his side, I put my hand on his arm to stop him from searching for a way to flee. "It's fine, Michael. I was just going to say I'll miss you too . . . more than I ever thought I would. I regret crashing, but I'll never regret meeting you. Being here with you . . . it's been wonderful."

His gaze snapped to where we were touching. A part of me wanted to pull my hand away, but I held firm. He should feel purposeful human contact; he'd gone far too long without it. Michael swallowed, then slowly slid his eyes up to mine. Maybe it was the alcohol, but my skin tingled everywhere his gaze lingered. When his eyes locked on mine, he opened his mouth, but no words came out. His silence made the room spin with anxious energy.

Feeling closer to him than I'd ever felt before, I slid my hand up his arm, wrapping it around his bicep. I felt his muscles flex, even under his thick shirt, and I instantly remembered how they looked, bare, casually slung over his tub. The visual did surprising things to my attention-starved body—my breath picked up, my heartbeat quickened, my lips parted in anticipation. I wasn't sure what I wanted to happen, but at the moment, I felt up for anything: a hug, a kiss . . . or maybe more.

"Michael . . . do you . . . ?" *Do you feel this energy, too, or am I in this alone?* Maybe I was. Maybe the cabin fever had finally driven me over the edge.

Or maybe I wasn't alone. Michael was still staring at me. His brows bunched, and he drew his bottom lip into his mouth like he was suffering from confliction. If I leaned forward, would he lower his lips to mine? "Do I what?" he murmured, looking lost.

Just when I felt bold enough to lean forward and test my theory, Michael took a step back. Inhaling a deep breath, he shook his head and slapped on a smile. "Do I want to get meat for dinner before it gets dark?" he asked. "Yes, yes I do. Good thinking."

Grabbing his jacket, he swiftly opened the front door. Chill seeped into the room, instantly killing whatever mood had been building. A shiver went through me as I clutched my elbows to keep warm. "That wasn't my question," I muttered, but Michael was already closing the door behind him.

I watched from the window, helpless and embarrassed, as he clipped himself onto the yellow line leading to the shed. The white squall outside swallowed him up seconds later, and he was gone from my sight. Disappointment flooded me, but it was almost instantly replaced with relief. Michael was right to firmly stop the building tension between us, before we both made a mistake. I knew I'd fall for him if anything happened, and I just couldn't fall for a guy who I'd probably never see again after the snow thawed.

Winter romances weren't my style, and I had a feeling they weren't Michael's either. We needed to be extremely cautious with each other, because despite everything out there that might hurt us—being mauled by a bear, frozen in a river, impaled by a felled tree, or lost for all eternity in the woods—losing our hearts to each other might be the deadliest of all.

Chapter Twelve

The whiteout conditions eventually eased into gentler snowfalls and even a few sunny days, not that the sunlight helped the temperature much. It was cold, damn cold, and Michael and I spent a lot of time warming up by the fire when we weren't working our butts off to keep surviving. It made me instantly realize just how much I'd taken for granted all of the modern conveniences that took the hardship out of everyday life. Electricity. Running water. Thermostats controlling the heat. Showers. Washing machines. Refrigerators. I made a vow to kiss every appliance I owned when I returned to my quaint little home in a few months.

I was having a really weird dream about marrying a microwave when I was aroused into awareness by the tantalizing smell of the most amazing meat on earth: bacon. My eyes popped open, and I was greeted by the underside of the logs forming the ceiling. Stretching out the kinks in my back, I looked over to the stove, where Michael was standing, tending to the frying pan.

He looked over when he heard me stir. "Good morning," he said, a warm smile on his face.

"Morning," I yawned in response. Tossing off my blankets, I gingerly stood from my hard couch bed and walked over to Michael.

"Bacon?" I said, glancing into the pan. "I didn't know you had bacon in the shed."

Flipping a couple of perfectly browned pieces over, Michael's grin grew as he said, "I was saving it for a special occasion."

Intrigued, I asked, "Oh? And what's the occasion?"

Michael gave me an odd, amused look before returning his attention to the bacon. "It's Christmas, Mallory."

"Oh . . . right." I'd known it was quickly approaching, but without a calendar to help pinpoint the days, the passing of time became a blur. Especially up here, when it was dark more often than it was light.

A thick knot of sadness threatened to take control of my stomach as I thought of my family waking up without me nearby, hoping I was alive but fearing I was dead. I firmly pushed the grief aside. Michael was trying to make today special for me. I wanted to focus on him, on how sweet he was being, and not dwell on the people who were missing me.

"What can I do to help?" I said, throwing on a smile.

"How about some Christmas pancakes to go with our Christmas bacon?" he said, his entire expression loose and easy. It was like for this one day, all his walls were down. I loved seeing the freedom in his eyes.

"I can do pancakes," I said, practically skipping as I got to work.

After our breakfast, I thanked Michael by offering to do the dishes.

"That would be great. It will give me time to finish up your present."

My jaw nearly dropped at his statement. "Present? I didn't know we were doing presents. I didn't get you anything . . . and what could you possibly have gotten for me around here?" There wasn't exactly a mall close to us.

Michael smirked at me as he finished putting on his boots. "You'll see." His face grew more serious as he stood up. "And don't worry about getting me something. Just having you here has been . . ." He cleared his throat after his voice trailed off, and warmth blossomed in my chest. Having me here was his gift? His loneliness was practically radiating around the room. He shouldn't keep staying out here by himself. He should go back home . . . once I left.

Like he knew where my mind had taken me, Michael pointed at the door. "I should get going."

I nodded and watched him leave, but my mind was spinning with questions. And concerns. Would Michael be all right once he was alone again? Granted, he'd been living this way for years, but somehow, things felt different, like it would be harder for him this go-round. While I was so grateful that I'd met him, I felt horrible that I'd caused him to be at all discontented with this solitary life he'd chosen. And I really wanted to know why he'd chosen it, because I still didn't understand.

When he returned a couple of hours later, I was slowly winning the battle with the always-dirty floor. Not by much, but there were places now that looked like they might be clean, and I was claiming it as a victory.

Michael poked his head in the door, clearly keeping something from view. "Close your eyes," he told me.

With a sigh, I did what he asked. "This really isn't fair. I didn't know we were exchanging gifts. And me being here doesn't count . . . I hadn't planned on that." Michael didn't say anything about my comment, just continued hauling something into the house. It sounded big and cumbersome, and I was dying to crack my eyes open and steal a glance. I refrained, but it was difficult.

Finally, I heard the door shut, and Michael said, "Okay, you can look now."

When I opened my eyes, I wasn't sure what I was looking at. "Ummm . . . thanks?" It looked like a couple of heavy sheets sewn together with something shoved between them. It kind of reminded me of a cloth beanbag chair, only longer, more rectangular.

Michael laughed, then moved the contraption over to the hard bench I was using as a bed. He started spreading it out over the wooden slab, and I instantly understood. "You made a mattress? For me?"

Smoothing whatever the sheets were stuffed with, Michael nodded. "Yeah. I know from experience that just sitting on that couch hurts after a while; I don't know how you've managed to sleep on it for so long."

I'd managed because I hadn't had a choice. It was either the couch or the floor, and at least the couch was relatively clean. From the woodsy scent coming from the sheets, I was beginning to believe they were stuffed with a ton of moss. And I knew from experience that moss was a natural cushion, about the best, most comfortable thing you could find out here. I finally might be able to get the ever-present knot out of my back.

"Michael," I said, running my hand over the mattress once he was done. "This is . . . the best thing ever. Thank you."

Michael sighed and rolled his eyes at me, but he smiled the entire time. "You're welcome, Mallory. Now when I watch you sleep, I won't feel sympathy pains."

"You watch me sleep?" I asked, surprised.

His eyes widened, and his expression grew uncomfortable. "Not watch . . . it's just . . . I can see you from where I'm lying down, and sometimes you fall asleep first, and I'm not tired, and . . ." He held his hands up. "I'm not a crazy stalker or something. I promise."

His comment made me laugh. "It's okay. I didn't think you were either crazy or a stalker. I just didn't know . . . you noticed."

A smile softened his face. "I always notice you." He looked away again, like the words had come from someone else.

"Come on," I said, easing his discomfort. "We should bring in some wood before it gets dark."

Clearly grateful for the escape, Michael's eyes returned to my face. "Good idea."

It was lightly snowing when we stepped outside, and the untouched woods around us made for a perfect winter wonderland. I had to concede that maybe Michael was right in letting his "yard" remain as intact as possible. It was always a sight to behold when there was fresh snow on the ground; it made me miss my camera.

"I wish I could capture all this," I murmured as we made our way to the wood stack.

"Capture it?" Michael asked, turning his head my way.

"With my camera," I said, nodding. "It's just so beautiful here. I'd love a memento of it, something to help me remember it forever."

I stopped walking to take it all in, and Michael stopped with me. "Yeah . . . you could always . . . come back? You said once this was an annual trip for you? You could spend a couple weeks here taking your pictures."

His voice grew softer the longer he talked, and I shifted my gaze to look up at him. The snow was speckling his hat and beard with light white frost, making him seem a natural part of the environment. His eyes were darting everywhere as he waited for me to say something in response to his suggestion. I knew this was another big admission for him—asking me to return, even if it were only for a couple of weeks. I couldn't deny the appeal, staying in a cabin instead of the woods, having someone nearby to help with chores, or just another set of eyes to look for tracks and keep an ear out for bears. It was definitely an attractive thought.

"I think I'd like that. Thank—" I stopped myself from saying the oft-repeated words and laughed instead.

Michael's smile widened as he gazed at me, and his eyes were blazing with joy. "Good . . . it's a date then." The smile fell from his lips, and his eyes widened in embarrassment. "Not date-date, just . . . it's a plan."

I laughed harder at his awkward stumble, and Michael's smile finally returned. "You have a great laugh," he told me.

His cheeks flushed with color, and I could tell he was mortified that he'd said that. Not wanting him to feel weird or awkward for complimenting me, I quickly returned his sentiment with one of my own. "You have a great smile."

He instantly smiled, then studied the ground as a small laugh escaped him. It was adorable, and it made me want to compliment him about everything I liked—his eyes, his strong hands, the solid chin I could just make out under his scruffy beard . . .

It took me a second to realize that our eyes had locked, and we were silently staring at each other while the snow softly fell around us. The minute I became aware of it, my heart started racing, and every inch of me became hyperaware of our proximity. Fearful that he'd break the connection if I moved, I stayed as still as possible.

The chill was beginning to seep inside me, but I didn't care. I'd get frostbite if it meant Michael didn't run away, if it meant this buzz between us could keep going. My eyes were the first to break formation as they drifted along his nose to the full lips nestled between the frozen beard and mustache he used as an extra layer of defense from the cold. The puff of my breaths started increasing as his mouth became my sole focus. I nearly gasped in delight when his lips parted and his tongue darted out to run over his bottom one. If I leaned forward, would he press his lips against mine?

I was too scared to move to test my theory. Waiting was working: he hadn't run yet, hadn't gotten all awkward and made an excuse to leave. And the breaths escaping his lips were just as quick as mine; he was feeling this too.

Anticipation rose inside me, filling me with need—a need for something, *anything* to happen. Standing still was no longer an option. I needed to move before I combusted. All I did was angle my head and tilt my chin up, but it was enough to snap Michael out of the spell holding him in place. He let out a long exhale and looked away, toward the cabin. "I . . . uh . . . I'm sorry. I don't know what . . ."

He stopped speaking as words failed him. Frustration rose in me. I'd wanted him to stop pulling away, to embrace the moment . . . but maybe he was right to cut it off before it began. He was being smart, and I couldn't blame him for that. "It's okay . . . I just . . ."

As an awkward tension built between us, I noticed Michael reach down and play with his ring finger like he was twisting a piece of metal that wasn't there. I knew where it was—in a plastic bag buried deep in one of his bins. "Your ring . . . you're still used to wearing it, aren't you? Is that why you kept it?"

I wanted to slap my hand over my mouth, but the words had already been set loose. There was no putting them back now. Michael's eyes were huge when he snapped his gaze back to mine. "What are you talking about?" he asked, his voice tight, like the words hurt him.

Wishing I'd just kept my mouth shut and let the awkwardness extinguish the moment between us, I quietly told him the secret I'd been holding on to for far too long. "I found your wedding rings . . . attached to a picture of your wife. She's very beautiful." *And I can see why you're not ready to move on from her. Especially with someone who isn't sticking around.*

Michael's eyes went even larger. "You found . . ." He looked around, then rubbed his bare hands. "We should get the wood before we freeze."

He took off without a second glance at me, and all I could do was stare in shock at his retreating form. I'd figured he wouldn't be happy that I'd been snooping, but I hadn't expected him to passive-aggressively brush it off and ignore me. Following him, I said, "I'm sorry. It was back when I first got here, and I just wanted to know something about the man who'd rescued me. You're not always forthcoming with information, so I—"

He spun around to face me then; his eyes were heated when they met mine. "So you took matters into your own hands, right? Is that why you asked me if I was married? If it hadn't worked out? You couldn't ask me directly about the rings without admitting you were spying on me, so you made sure it came up in conversation?"

I tossed my hands into the air. "Yes, that's exactly what I did. I'm sorry I went through your stuff, but can you really blame me for wanting to know who I was living with?"

The spark in his eyes died, and his voice dropped. "No, I can't blame you for that. I get it . . . and it's fine."

It didn't feel fine as I watched him continue walking to the shed to load his arms up with wood, but he was dropping the conversation, so I decided to drop it too. I never should have brought it up anyway.

Things were silent between us as we collected some logs and trudged back to the cabin. All of the beauty I'd admired earlier seemed to be gone now, swept away by my word vomit. I hadn't meant to admit my faults, hadn't meant to cause him pain, hadn't meant to ruin Christmas. As Michael stoked the fire in the stove, I tried to somehow salvage the remainder of the day.

"I really am sorry, Michael. Please don't be mad at me all night. It's Christmas." I smiled at the end like I believed those two words were enough to solve any dilemma. And they should be. Temporarily, at least.

Michael looked over at me on my new ultrasoft mattress and let out a low sigh. After closing up the stove, he walked over to sit beside me. "I'm not mad. It's just . . ."

"Just what?" I asked, grateful that not only was he still talking to me, it seemed like he wanted to open up to me as well.

"I just . . . it's hard to think about those rings. Hard to think about what they symbolized . . . what I had. You poked a tender spot is all." When he looked back at me, his eyes were full of age-old pain.

Knowing I'd brought this remembered sorrow upon him made guilt swell inside me. "Because you two didn't work out? I'm so sorry to remind you of that . . . especially on a day like today. That was callous of me."

I hung my head in shame, and Michael let out another sigh. "We *did* work out, Mallory. We were . . . great together. Amazing even . . ."

There was so much pain in his voice that shivers raced down my back. "What happened then?" I asked, lifting my head to look at him.

As I watched, his eyes misted over. "She . . . died. She meant everything to me, and one minute she was there beside me, and the next she was gone. Forever."

That certainly explained the rings, the picture . . . even the isolation suddenly made sense. He was still in mourning. I had no idea what to say to that, what could possibly ease his pain, so I said the only thing that I could think to say. "I'm so sorry, Michael."

A tear rolled down his cheek before he hastily wiped it away. "It's fine, I just . . . I don't want to talk about my past anymore, okay? It's over—it's behind me—and I have no desire to reminisce about it. Deal?"

He stared at me unflinchingly, but I could see the turmoil and emotion rampaging through his eyes. It wasn't over, not for him. There was nothing I could do to help him, though, except agree to let him keep his privacy. "Okay . . . deal."

Chapter Thirteen

Michael was right about feeling better once the holidays were over. It was like a weight had been removed from my chest, and I could breathe again. Or maybe that feeling was because living at the cabin with Michael was going really, really well. Every day we seemed to get just a little closer; as the temperature was dropping outside, things between us were warming up, and there was a deep well of friendship between us now.

I had acclimated to the rigors of wilderness living, and I was even starting to have fun doing my chores. Well, not so much the water gathering. Walking right up to the edge of an ice shelf on a swiftly flowing river never became less nerve-racking. I kissed my cross and said a prayer of thanks after every successful trip. I'd become such an expert at wood chopping, though, that—in addition to having the sexiest arms of my life—I also had time to spare most days. Michael let me join him on his trap run when I was all caught up and didn't have anything else to do.

Walking through the quiet, snow-laden forest with Michael by my side, I began to forget that this wasn't a typical existence. Being out here with him just seemed so incredibly natural. As we approached our third trap of the day, I spotted a lump of fur inside the sprung device.

Grin on his face, Michael carefully pulled the hinge back so he could remove the dead animal.

"What is it?" I asked, trying not to look directly at the face of the deceased creature.

Slipping it into the basket backpack he was wearing, Michael said, "It's butter, flour, toothpaste, and fresh batteries. That's what it is."

I had to smile at his answer. Michael wasn't doing this for sport; he was doing it for survival. There were things he needed that the land here couldn't provide. Like in the pioneer days, trade was essential, and in the wilderness, furs were gold. "Good," I told him as he reset the trap. "Let's see if we can find some chocolate, toilet paper, and pillows to go with it."

Michael laughed at my requests. As I watched his lips curve into a smile, a bit of melancholy slipped into me. If he actually did purchase those things, I wouldn't benefit from them. I'd be gone. Back home with my dogs and my family. Michael would have to enjoy them without me.

Seeing my expression fall, Michael asked, "What's wrong? Are you too cold? We could take a break—I could make a fire."

He was scrutinizing me, trying to see if that was my issue. It wasn't, but his thoughtfulness was sweet. Yet another thing I'd miss. "No, I'm fine . . . we don't have to stop. I'm actually enjoying this." *And enjoying you.* I didn't mention that, though.

He smiled. "Good. It's nice to have company." His grin turned sheepish, and he looked away.

The embarrassment of his smile perked my spirits back up. "Where's the next one?" I asked.

Flicking a glance my way, he nodded to our left. "Up that way."

Adjusting my own basket backpack, I began trudging in the direction he'd indicated. "Let's go then. Lots to do before the daylight fades."

Michael laughed as he fell into step behind me. "Yeah, and we don't want to miss the fireworks."

That made me stop in my tracks. "Fireworks?" I asked, confused. Unless he was lighting stuff off, we were way too far from civilization to see anything. And why would there be fireworks anyway?

He grinned as he adjusted his pack. "Yeah, fireworks. Can't celebrate New Year's Eve without them."

I blinked in surprise. He was so good at keeping track of time; I'd already lost count of the days on multiple occasions. "Oh . . . that's right."

Shrugging, he said, "There won't be any actual fireworks, of course, but I thought we'd sit outside for a while and see if we can catch Mother Nature's show."

He looked up at the sky, clear for once instead of a hazy gray, and I instantly knew what he meant. "The northern lights?" My grin was unstoppable.

Michael nodded. "Yeah. It can be tricky to see, and we'll have to stay up late to get the best chance, but if we're lucky . . . it's pretty spectacular. Best show on earth."

Even though it would be late and cold, I couldn't think of a better plan for tonight. It sounded . . . wonderful, and I was instantly filled with contentment; right now, there was nowhere else I'd rather be. Not even home.

It took us the rest of the day to check the remaining traps, and there were quite a few surprises waiting for us when we did—powdered milk, canned vegetables, dried beans, candles, and matches. Assigning every fur we collected a commodity value made the day kind of exciting. And even though I wouldn't be partaking in the spoils, I was still happy for Michael. He needed this.

Later that evening, after the furs had been prepared and stored for the night, Michael and I sat down to an amazing venison stew dinner. There were candles on the table and the last of the moonshine in our cups. Maybe because today had been truly productive, maybe because of the holiday, maybe because of the event we were going to try to witness, I was full of good spirits. For this brief moment in time, everything was perfect.

"Have you ever seen the northern lights?" Michael asked, stirring his spoon around his bowl.

"Surprisingly enough, no. I've never managed to catch it on my trips up here. Of course, I was trying to make the most out of my daylight, so I went to bed early, got up early."

He nodded like he understood. "I've only seen it twice myself. I'm looking forward to seeing it with you," he added, a sparkle of joy in his eyes.

For once, he didn't look away after his sweet comment, and our gazes locked. A contented sigh escaped me, and Michael's smile grew. The peace I saw on his face mirrored my own, and I loved that he was happy . . . loved that I was happy. I desperately didn't want to do anything that might kill the hopeful spirit in the air, but sometimes it was difficult to know what to do and what not to do. Bringing up the past altered Michael's mood, while mentioning the future dampened mine. Staying in the here and now was the only way to ensure the vibe between us didn't change, and that was tricky, like walking an emotional tightrope.

Studying Michael helped keep me grounded in the present. The way his lips moved when he talked, the way the candlelight flickered in his pale-blue eyes, the way he ran his hand through his scraggly beard . . . a beard I was dying to cut.

Disarmed by my errant thought, I asked him a question I probably shouldn't have, since it had nothing to do with the moment we were currently experiencing. "Will you let me cut that when the weather warms?"

Michael's eyes widened in alarm. "My beard? You want to cut this work of art?"

I nodded as fervently as I could. "Yes, yes, and yes."

He frowned, then laughed. "I usually cut it in the spring. My hair too . . . so I guess that's fine. It will save me a trip to the barber."

A barber. A town. An impending goodbye. It all hit me so fast I sucked in a breath like I'd been punched. "I'll do the dishes tonight," I murmured, rising from my chair.

Reaching out, Michael grabbed my hand as I walked by. The contact instantly sizzled my skin with comforting heat. "Mallory?" he asked, searching my face.

Feeling melancholy enter our happy place, I made myself smile. "I'm fine. I just . . . want to help."

He searched me a second more, then released my hand; I instantly missed the contact. "Okay . . . let me know if you change your mind." He flashed me a grin that made my heart beat faster. That smile could unfreeze the Arctic, I was sure.

After I was done with the dishes, Michael and I killed time by playing a few rounds of cribbage. Just when I was yawning so hard I never thought I'd stop, Michael indicated the door. "It should be getting close to time. Want to go outside?"

Nodding enthusiastically, I started getting on all my extra layers. It was nice and toasty in here with the stove, but it was downright frigid out there. When we were both bundled up, we headed outside. I scanned the skies right away, expecting to see a vibrant display of color. But all I saw was a beautiful speckling of stars. Not bad, but not what I'd been wanting to see.

Michael didn't look surprised when he joined me. "Shouldn't be too much longer," he said, sounding confident, like he was wearing an aurora borealis watch.

I smiled up at his presumptuous answer, then stepped closer to his side. Our shoulders touched, and even through our thick jackets, it was a delightful feeling. My gloved hands were dangling close to his, tantalizingly close. I wanted to reach out and share that connection with him, but I didn't want to scare him away either.

Wanting to do something but not being able to do it was maddening, and the feeling only worsened as time went on. I was just about to say *Screw it* and grab his hand when I suddenly felt his gloved fingers wrap around mine. A smile I couldn't contain lit up my face, but I made sure I didn't twist my head to make eye contact. He might change his mind and run if I pointed out what he was doing. All I allowed myself to do was squeeze his hand and lean into his side; another contented sigh escaped me. I could stay like this forever.

And then, as if to make the moment even more picture perfect, a faint greenish-white light brushed the sky. I held my breath and gripped Michael's hand tight as the light grew wider and more pronounced. As the curtain of color intensified, it began undulating, deforming, turning into arcs and spirals. It was the most amazing thing I'd ever seen, better than any New Year's fireworks show.

Blown away by the beauty of nature and wishing once again that I had my camera, I finally looked up at Michael. He looked down at me when he felt my eyes on him, but he didn't break contact, didn't go running back into the cabin. He just gazed at me with warmth in his eyes.

"Happy New Year, Michael," I whispered, my heart in my voice.

"Happy New Year, Mallory," he answered. Then, inexplicably, his lips started lowering to mine.

I thought I was dreaming. I was so certain that I nearly pulled off my glove to pinch myself. Because there was no way Michael was about to kiss me. He could barely touch me without pulling away. But I wasn't asleep, and he *was* making a move.

My heart was pounding now as his face inched closer and closer. It was hard to stay still as he made his slow descent. I wanted to reach up and pull him into me. *Yes . . . please kiss me.*

He was so close I could feel his light breath on my face. I closed my eyes in preparation; my every nerve ending was on fire, waiting for the moment. And then his cool lips pressed . . . against my cheek.

Surprise shot my eyes open, and I could see him quickly pulling away in the moonlight. "Michael?" I asked, unsure what that had meant.

"We missed midnight," he explained, his eyes darting back and forth from my eyes to the ground. His breath was harder, his voice shaky, like he was embarrassed . . . or like he was struggling to resist me.

"Oh . . ." I swallowed in a vain attempt to dislodge the rush of desire that had begun to sweep over me. Michael's eyes flashed to my lips, making it even more of a challenge to subdue the feeling. "I thought maybe you wanted . . ."

I stopped talking as embarrassment washed over me. Mentioning my misunderstanding would only make this moment even more mortifying. Thinking I should let go of him now, I eased my hold on his hand. Michael's eyes were still glued on my face, though, and his grip on my hand hadn't changed any. If anything, he clasped on tighter when I let go.

"Michael?" I asked again, confused.

His face scrunched as he stared at me. "I did . . . I do . . . want . . ."

Something changed in his eyes, like a decision had been made. Then before I knew what was happening, his lips were again lowering to mine. They didn't deviate at the last minute this time, and we connected just seconds later. His lips were so soft, so gentle, but full of so much restrained passion too. I just wanted him to lose control, wanted him to let down every wall he'd erected around himself, and let me in. I just . . . wanted him.

As our mouths moved together, as his beard lightly tickled my face, I changed my earlier thought—*now*, this moment could last forever, and I'd be happy. There was just something about Michael that spoke to me—his courage, his independence, his thoughtful nature, the pain he tried to hide. This was a person I could see having a future with . . . if our circumstances were different. But as of right now, it seemed impossible. He was staying. I was leaving.

I shoved that thought aside as our light, tender kisses slowly began turning to something more . . . passionate, and I felt myself getting caught up in the bliss—mindless, unworried, and untroubled. Michael's free hand ran around my waist, pulling me in tight, and my free hand curled around his neck. I wasn't sure what I wanted, what could happen between us that wouldn't scar us both, but at the moment, I didn't care about the approaching pain. I never wanted this moment to end.

But of course, it had to. If we stayed out here, we'd eventually freeze solid. We needed the comfort and warmth of the cabin enveloping us. Weighing the pros and cons of breaking this magical moment with Michael, I pulled away far enough to ask him, "Want to go inside?" My breath was fast; my smile was huge . . . but Michael's expression instantly changed.

Once realization of his lapse in judgment hit him, he took a step back, releasing me. I could almost see him shutting down, and pain pierced my chest as I watched the walls reforming. "Michael, don't . . . it's okay," I said, trying to be encouraging. It was more than okay. It was . . . amazing. Possibly the best kiss I'd ever had. One I wanted to have again, even if it was a bad idea, even if we weren't going to last long. Couldn't we have that bliss for the brief time we were slated to be together?

Michael seemed to feel that it wasn't worth the risk. "No, it's not okay. I shouldn't have . . . we can't . . ."

Stepping forward, I grabbed his hands. "We can. We're adults. We both know the situation. I know you're trying to protect me . . . like you always do . . . and I adore you for that, but there's no need to protect me from this. I accept it's short term, and I'd rather have a brief time with you than—"

Looking at me with sad eyes, Michael interrupted my declaration. "No . . . *I* can't. I can't give you my heart when I don't have one. And I can't let you give me yours. I won't break your heart, Mallory. I just won't. That shouldn't have happened, and nothing like it will happen again. You have my word."

He turned and left me, and I stared at the spot where he'd been standing, gaping like an idiot while the northern lights above me faded into nothingness.

Chapter Fourteen

The air was thick with tension when I returned to the cabin. Michael ignored me as he got ready for bed, although he did it in such a way that it wasn't obviously apparent that he was ignoring me. He just seemed preoccupied with his tasks. Finishing quickly, he climbed into his bed and rolled over so his back was facing me.

It killed me to see the disconnect, especially since the feel of his lips was still burned into my brain. I wanted to go over to him, put a hand on his shoulder, roll him my way, and beg him to talk to me. He did have a heart; I know he did. He was just trying to protect me—or himself, since we both knew this was temporary. And while a part of me agreed with his decision, the rest of me knew I couldn't spend months here with him . . . and not fall in love with him. I was doomed either way, so couldn't we at least be happy before the pain set in?

As I climbed into my own bed—comfortable now, since Michael's thoughtful gift—I wondered what things in the cabin might be like after this. It was such a small space that it was impossible to avoid each other. Even if he left all day to go trapping, he had to return when it got dark, and the nights were long here. We had endless hours of uncomfortable awkwardness ahead of us, unless I could somehow convince him to give us a chance. To give *me* a chance.

Waking up the next morning didn't bring me any insight on how to do that, especially when I looked over and saw that Michael had sneaked out while I'd been sleeping. We usually spent time together in the mornings, having something to eat and making small talk before heading out to do our chores for the day. It hurt that he'd disrupted that pattern because of what had happened last night . . . because of that kiss. The memory of that kiss that still made my toes curl . . .

Thinking of that moment as I began my chores made sadness well up inside me. Michael's words before the kiss, the look in his eyes when he'd been debating whether to change our relationship. The fateful moment when he'd finally said *Screw it* in his mind and taken a chance. Emotion had been thick in the air between us, so him telling me that he didn't have a heart—that he'd felt nothing—was complete and total bullshit. He'd felt something for me; that was why it had been so hard for him. But then he'd chickened out and given me an excuse so he could back off with a clear conscience. And the more I thought about that, the angrier I became.

I was sitting at the kitchen table waiting for him when he finally came home an hour or so after full darkness. He glanced my way, tilted his head in some sort of nod that was supposed to be a greeting, then shuffled over to the basin to wash his hands.

"Hello, Michael," I said, my voice crisp. "How was work?"

Eyes on his hands, he gave me a one-word answer in response. "Good."

Frustration made my eyes well with tears. We'd been on the road to getting really close, and now there was a dam-size wall between us. And he was putting it there, erecting it brick by brick with his frosty attitude and feigned indifference. Clenching my hands into fists, I slowly stood from the table.

"If this is the way things are going to be from now on, then why don't I do us both a favor and leave. I'm sure you'll appreciate my absence." I knew it was a ridiculous statement—I wouldn't last a week out there on my own with practically zero supplies. Michael knew it, too, and he looked up at me with shock on his face . . . and a trace of fear in his pale eyes.

"What? No, you can't go out there by yourself. It's too dangerous." Drying off his hands, he came over to stand in front of me. He'd been avoiding looking at me since last night, and now, having the full force of his gaze upon me was almost overwhelming. I just wanted to wrap my arms around him, tell him he didn't have to be scared of this . . . of us.

Crossing my arms over my chest, I stared him down. "Then stop giving me the silent treatment. You wanted to kiss me, so you did. And it was wonderful." My voice grew soft as the memory flooded through me.

Michael sighed and hung his head. "It was," he admitted, his voice equally soft. Feeling bolstered by his admission, I took a step toward him. His eyes flashed up to mine, and he held his hand out to stop me. "But it can't happen, Mallory. I can't let this happen."

He indicated the two of us with his hand, and I frowned. "Why?" I asked, tossing my hands into the air. "Because I'm leaving? I know that. You know that. Can't we enjoy this while it lasts?" He looked away, and I took a step toward him. "I didn't think I would ever want a winter romance, Michael. I didn't think I could handle it . . . but then, the weirdest thing happened."

When I paused for effect, he returned his eyes to me. Curiosity swam in them. Gently, carefully, I laid my hand on his arm. "I realized that I couldn't stop myself from liking you, couldn't stop myself from caring about you. Whether or not I acted on it, I was already having a winter romance with you. I *am* having a romance with you. Right now . . . because I like you . . . so much."

Michael swallowed, and his pale eyes were suddenly bursting with pain. "You shouldn't," he whispered.

"Why?" I answered. "Because you don't want to leave here? I understand that, and I'm not—"

He shook his head, interrupting me. "No . . . because I meant what I said . . . about not having a heart. Or maybe I do . . . it's just . . . taken."

I blinked in confusion, not understanding. "Taken?"

With a sigh, Michael grabbed both of my hands. His were cool from the water, calloused from his hard life, but they felt incredible around mine. "I'm in love with my wife. Still. I came out here to get over her . . . but I don't think I ever will. She's all I see, all I think about, and there just isn't anything left of me to give to you. I'm a shell . . . and you deserve better than that."

If he had intended his words to push me away, they had the opposite effect—my heart surged with compassion, and I felt even closer to him. It wasn't that he didn't have a heart; it was that his heart was broken, shattered . . . and all I wanted to do was fix it. Love on him until he healed, until he could feel again, because I was certain that he could love again in time. But time was a luxury we didn't have.

"But you feel something for me?" I asked, my voice a whisper.

"I feel . . . guilty," he answered, his eyes drifting to the floor.

Guilty because he couldn't have feelings for me? Or guilty because he did? Biting my lip, I took one more step toward him so our chests were almost touching. "Your wife would want you to be happy again," I told him. "She wouldn't want you up here, hiding from the world in solitude. She would want you to live."

His brows creased, and a myriad of emotions flickered through his eyes. He pulled away from me, yanking his hands free from mine. "And I wanted *her* to live, but sometimes we don't get what we want."

I sighed as defeat filled me. But he'd been holding on to this pain for so long. I knew he wouldn't release it just because I told him to. Hoping I could help him heal by encouraging him to talk about it, I asked, "What happened to her? Did she get sick?"

His pale eyes grew hard and cold as ice; the snowbanks outside looked warmer. "No . . . she got shot."

I hadn't expected him to say that, and I blurted something before I could stop myself. "She was murdered?"

Michael's expression cracked, and the anger shifted into pain. "Some gang-banger shot her for twenty bucks in her purse. I lost the love of my life . . . for twenty dollars." He collapsed into a chair next to the table like his legs refused to keep him upright. I didn't know what to say to that, didn't know what string of sentences could possibly ease the pain of that kind of senseless loss.

"I'm so . . . I'm so sorry, Michael."

He looked up at me with haunted eyes, like he was reliving the moment over and over. My chest constricted as I watched his pain. "Want to know the worst thing . . . the part that makes all of it so . . . unbearable?"

I couldn't speak, so I merely nodded for him to continue.

"She didn't die right away," he said. "He shot her in the stomach, nicked her spinal cord, so she couldn't walk, couldn't get help. But she yelled. She was just a few feet from a busy street, and she cried out for help over and over, but no one did anything. Some of them told the police later that they were too scared, too unsure. They didn't want to risk getting involved, so they didn't do a damn thing to help her . . . until it was too late."

My eyes filled with tears, tears that slid down my cheeks. Michael watched the drops rolling off my skin with a face devoid of emotion. "That's why I won't ever go back," he murmured.

Wiping my face dry, I knelt in front of him. "Won't go back . . . to New York?"

His eyes refocused as he reconnected with the present. "That's why I won't go back to anywhere people are. Humans are the worst species on this planet, and I don't want to be among them again. *Ever* again."

The heat in his tone and the vitriol in his words took me aback. "You can't really feel that way. Not about everyone."

He twisted his lips as he considered that. "There are a few . . . exceptions . . . but by and large, humans are not good, decent people. They're selfish, conniving . . . cruel. I'd rather live out here with the animals than there in the thick of them. At least you know where you stand with animals. People, though . . . they're just crazy."

While I understood where his world beliefs stemmed from, I couldn't agree with them. Not with his unrelenting ferocity. The human race was flawed, yes, but there was goodness to humanity that couldn't be found in the animal kingdom. We were unique, special, and cutting our *entire* species out of his life seemed too extreme. Balance was everything; it ruled the world. "I understand that people let you down, and what happened to your wife . . . that was just . . . awful. But giving up and hiding out here isn't the answer. I could show you a better side of people, something to give you hope again."

His eyes seemed to deaden as he stared at me. "Hope is an illusion, as insubstantial as rainbows in the sky. I worked in the emergency room at a major hospital right in the heart of New York. I know what life is all about. I know what humanity is all about . . . and I want no part of it." He pointed to my cross necklace. "Your Maker there, he messed up somewhere along the line when he created us. And if we were created in his image . . . then I want no part of him either."

He'd said yesterday that he hadn't wanted to break my heart, but every word he was saying was slicing me open. How could I help someone so torn apart? "Michael . . ."

Holding a hand up, he stopped me. "We're not going to agree about this . . . I can tell. You have your beliefs, I have mine, and we just . . . we shouldn't talk about it, okay?"

I felt crushed, saddened, but I knew he was right. Until I could convince him to give humanity another chance, we'd never agree on this. Nodding, I told him, "Okay." Then I stood up and headed for the door. I needed something to do after that conversation. Might as well start dinner.

The chill in the air felt good on my face as I walked to the shed to get some meat out of storage. The entire time I worked, I contemplated Michael. Grief had hardened him, turned his insides to stone. I wasn't a therapist like my sister; I didn't know how to help someone in that way. All I knew how to do was take pictures, and that seemed like a woefully inadequate skill at the moment. Michael needed true help, and I didn't feel capable of giving it to him. It killed me to know that I would leave here with him still broken, that I would have failed in trying to help a good man. And I truly believed Michael was a good man—that was why he was in so much pain.

Gripping my necklace tight, I said a prayer for him. It was the only thing I could think to do.

When I returned to the cabin, Michael was pacing the room. He locked gazes with me when I closed the door, and his eyes were laced with regret and sadness. "I'm sorry," he immediately said. "I know that was a lot to take. Sometimes I wish I didn't feel this way . . . but I do, and I think I always will. And even if I . . . I like you too . . . between my feelings for my dead wife and my views on society and religion, I just don't see any possibility of us . . . working."

Even though hearing him say that he liked me too thrilled me in a way that nothing else had recently, I kind of agreed with him. He was too broken for me to fix. The two of us falling into a passionate relationship . . . it wouldn't just be a bad idea. It would be catastrophic. "I know . . . and I think I understand now. But I can't handle months of us ignoring each other. I really would rather live in the forest than face that every day. Can we still . . . be friends?"

A slim smile curved Michael's lips. It was my favorite smile, the one that made my heart race. And looking at it now, I still felt flutters in my stomach . . . I probably always would. But right now, he was beyond my reach. His heart and mind were locked up tight, rusted shut from years of disuse and distrust. It would take a miracle to pry them open again, and I wasn't sure that I could be that miracle for him. But I prayed that

I was, because if Michael was ever going to be a whole human being again, then he desperately needed divine intervention.

He held out his hand to me like he'd done when we'd first met. "I really enjoy your friendship, Mallory, and I'd love it if we could keep . . . what we have."

Confusion passed over his face after he said that, and I knew he looked that way because he wasn't entirely sure just what we had. All he seemed to know was that, like me, he didn't want what was between us to end. That gave me hope, because I was sure, in the deepest recesses of my soul, that what we had went deeper than friendship, and if he wanted to keep that alive, then a part of him wanted to live again, wanted to love again. His light hadn't entirely been extinguished yet, and as I shook his hand, I could see the smallest kernel of a miracle begin to grow.

Chapter Fifteen

It was difficult to be around Michael after that day. Not because of what he'd said, not because of his thoughts on humanity, but because . . . I couldn't stop thinking about that kiss. I also couldn't stop thinking about his wife, a woman he was still in love with, bound to for eternity by guilt and regret. I couldn't believe that his wife would want him to be this closed-off person, though. She'd want him to live, to be happy, to love those around him, not to hide away from everyone and everything. Hearing Michael's views broke my heart, so I had to believe it would have broken hers too.

It made me miss my sister even more. I wished I could talk to her, ask her advice. She occasionally worked with veterans and had experience dealing with PTSD, and that seemed to me to be the closest thing to what Michael was going through. He'd been ripped open by a traumatic event, one he hadn't even been present for, and the wound went deep; there was no sure way to stitch it, except time. And that was part of the problem. This isolated life that Michael was living—it was like being stuck inside a bubble of time. The seasons changed here, but nothing else. Every time the sun rose, it was like hitting the repeat button, and while the simplicity of that was refreshing, I had a feeling that it was also prolonging Michael's grief. Without feeling time moving forward, there was no real way to heal. He was killing himself here. But I didn't think I'd ever convince him of that.

In Michael's mind, the outside world was an empty, cruel, heartless place . . . a war zone, one he didn't wish to return to. If I felt the same way, I could understand and support his decision, but he was oversimplifying the human race. For every ounce of vileness, there was an equal—if not greater—amount of goodness. Sometimes you just had to look harder to find it. For some reason the negative aspects of life were abundant, prevalent. It was almost a daily assault on the senses: *Here are all the horrible things you missed while you were away!* You had to reach through the garbage to find the golden nuggets of pureness and light. I truly wished it were the other way around, but human beings tended to be intrigued with grief. While good deeds were praised, then forgotten, horrific deeds were forever etched on our psyches.

But that didn't mean we were a lost cause. Like wayward children, we just needed . . . guidance. And I desperately wanted to be that shining light for Michael to follow. I just didn't know how.

"How are you doing?" Michael asked one afternoon, his light eyes inquisitive. I was helping him with the trapline today, like I usually did when I didn't have enough chores to keep me busy for a full day. Michael had asked me something similar to this question almost every day since our conversation, like he was afraid I viewed him differently now. And I supposed I did see him in a different way. It just wasn't in a negative way like he probably thought.

Trudging through the thick drifts of snow, I shrugged. "My toes are a bit on the cold side, but other than that, I'm fine."

He frowned at my answer; clearly he hadn't been wondering about my physical discomfort. "Are you . . . do you . . . ?" With a sigh, he stopped talking. We'd both decided we'd never see eye to eye on certain subjects, so we shouldn't talk about them, but he looked like he was having second thoughts. Or maybe doubts.

"I really am fine, Michael. I'm more . . . worried than anything."

That made his eyes open wider as he looked over at me. "Worried? About me?"

"Yeah . . . I worry about what's going to happen to you once I leave." The truth of that statement settled on me like a cold stone upon my shoulders. How long could he continue like this? What would kill him first—the elements or the loneliness?

Michael stopped and turned to me. The snow falling around us was getting thicker, and heavy, fat flakes partially obscured his face. "I'll be just fine, Mallory. I've lived this way for a while now . . . I'm not scared, so you shouldn't be."

Yes, but it wasn't just where he was living that worried me. Not wanting to get into it, I gave him a small smile. He saw right through my attempt to be cheerful, and his eyes saddened. "I'll be okay, Mallory. You don't need to worry about me."

"That's just it," I said. "I don't *need* to worry about you, but I still do. I think a part of me will always worry about you."

A slim smile curled his lips. "And a part of me will worry about you. I guess in that small way, we'll always be connected."

A very small way. Much too small for my taste.

The wind picked up, sending a slice of cold right through me, and the heavy snowfall suddenly became a near blanket of white. I could just barely make out Michael's outline as he looked around. "This is starting to get really bad. We should go back."

I turned around to get my bearings, but all I saw was white. It was disorienting, and panic began seeping into me as I realized that I had no idea what direction to go. Where was the cabin from here?

Afraid I'd lose him, too, I reached out for Michael's hand and took a step toward him. "Where?" I asked, above the sound of the wind.

Michael looked lost, too, as he turned his head this way and that. He clenched my hand tight like he thought I might wander off if he released me. "Uh . . ." We both searched the ground, but the snow and wind had already erased our trail. We were lost . . . it had happened so fast, without warning, but I supposed that was how these things usually happened.

As my heart began to surge with anxiety, Michael took off his glove and dug into his pocket. "Shit," he muttered; then he searched another pocket.

He seemed unsatisfied with every pocket he checked, so I finally asked him, "What are you looking for?"

"My compass," he answered. "I usually keep one with my pocketknife and my lighter, but . . . I guess I wasn't as prepared as I thought. I don't have one on me." He frowned after he said it like he didn't know what to do now.

For a moment, I wondered if he hadn't been prepared because of me. Were we about to die because he'd been so worried about me that it had distracted him from taking the necessary precautions? That seemed like a cruelly ironic fate, and I began to shiver as fear settled into every pore. I didn't want to freeze to death in a snowstorm.

Exhaling heavily, Michael put his glove back on and looked around the forest again. "Look, Mallory . . . I don't think we can make it back to the cabin. The storm's picking up, and if we go the wrong way, we'll get so lost out here we'll never get back. Our best bet is to stay here. Once the storm passes, I'll be able to read the land again—I'll be able to find the trail home."

"Stay here? We can't stay here, Michael. There's no way to build a fire in this. We don't have shelter. We'll freeze. We'll die." My voice was coming out shaky, but I couldn't help the reaction. Once again, I was facing my mortality. I was really tired of doing that.

Michael seemed more okay with facing the end, probably because he was facing it on his terms . . . and not like his wife had, at the end of a barrel being wielded by someone else. He squatted in front of me and clasped both of my forearms. "We're not going to die. We just need to ride out the storm. We just need shelter."

I raised my hands to the empty woods around us. "What shelter? There's nothing here we can use, Michael."

A small smile cracked his lips; it seemed wholly out of place, given the circumstances. He lifted a finger to the sky. "We're being provided with more of a shelter every second, Mallory."

My eyes widened as I grasped what he was saying. "You want us to bury ourselves? Under the snow?"

"It's actually a great insulator. Igloos hold a surprising amount of warmth," he stated.

"Except I don't know how to build one," I inadvertently snapped. "Especially without any tools. Do you?" *Please say yes. Please tell me you took survival training courses before you came out here, and that was part of it.*

Michael shook his head, dashing my hopes. "No, I don't know how to build one . . . but I can build a cave. We just need a deep-enough drift."

A cave? A snow cave? God, we really would be buried under the snow. But I supposed that was better than becoming human icicles. "Okay . . . what do we do?"

Clasping my hand again, he nodded ahead of us. "We search for something deep enough to hold both of us. Then hope we can dig it out before dark."

Swallowing the lump of dread in my throat, I let Michael lead me onward, into the blizzard. The snowfall intensified as we walked, so much so that I could barely see Michael's body as he stretched out in front of me. I clasped his hand like the lifeline it was; if I let go, if we separated, that might be it for me. Staying together was our only chance, and knowing that strengthened my belief that good or bad, right or wrong, humans needed each other. We weren't designed to spend a lifetime alone. I had to make Michael see that.

Just a few shambling feet from where we'd been, we came across a fallen tree surrounded by a snowdrift. Michael was smiling at me through his frosty beard when I stepped close to his side. "We can use this. We dig a hole until we reach the tree; then we carefully scoop out the inside, making it bigger. We can't break the ceiling, though—otherwise it won't work as insulation."

I nodded like I was in complete agreement with him, but I had no idea how to do everything he'd just said. Closing my eyes, I prayed for strength and luck. I had a feeling we'd need both for this.

Removing our basket backpacks, we lowered to our hands and knees and began digging into the snow. It was icy, easily compacted, and that boosted my spirit. We might be able to scoop out the insides while leaving a sturdy shell that would block us from the elements. Michael wanted to keep the opening as small as possible, so once we had a space big enough to crawl through, he ducked inside to scoop out the rest. Fear and the chill assaulted me the entire time he was half-buried in the bank. I didn't think it would hurt him if the cave collapsed, but it would mean we'd have to start over, and I didn't want to scour for another place and try again. I wanted this to work. I wanted us to be safe.

Finally, after what felt like an eternity, Michael scooted out of the hole. Looking up at me, he nodded at the opening. "I think it's big enough for both of us. Go ahead, but try not to touch any of the walls. You might accidentally break through."

Hoping against hope that this actually worked, I slid into the slim circle. There wasn't a lot of room in the tiny cave or a lot of light. But it was protected from the wind and the snow and noticeably warmer. I pressed myself to the side to make room for Michael, being careful to not puncture anything. When he began scooting inside, I wasn't sure how we'd both possibly fit. I was already curled into a tight ball. But Michael managed to squeeze into the space beside me. Every inch of us was touching, though, and for us to both fit, we had to tangle our legs and lean against each other's torsos. We were cuddling for survival, and even though I was scared and feeling extremely claustrophobic, being this close to Michael was comforting.

Taking off his gloves, Michael grabbed my hand. It was dark in the cave, but I could make out his outline clearly enough. He gave me a small, warm smile. "It's going to be okay. It will probably blow over enough by the morning that I'll be able to tell where we are."

I nodded, then pressed my head against his shoulder. As I watched snow cover the opening where we'd entered this tiny sanctuary, Michael rubbed his thumb over my glove. Adjusting my position, I removed my glove so I could feel our skin press together. I needed the contact and the reassurance that came with it. Michael let out a sigh that was strangely relaxed, then laid his head against mine. Our little space was so warm that I was no longer shivering. In fact, I almost felt too warm, but there wasn't enough room to start removing clothing, so I just dealt with it.

Pulling back, I looked up at Michael with a smile. "You were right about the cave. I'm actually getting hot."

Michael returned my grin. "Yeah, our body heat has a lot to do with that. I'm sorry I couldn't make the cave a little bigger. I didn't want to risk the walls caving in."

"It's fine," I said. "Cozy even. I think we should consider moving here."

He laughed, and the sound evaporated the rest of my anxiety. "Sure, if you don't mind moving again in the spring when the snow melts."

Considering the fact that I *was* moving in the spring—moving home—his joke struck a nerve of sadness. "Yeah . . . spring . . ."

His smile fell, and melancholy settled around us just as surely as the snow above was settling on the earth. Our gazes locked as I wondered what I could possibly say to this man. How could I convince him to leave? And how could I be okay with him staying? He'd die out here all alone. Maybe not right away, but eventually. Leaving without him felt like his death sentence, and I just couldn't bear the thought of anything happening to him. My vision grew hazy as I contemplated that very real possibility.

Michael sighed as he searched my face. "Are you still scared?"

"Only of leaving you," I whispered. I bit my lip after I'd said it. I hadn't meant to confess that, hadn't meant to bring up the conversation that we were both avoiding.

As his pale eyes continued examining my face, his hand tentatively reached up to touch my cheek; his fingers were surprisingly warm, and I closed my eyes at the wondrous contact.

"I wish this were easier," he whispered.

Reopening my eyes, I saw the confusion on his face. "Wish what were easier?" I asked, my heart fluttering in my chest.

Instead of directly answering my question, he said, "I wish I didn't feel . . . this . . . for you . . . when I know I shouldn't." His gaze drifted down to my lips. "I'm still in love with my wife, and you . . . you're going home. I don't want to hurt you, but I can't stop wanting . . ."

As his thought drifted off, he pulled his bottom lip into his mouth. My heart was racing now, and all I could think about was his mouth on mine again. I leaned forward into the darkness, hoping I would find his lips, warm and responsive. Like him, I knew it was wrong . . . for both of us . . . but I couldn't stop myself from wanting it too.

When I felt his breath against my lips, faster than before, his hand on my cheek shifted to my neck. I thought he might push me away, but he didn't. He pulled me into him. He wanted me, wanted this, possibly just as badly as he didn't want it. Our mouths met in the darkness, and an explosion of sensation struck me. The heat, the enclosed space, knowing that there was no place for us to go—no escape—it amplified everything inside me, made the kiss feel like a thousand sparklers were igniting inside my body.

The kiss intensified, and nothing was going to stop it this time. Not ghosts of the past, not the bleakness of the future. All we had was this moment, and as my hand reached up to cup his face, I felt something crack inside me. Walls I hadn't even known I'd been erecting were crumbling to pieces, shattering into oblivion, and all I was left with was . . .

feeling, emotion . . . love. I cared for this man more than I wanted to admit, and broken and bruised as he was, I desperately wanted him to care about me too.

As the passion tapered off and our kiss dwindled to soft pecks, I waited for him to tell me what a mistake he was making. The fear of his rejection tightened my throat, and I couldn't speak; I could only search his eyes in between light kisses and pray that he wouldn't hurt me. All I saw in his expression, though, was confusion and desire and something else, something stronger than interest. He cared about me—I could see it.

After a few more soft kisses, the tightness of the space forced me to move. That tiny adjustment broke the spell, and Michael turned his lips away from my reach. "We should . . . rest . . . try and get some sleep. It won't be easy . . . like this . . . but the more energy we conserve, the better off we'll be."

I wasn't sure if he was talking about our current situation . . . or the long run. And I didn't want to think about it, didn't want to piece together the hidden message. I just wanted to enjoy the fact that we were stuck together in this close proximity, and neither one of us could flee from it.

Telling him, "Okay," I scooted even closer and laid my head on his chest.

He sighed again, then removed my hat so he could run his hand through my hair. I fell asleep with the sound of his heart in my ear, the feel of his touch on my head, and the memory of his taste on my lips.

Chapter Sixteen

Everything ached when I woke up the next morning. Every muscle was sore; every tendon was tight. I wanted to stretch out more than anything, and I began straightening my legs before I remembered where I was and why I was scrunched up like a sardine. Fear instantly replaced the need to move. I had no idea how much it had snowed last night. I had no idea if it was still snowing. All I did know was I was buried inside a drift . . . buried alive.

Panic started clawing at my body, begging for release. Keeping it at bay took a tremendous amount of willpower, and I think I was only able to do it because I felt Michael's warm body snug against my side. I wasn't alone in my misery. And that made all the difference.

"Michael," I choked out, stress making my voice tight. "Are you awake?"

He stirred in the small space allowed to him and let out an equally pained grunting noise. "Yeah." Thoughts of last night tried lifting to the surface, but anxiety beat them back. Now wasn't the time to dwell on the memory of his lips.

"What do we do?" I whispered. We couldn't stay here forever. It was morning, I had needs that had to be met. And as soon as my anxieties melted away, I was going to have to move. It wasn't optional at this point.

Michael tapped his foot against the opening that we'd crawled through last night. It looked like a solid sheet of snow, but it gave away at his touch. Just seeing a sliver of daylight made a rush of relief go through me. We weren't buried alive, not truly. We had a way out.

As Michael cleared more of the snow away, I listened for the telltale signs of a still-raging storm. Everything seemed quiet, though. Peaceful. "I think it's stopped. I think we can go home."

Home. Nothing had ever sounded quite so wonderful. When it became obvious that the storm had indeed stopped, Michael began attacking the entrance with abandon. I reached out with my legs to help him, and it felt so good to finally get some blood flowing to my limbs. Once the opening was clear, Michael shimmied his way out; then he reached back inside the cave to help me. I was partially blinded from the glaring sunlight when I got all the way out, and when I could see, I was stunned. The amount of snow that had fallen last night was astounding. If we hadn't made a cave, we most certainly would have frozen to death lumbering through the steep banks. For what felt like the millionth time, I owed Michael my life.

Before I could truly think about what I was doing, I wrapped my arms around him in a gigantic hug. He staggered back from the force. "You saved us, Michael. Thank you."

He seemed unsure what to do in response to my fierce grip, and thoughts of our heated moment last night filled my brain. Wondering how he felt about that kiss, I looked up at him. "Are you . . . ?" Was he what? Okay? Physically, he was fine; emotionally, I was sure he was just as much of a wreck as I was. Maybe more of one. He was still grieving, after all. Pulling back, I felt like I should apologize. I'd gone too far again, and almost directly after he'd asked me not to.

Like he understood my expression, Michael sighed as he took a step back. "It's okay, Mallory. We made it, and we're both . . . okay."

I wanted to ask him if we were more than okay, if we were more than . . . more . . . but I had a feeling I knew exactly what he would say if I asked, so I dropped my arms, stepped away, and didn't bother asking.

When it became obvious that I wasn't about to start an awkward conversation about what had happened between us, Michael visibly relaxed. He looked around us with the eyes of a hunter, and I knew he was searching for clarity—some sign that would magically tell him where we were in relation to the cabin. It all looked like one giant cloud of white to me, so I hoped his years of exploration helped him successfully sift through the oneness.

And it seemed to. With a smile, he tilted his head and studied a pair of trees leaning toward each other like lovers embracing. Looking back at me, he confidently said, "It's this way." Since I was completely lost, I took his word for it.

After unburying our stuff, I followed Michael as closely in his footsteps as I could. The entire trek home, my mind was on the kiss we'd shared in the dark. Once again, it was the best kiss I'd received in my entire life. The softness of his lips, the tightness of the space, nothing but the sound of our quiet breaths filling my ears, the way my heart had pounded in my chest. Even though the situation had been completely wrong, the moment had felt so right. It made me ache for more. I just wanted to feel his tender embrace, to be consumed by this feeling for him that was growing steadily stronger. But he didn't want that. And we weren't meant to last anyway. But still . . . I wanted it. Desires weren't easily shut off, especially not by logic.

When we got back to the cabin, I was thrilled to see it and sad. Scary as it was, our adventure had brought us closer together. I didn't want that part of it to be over with. I didn't want to distance myself from Michael. I wanted to draw him closer, hold him tighter, cherish every last moment we had together . . . then convince him to leave here with me. He was just too wonderful to be alone for the rest of his life.

Michael sighed as he took off his hat. "I'll make something to eat. Are you hungry?"

I was *everything*. Hungry, tired, thirsty, happy, sad, confused, conflicted. "Yeah . . . I'll go get some water." Michael opened his mouth like he was going to object, insist he would do all the chores today or something, but I interrupted him before he could. "It's fine—I need to use the bathroom anyway."

Grabbing an empty five-gallon bucket, I trudged off before he could stop me, but I felt disappointed and disheartened. As great as it was, that kiss shouldn't have happened, because now I wanted something I couldn't have, and it sucked. It sucked hard.

There was smoke releasing from the small chimney when I got back from my errand. The lazy curl drifting into the hazy-gray sky promised warmth, a treat that sounded heavenly. Clutching the handle tight, I opened the cabin door and hustled through. I was breathing heavier when I sloshed the bucket into its place in the corner.

Michael looked concerned as he rushed to my side. "That could have waited until you had something to eat."

"It's fine," I told him. "I needed air anyway."

I hadn't meant to say that last part out loud, but I did. Michael's eyes filled with guilt, and his gaze drifted to the ground. "Because of me. Because I . . . because we kissed again? I'm sorry," he said, returning his eyes to mine.

Removing my hat, I walked over to my bed and set it down. "I know you are, Michael, but that doesn't . . ." I turned to face him. "Being sorry doesn't stop how we feel about each other. I know you think your heart is missing, or . . . it's somewhere else, but from where I'm standing, it's not as far gone as you think." Walking over to him, I searched his face. "You said so yourself . . . you like me. You feel something for me. You want me. So your past aside, what's going on with us?"

Michael bit his lip, discomfort clear on his face. He nodded over his shoulder to the food steaming on the table. "Breakfast is ready—we should eat."

The smell of pancakes was making my mouth water, but a meal wasn't what I wanted right now. "Don't change the subject, Michael. Answer my question."

The look on his face grew frustrated. "I don't know, okay? I don't want anything to happen between us. I just want to be friends. But then, when I'm around you, when you're close to me . . . you're so . . . the way you smell, the way you talk, the way you move . . . I can't help wanting you . . . even though I know it's wrong."

He was breathing heavier as he stared at me, and my body practically purred in response. "Why is it wrong? Your wife wouldn't want this life for you. She wouldn't want you to hole up in this . . . prison that you've created for yourself, distant from everyone and everything. She would want you to live."

His lip trembled as he held my gaze. "How do you know what she would want?" he asked, heat in his voice.

"Because I know what *I* would want," I answered. "And I would want you to live. You're too incredible for anything else."

The fire in his eyes died as his gaze drifted to the ground. "You barely know me, Mallory. How can you say I'm incredible? I could be the worst person in the world for all you know."

"Don't think I haven't considered that," I told him with a smirk. "Remember when I ransacked your house? I was worried you were a serial killer in hiding." A small smile curved his lips, and some of the tension in the room drained. Shaking my head, I stepped closer to him. "Give me the chance to get to know you. Stop closing yourself off and pushing me away."

His eyes scanned how closely we were standing, but he didn't retreat. "Why? What's the point? You're leaving. All of this . . . is temporary . . .

so why let it happen?" His voice lowered into a sultry tone that sent goose bumps racing along my arms.

"I know I'm leaving," I said, stepping in to his body, closing the space between us. Looking up at his face, I murmured, "I know this is short term . . . but my feelings aren't. And I can't keep ignoring how it feels to kiss you, to hold you . . . to be near you. I don't want to."

I pressed my body against his, and I felt him shudder as he closed his eyes. "So we what? Satisfy ourselves now so we can be miserable later?" When he opened his eyes, there were both sadness and intrigue in the pale depths.

"Weren't you already miserable?" I asked. "I'm offering you . . . I'm offering *us* . . . a reprieve from that misery. A temporary shelter to keep us warm from the cold, even if it's just for a little while."

He stared at me for so long I was positive he was brainstorming ways to tell me no, that what I was asking was beyond his capabilities. And honestly, it felt a little outside of my own capabilities. I just wanted to pursue this enough that I was willing to close my eyes to the runaway train screaming toward us.

After long, agonizing seconds, Michael finally responded to my statement, and his answer wasn't anything like what I'd been expecting. "Okay," he simply said.

I blinked in surprise. "Okay?" What did that mean? What was he agreeing to? What about me leaving—what about his feelings for his long-gone wife? How far were we taking this? And just what was "this" now? My heart started surging with hope and happiness as I waited for clarification.

A small smile crossed Michael's lips as my bewilderment flew out of control. "Okay, yes, we won't fight this . . . but . . ." He frowned, and my momentary thrill diminished. "This is going to sound crass, but I can't have sex with you. With the way I still feel about . . . my wife . . . and with you going home soon, I just . . . I can't go there. I hope you understand."

Endorphins flooded me, and I couldn't contain my smile. Wrapping my arms around his neck, I coyly told him, "I was asking for your heart, Michael, not your body."

A charming flush brightened his cheeks, but then he sighed. "I don't know if I can go there either, Mallory."

I understood completely, but still, a part of me was disappointed. "You can try, though, right?"

"Trying is about all I can do," he said with a brief smile. "But I can't promise you . . . anything."

"Whatever you can give, I'll take. Just don't hide from me. Don't leave me alone in this."

Threading my fingers through his thick hair, I pulled him into me as close as I could. Michael sighed, then lowered his forehead to mine. "You know we're making a mistake, don't you?"

I did, but I still couldn't stop myself from doing it. In answer to his question, I angled my head and found his mouth. As our lips moved together, that same feeling of rightness and sadness washed over me. Knowing this was going to be short lived made it bittersweet, intense in a way I'd never felt before. I felt my heart opening to a point where it was nearly painful, and I hoped Michael felt it too. He deserved to feel love again, even it was just for a moment.

Wanting to feel closer to him, like we'd been in that snow cave, I pulled him to my bed. He went freely, even letting out a soft laugh as we landed on the moss mattress, but I could feel the tension in his body. He didn't want this to go too far. I didn't either.

"It's okay," I murmured. "I just want to kiss you." His body melted into mine after I reassured him that I wasn't trying to break his *one* rule. Then we readjusted ourselves so we were lying side by side.

Our breakfast was forgotten as we reveled in the bliss of each other's embrace. His strong hands felt along my body, and my smooth fingers traced his curves. He was smiling between kisses, and I finally saw true joy in his eyes. As much as he'd been avoiding this, he'd wanted it too. We were both finally content.

His beard tickled my face as we kissed, and with a laugh, I playfully pushed him away. "Can I finally cut this? At least trim it into a more manageable . . . piece of art."

Michael laughed as he leaned in for my mouth. "As long as you keep kissing me, you can do whatever you want."

God, I loved how that sounded. And felt. As our lips languidly connected, I thought I could kiss this man forever. "Okay . . . after . . . this . . ."

He laughed, deep in his throat, then kissed me deeper, harder. Something flared inside me, an inferno of desire and need, and I returned his kiss just as hungrily as he sought mine. His lips wandered from my mouth to find my neck, and the fire inside me tripled. His free hand was resting near my hip, and I thought I might die if he didn't do more than kiss me.

But no, we weren't going there. And that meant this needed to stop, right now.

"Michael," I breathed, my words laced with desire.

"Yeah," he whispered in my ear, stoking the blaze inside me.

"I think we should go have breakfast now." Food was about the last thing I wanted, but I needed to cool down.

Michael pulled back to stare at me. "You finally get me to agree to kiss you, and now you want me to stop?"

Grabbing his hand, I placed it over my racing heart. "No, I don't want you to stop . . . and that's why you have to." I smiled so he would know that I was still happy about all of this.

He grinned in return, then leaned down to give me a chaste kiss on the cheek. "Sorry, I didn't mean to tease you." As he pulled back again, his expression grew more serious. "I want this to work for both of us, Mallory. If it's too . . ."

"I know," I said with a nod. "That's why I let you know you needed to stop. We can do this, Michael. It's going to be fine. It's going to be better than fine, because we're finally on the same page. And if it gets to be too much—for either of us—then we can stop anytime."

He flashed me a brief smile, then stood from the bench and helped me to my feet. I wrapped my arms around his neck, holding him tight, and softly let my lips collide with his. The spark of desire was still there, goading me for more, but the pure ecstasy I felt when I was just lightly kissing him was enough to calm the urge inside me. We could stop ourselves, we could keep this light and romantic, and when the time was right, we could say goodbye and hold the memory of this moment deep within our hearts. Forever sealing it in place with every tender touch. No matter what happened from here on out, I would never be able to forget this man. Brief as it might be, I would cherish this memory for the rest of my life.

Chapter Seventeen

I was nervous when I woke up the next morning. Nervous that Michael would say he was wrong and try to take it all back. Nervous that he would say we had to keep our distance. For our own good. But I didn't want to keep a distance between us. I meant what I'd said: I was going to have a romance with him regardless, and I'd rather act on our feelings, encourage the fondness to grow, than stomp it in the mud and try to destroy it.

As I looked around and noticed that Michael wasn't in the cabin, my nerves tripled. Was he ignoring me again? Would he go back to how he'd been after that brutally honest conversation regarding his beliefs? Would the awkwardness return? I'd really hoped we'd finally moved past that.

With a sigh, I tossed off the warm covers and stepped onto the chilly floor. I was just slipping on my boots when the front door banged open. I startled in surprise, then smiled when Michael walked inside. He was covered in a light dusting of snow, and I wondered if we were in for another snow day. God, what would that be like, now that our relationship had shifted? Or had it? Was he still on board, or were we back at square one?

I tried to gauge his mood as he shut the door, but with his back to me, it was hard to tell anything. "Good morning," I tentatively began. "How . . . are you?"

He twisted to look at me, and a smile instantly erupted on his face. I let out a relieved sigh at seeing it. "I'm . . . okay . . . I think." With a laugh, he shook his head and set some meat for breakfast on the table. "I honestly don't know, and I'm trying not to think too hard about . . . things, but . . . I feel good, and that's something."

Yes, that was everything. Pure joy radiated through me at the thought that I'd made him happy—genuinely happy. Standing, I practically skipped over and tossed my arms around his neck. He stepped backward like I'd caught him off guard, but then he put his arms around my waist, and his smile stayed constant.

Not truly sure if I was still allowed to do this or not, I leaned up and lightly pressed my lips to his. He stiffened in my arms but then softly returned my affections. "Are you okay with this?" I asked between tender kisses.

Michael paused, then pulled away from me. His expression changed, grew confused, troubled, like he'd just remembered all the reasons we shouldn't allow this momentary happiness to continue. My heart began to surge as I studied his face. Had I pushed him too far? I wanted to tell him it was okay, that we could do this, that we could have this, and it would be all right, but he spoke before I could. "Yeah," he said, his face softening, "I'm okay . . . with this small . . . your company means the world to me, Mallory."

While he was being vague with his words, his message was as clear as if he were shouting: *Friendship and these small kisses are all we can have.* There would never be more between us. Ever. My heart squeezed in sadness with the truth of that, but I chose to accept it, the same as he was accepting this. We could never be more than we were right now; it just wasn't possible. But "now" was enough, and I vowed to do my best to never ask him for anything more.

Even though I wanted the oh-so-soft kisses to continue, I let Michael go and took a step away from him. It thrilled me to no end when he stumbled toward me like he wasn't ready to give up our connection. "We should get started on our chores," I murmured, putting on my most sultry expression.

Michael's gaze turned heated as he stared at me; then he swallowed and looked away. "Yes . . . you're right." Running his hand through his hair melted the remaining flakes sticking to the unkempt mess. "We'll have breakfast before we go," he said, pointing to the meat he'd brought in from the shed. Almost as an afterthought, he turned to me and said, "When you're out gathering water, could you get some extra for me? I'd like to take a bath."

Right after he said it, he looked away, seemingly embarrassed. We hadn't bathed since our newfound agreement—since we'd decided to accept the physical part of our relationship. Bath days had always been awkward before, with the person not in the tub always escaping to the outside, but now they seemed especially . . . tense. Like a sexually charged bomb had been set, and it would go off the minute one of us stepped foot in the water.

I swallowed a hard lump. "Yeah . . . sure. Maybe I'll finally cut that beard," I added with a smirk.

He smiled at my oft-repeated attempt to tame his mane. "Yeah . . . maybe I'll finally let you." I wasn't sure how that would work with the chemistry bouncing between us, how I would be able to peek into the tub at all his naked glory, and not get . . . carried away . . . but if he was willing to try . . . then I would try too. And I'd pray for strength the entire time.

After breakfast, Michael went his way, and I went mine. The snow had eased up, and only small, light flakes were falling from the sky. Thank God we weren't going to be stuck inside all day with this bottled spark between us. Just thinking about the bath later had me on edge.

I thought about it the entire time I was doing my chores. Pictured that the water droplets rolling down the side of the bucket were sliding down his skin instead, fantasized about the satisfied sounds he would make when the steaming water eased every ache in his body, imagined the look on his face when he rolled his head to the side of the tub and gazed at me. Remembered words filtered through my brain, heating my skin even though the air was chilled: *Your company means the world to me.* It was a sentiment I strongly shared; being with him meant the world to me too.

I was so entranced in my visions of Michael bathing that time leaped ahead in bounds, jumping forward in bursts of hours instead of dripping forward second by second. When I noticed the daylight fading and darkness starting its inevitable descent upon the woods, I was surprised; I was usually well past done with my work before nightfall, and while the bears were sleeping, other animals were quite awake.

Hurrying back to the cabin with my arms full of wood, I wondered if Michael was back from the trapline yet. I usually heard him when he returned, but I'd been so caught up in my thoughts today that I had a feeling he could have easily sneaked past me or noisily lumbered past me, and I wouldn't have noticed. My smile was huge when I nudged the door open with the toe of my boot. I only had a millisecond to consider how odd that was—I usually had to set down my stack and wrangle the door open; the lever often stuck—before I realized something was very wrong.

A soft, menacing growl echoed around the small cabin, and every hair on my body stood straight up. I knew that growl, knew it to the very core of my bones. Similar to a dog's, but wilder, more feral. A wolf. In the cabin. I only had a heartbeat to wonder how that had happened before I spotted the furry beast. Our eyes locked, and my blood went as frigid as the icy river where I'd pulled out our drinking water.

The heavy logs fell from my arms as fear sapped all the strength from my limbs. My legs felt like rubber. I couldn't keep them straight, but I somehow remained standing. While the creature let out another terrifying snarl, I scanned the cabin. Had the animal gotten a jump on Michael? Was he already . . . gone? I didn't see a prostrate, bloody body, though. There was relief in that, but what I did see filled me with anger. Everything in the cabin was ripped apart like the beast had been on a wild rampage. Containers had been chewed open, their contents strewn everywhere. Dishes had big gashes in them where they'd been gnawed on; my new mattress was torn to shreds, the mossy interior in bits and pieces around the cabin; and every piece of nonperishable food had been consumed—only the empty packages remained. In just one afternoon, this lone animal had destroyed almost everything Michael had worked so hard to put together.

My eyes flashed back down to the creature, a vile curse on my lips, but it took a step toward me, silencing me before I even spoke. Knowing I couldn't stay in a startled state, I jerked my shoulder, swinging my rifle around to the front of me. Chambering a bullet, I pointed the weapon directly at the wolf. I expected it to lunge at me, go for the throat, but it hesitated, like it knew what I was carrying and knew exactly what the gun could do.

Fingers shaking, I jerked the barrel of the gun at it. The wolf flinched but didn't back down. "Go!" I shouted. "Get out of here! Don't make me hurt you." Weapon still trained on it, I moved away from the door so the wolf could go outside. "I don't want to kill you," I murmured. "But I will, if you leave me no choice." I was hoping it was full, having gorged itself on our food, and wouldn't want to try to take me for dessert or because it was scared.

With its teeth bared and low rumbles emanating from its chest, the wolf took another step forward, but toward the door this time. Relief filled me at seeing that it was heading for retreat, not attack. "That's a good doggie," I said in singsong. "Move along."

The wolf stopped, and the sound coming from it grew in intensity. I retreated a half step, quickly telling the creature, "Not dog . . . sorry. Wolf . . . pretty wolf. Now *please* go home."

It snarled at me once, then turned and fled out the door. I slumped over in relief, then ran to the door and threw my weight against it, slamming it shut. I fell to the ground with my back to the door, keeping it securely closed. My entire body started shaking with nerves. That could have gone so differently. I could have been ripped to shreds, lost for good, and all because I hadn't made sure the door was securely latched. Life here was so fragile—one second you were fine, safe, and secure. The next you were on the edge of death, fighting for survival. It was like constantly balancing on the edge of a precipice, hoping you didn't fall.

I wasn't sure how long I sat there on the floor, recovering. The rifle was stiff in my hands, and my arms ached from keeping it taunt, rigid, ready for action. Even though I knew I was probably safe now, I couldn't relax. I was too scared that the wolf would return, find some secret hole, or chew through a wall. Or maybe there was another one in the cabin, hiding, biding its time until I let my guard down. I knew wolves didn't work that way—if there was one still in here, I'd know it—but my brain couldn't convince my body to calm down. My sanctuary had been violated, and nothing felt safe.

As I ceaselessly scanned the room, looking for danger, I felt my back being shoved by the door. Panic surged through me. Had the wolf figured out how to open it? Was its strength so great that it could push the door back—and me with it—with pure brute force? Or were there more of them now, working together? Instinctively, I pushed against the door, digging in with my heels to keep it closed.

The weight against the door increased in strength, then a voice said, "Mallory? Are you blocking the door?"

I immediately scooted away so Michael could open the door. The loss of resistance was so sudden that Michael burst through the door like a bullet being released from a gun. He ran into my legs and nearly tumbled to the ground on top of me, but thankfully, he managed to save himself at the last minute.

Concern darkened his expression as he spotted me huddled on the ground, clutching my rifle to my chest. "What happened?" he asked. "Are you okay?"

Nodding, I struggled to my feet. Every inch of me still felt doughy, insubstantial, like I was a doll and not a real person. "Yes, I'm fine. I came back to the cabin, and there was a . . . a wolf. I guess I didn't secure the latch well enough. I'm so sorry, Michael. It wrecked . . . everything."

Michael's eyes shifted to take in the chaos surrounding us. When his gaze returned to me, I expected to see anger, but all I saw was relief. "This is just stuff, Mallory. I'm just glad you're okay. *You're* the one thing I can't replace," he said. Then his arms slid around me, and he was holding me tight to him.

His words warmed me as much as his embrace, and slowly, I felt the terror subsiding. I was tired, though, tired of having survival so close to the surface, tired of facing my mortality at every corner. Like he could sense my bone-chilling exhaustion, Michael ran his hand up and down my back, murmuring encouragement. "It's okay. You're okay . . . we're okay."

I could feel the tears welling, could feel the sadness and homesickness seeping in, but I fought it off as best I could. "We should . . . clean this up." My voice felt tight, like any moment it might snap.

Pulling back, Michael shook his head. "I've got this, Mallory." Taking the gun from my stiff fingers, he softly said, "I'll make you a bath, and while you're relaxing, I'll clean this up."

I skewed my lips at him. "How is that fair? I'm the reason the wolf got inside. I should clean this up." Then I should replace everything I'd allowed to get destroyed. Somehow.

Michael smiled at me. "It's fair because you're the one who is upset. You're the one who faced down a wolf. I'm fine, and I'm more than happy to relinquish my bath night for you, if it will ease your mind."

Rubbing my arms, he added, "And besides, this way I'll be able to keep my beard another day." He stroked the long strands while he gave me my favorite uninhibited smile. I couldn't help but return his infectious grin.

"Fine, but don't get too attached to that thing. You, me, and that beard have a date with a pair of scissors soon." Saying the word *date* made me want to cringe, but Michael didn't react to my choice of words. He just kept smiling at me like all was right in the world, even though everything was in some state of disrepair, if not total destruction.

Before we separated, Michael bent down and gave me a soft kiss on the lips. It sent a rush through me, the good kind, that made facing down a vicious animal almost seem worth it. Almost. I didn't want him to walk away, didn't want to give up the comfort of our connection, but Michael was on a mission, and it was clear nothing was going to stop him until he had me soaking away my worries in a tub.

While he warmed pot after pot of water, I tried to help clean up the cabin. He shooed me away each time with a gentle slap on my arm. "Stop it, or I might have to spank you," he told me.

My face heated at his words, and Michael instantly looked away. "I mean . . . never mind," he said, clearly embarrassed. It made an ooey-gooey sort of feeling go through me whenever he was embarrassed by his words. He could be fierce and protective one minute, then wholesome and adorable the next. It was an intriguing combination, one I had to admit that I really, really liked. It made the thought of leaving him all the harder. If only he rubbed me the wrong way . . . instead of all the right ways.

Once the tub was full of steaming water, Michael gave me a triumphant smile. "Your bath, milady."

Rolling my eyes, I giggled at his sweet, outdated phrase. "Thank you, sir."

He was intently staring at me, his eyes locked on mine, and the longer our gazes held, the more I felt a wondrous warmth blossoming inside me. It was difficult to keep my distance, difficult not to kiss him, but I had a feeling if I did, I wouldn't want to stop. Forcing myself to look away, I murmured, "I should change before the water gets cold."

I hoped he got the hint on his own, and I wouldn't have to ask him to leave; after everything that had happened today, I didn't think I could utter the words. Michael cleared his throat before speaking. "Right, I'll just . . . step outside."

He turned to leave, and I grabbed his arm. "You don't have to stay . . . out there. There's a lot to do in here, and we haven't even had dinner yet. You can come back . . . if you want to get started on that stuff."

I felt dumber with every word leaving my mouth, but I hated the thought of him killing time outside when there was so much to do—stuff he wouldn't let me help him with. And besides, if I was going to cut his hair in the tub, then we were going to have to get used to this. Might as well start today.

Michael looked me over, and I could see the confliction in his eyes. He wanted to stay, but he didn't want things between us to progress any further than they had. He wanted to stay the course. I did too. For now. After another moment's consideration, he finally nodded. "Okay, Mallory. I'll be back in ten minutes."

Another giddy rush swept over me as he stepped out the door. He'd be back. And I'd be naked. And just the thought of him being in the the same room with me when I was that exposed had my body tingling with anxious energy.

Chapter Eighteen

Placing my toe into the tub was like stepping into a vat of lava, but in a good way. It soothed every ache, eased every scrap of residual fear, made life seem glorious again. The feeling amplified in intensity as I lowered the rest of my body into the water. Nirvana.

As I was laying my head back on the rim, getting as comfortable as I could and letting the stresses of the day melt off me, I heard the door slowly creaking open. A slight tremor of fear rippled through me, as the wolf encounter was again at the forefront of my mind, but Michael's voice quickly broke the stillness.

"Are you . . . decent? Can I come in?"

Considering that my legs were hanging out the other side of the tub and my chest was barely covered by the startlingly clear water, I didn't feel very decent, but I let him enter all the same. "Yeah . . . come on in."

My heart started beating harder when he stepped through the door. Even though we weren't about to go there, I felt like I was celebrating my wedding night or I was about to lose my virginity again; the air was thick with tension.

Michael avoided looking directly at me as he came inside, but his eyes made quick flashes my way every so often. Knowing he was seeing bits and pieces of my bare flesh made my skin feel electric. "I'll just be . . . cleaning. Don't mind me."

The way every inch of me felt alive, I knew that ignoring his presence would be about as possible as ignoring the wolf earlier; he just seemed to fill the cabin. Closing my eyes, I tried anyway. Eliminating my vision amplified my other senses, and I could hear every bump, scrape, and grunt that came from his direction. With the aural play-by-play, it was almost like I could see him, and I smiled as I relaxed into the water. This wasn't so bad.

But then a few short seconds later, I felt his hand touch my arm. "Mallory?"

Jerking away, I instantly crossed my arms over my chest and looked up to see him right beside the tub, doing his best not to look in the water. "Michael?" I asked, my heart thudding in my ears. Why was he so close to me? While I was naked? Wasn't that against our . . . guidelines?

"You fell asleep in the water," he said, his eyes only briefly flicking to my face. "I tried to make as much noise as I could, but you were really out. I didn't want the water to freeze on you, so I thought I better wake you up."

"Oh," I said, stretching muscles that I was surprised to find were tight. "I guess I was more exhausted than I thought." Peeking around, I saw that the cabin was mostly put back together. The water in the tub was also just below lukewarm. How long had I been out? "I guess I should . . . get out," I said, tightening my grip around my chest.

Michael flashed me a brief smile, and his cheeks heated in such a way that I began to have a sneaking suspicion that he hadn't been as cautious with his gazes when I'd been asleep. Just the thought of his eyes on me made that glorious tingle return in force. "I'll go wait outside," he murmured.

"Okay," I whispered, kind of wishing he'd stay.

Once he was gone, I let out a yelp and dunked my head under the water. It was way too cold now for that, but it helped clear my head.

I couldn't want those things with Michael. Or at least I *shouldn't* want them. I also shouldn't want a gigantic hot fudge sundae with a mountain of whipped cream and sprinkles on it, but I did. Some desires just couldn't be helped.

Not wanting Michael to catch me while I was changing and also starting to get really cold, I hopped out of the tub and quickly got into dry clothes. I was just using the tub to clean a few of my dirty outfits when Michael came back into the cabin with some moose steaks and potatoes. "At least the wolf didn't break into the meat shed," he said. "That would have been a disaster."

Hearing him say that made me cringe. "I hate to sound like a broken record, but I am so, so sorry. I promise that won't happen again."

Michael gave me an easy grin as he set the meat down. "I know. I let a couple of squirrels in once. That's how I learned to triple-check the latch."

"Lesson learned," I told him with a smile. Lesson definitely learned.

The next few days were some of the best days of my life. Even though half of Michael's stuff was ruined, and most of the rest was in poorer shape than it had been before the wolf attack, things in the cabin were . . . wonderful. Michael was warm, funny, thoughtful. He always invited me to go with him on the traplines and always said he missed me when I couldn't go. Each day that I had with him was opening something incredible inside me, something I wanted to share with him and keep sharing with him. And even though I was pretty sure what his answer would be, I had to ask anyway.

"So . . . ," I began while he dealt us a round of crib one evening. "My plane was destroyed in the crash, as you know. I won't be able to afford another one for a while."

Michael frowned as he set the last card down; it had puncture marks through it. "Yeah . . . I figured that would be something you'd have to save for. I wish I could help you."

I gave him a bright smile. "You *can* help me."

His face instantly grew suspicious, but it was a playful look, almost amused. "I hope you're not about to ask for my plane. Because I do need to run into town a few times a year, and having to call you every time I need to borrow it would be damn inconvenient. I don't exactly have a phone, and my smoke signals are hit and miss." He smiled, and his pale eyes sparkled with joy.

With a small laugh, I shook my head. "No . . . I was thinking you could fly down and visit me sometimes. My town has supplies too." His bush plane was far too small for a trip that long, but he could fly to Fairbanks and take a commercial flight to me.

The look on his face instantly changed, morphed into one of pain . . . and anger. "You know why I can't do that, Mallory."

He picked up his cards and studied them, like the conversation was over. I knew I shouldn't press him, but I hated the thought of this peace we'd found ending soon. Spring would begin thawing the earth around us in just a handful of weeks, and I wasn't ready to say goodbye. "I'm not saying you have to stay, Michael. I live in the country. You wouldn't even have to talk to anyone but me . . . except at the airport, but that's a small price to pay to—"

Snapping his eyes up, he cut me off. "I won't leave the state, Mallory. Wherever you want me to go, no matter how isolated you think it is, it's still too many people for my taste."

"Even if it means seeing me?" I asked, my heart ripping.

A worn sigh escaped Michael as his head dropped. "I knew we shouldn't have started this. I knew I'd hurt you . . ."

Panic made me force brightness into my voice. "I'm not hurt. I don't regret us, and I don't want this to end." Fearful that he was retreating from me, I reached out and grabbed his hand. "I was just hoping . . . you would visit me. It was just a question—that's all."

His penetrating eyes studied me, searching for a lie, and I worked as hard as I could to keep my expression the same. *Don't notice the crack forming in my heart. Don't say something that will make it expand even faster than it needs to.*

After a while, he finally nodded. "Then I guess . . . to answer your question . . . no, I'm sorry. I won't be visiting you." A sad smile cracked his lips. "Although I can already tell there will be nights that I'll want to. Most nights, I think."

My heart started seizing and beating harder all at the same time. He looked so sad, so desperate to connect, and yet at the same time, he absolutely refused to step foot outside his social comfort zone. It broke my heart even more than the idea of our upcoming separation. *Who will make your eyes glow when I'm gone?*

I fingered my cross necklace, saying a silent prayer for this broken man who meant so much to me. Michael's eyes followed my movement, and like he knew what I was doing, he quietly said, "Do you pray for me?"

"Every day," I said with a nod. Michael bit his lip, and I could see the questions brewing in his eyes. "What?" I asked.

He pointed a finger at my necklace. "What do you pray for when you pray for me?"

"I pray for a lot of things. Your health, your safety . . . your happiness . . ."

I could almost see the irritation rolling up his spine, his hackles rising like a wolf's. "You think God cares about our happiness?"

Inhaling a deep breath, I nodded again. "Yes, I do."

Michael looked away, and I thought he was going to drop the topic he hated discussing. He surprised me, though, by returning his eyes to mine. "Then why does he let so many bad things happen? Why does he tolerate thieves, rapists . . . killers?" His eyes hardened with every word he spoke. "Why does he allow such horrible things to happen to such good people?"

I slowly let out the breath I hadn't even realized I'd been holding. "Because he gave us free will. Because he didn't want mindless automatons who loved him simply because we were told to love him. He gave us the freedom to *choose* to love him and his creations . . . or not to. And maybe that was a mistake, but if you think about it, what else could he do?"

Michael looked away again, but I could see him swallowing the lump in his throat; he was on the edge of an emotional cliff, about to go over, and I didn't want him to go over alone. I clasped his hand tight, tears stinging my eyes. "Trust me, Michael: he is mourning what happened to your wife right along with you . . . and he's taking very good care of her for you."

His eyes returned to mine, and a single tear rolled down his cheek. "Do you think so?" he whispered.

Leaping out of my chair, I tossed my arms around his neck. "Yes," I said into his skin. "I believe it with everything inside me. She's safe and happy."

Michael sighed as he held me back, and I felt a world of tension releasing from him with the exhale. He was silent for several long minutes, and even though my back hurt and my legs started cramping, I didn't let him go. Finally, when I thought I was about to get a charley horse I wouldn't be able to ignore, Michael pulled back. "Thank you, Mallory. That was surprisingly . . . therapeutic."

Smiling, I straightened and massaged my back. "I don't suppose that changed your mind?"

Michael stood with me, his face reflecting his inner peace. Twisting me around, he pushed my hands away and started rubbing my back for me. "No . . . it didn't," he said, his voice equally calm.

A small laugh escaped me as I enjoyed his ministrations. "Didn't think so . . . but I had to ask." A deep laugh rumbled through his chest, and then his arms wrapped around my waist, pulling me tight.

The heat emanating from his body was as soothing as the steel strength of his arms. Even though the world we were immersed in was treacherous, I'd never felt so safe. Thinking of the lurking beasts waiting in the darkness for their chance to devour us made me think of the wolf who'd penetrated our defenses. Worn dishes and broken containers were a constant reminder. A thought occurred to me while that moment swam through my head, and I twisted in Michael's arms so I was facing him. "Did your photo survive the . . . wolf invasion?"

Biting my lip, I hoped he knew which photo I meant. I also hoped the creature hadn't destroyed it. I didn't think I could survive that level of guilt. Michael's warm eyes drifted over my face, his smile serene. "Yeah . . . it's fine."

Relief flooded me so fast my knees felt like they might buckle. "Oh good . . . I didn't think I could deal with something—"

Before I could finish my sentence, Michael lowered his mouth to mine. "The way you care for me . . . makes it hard to resist you," he murmured, his lips barely brushing against me as he spoke.

A rush of desire sprang to life inside me, nearly burning me with its intensity. "Then don't." I wasn't sure what I meant by those words, but it was too late to take them back.

Michael minutely pulled away to look me in the eyes, and I saw the same desire heating in him. It scared me a little, but it excited me more. We couldn't cave—we shouldn't cave—but God . . . if we did, it would be . . . explosive.

I leaned up, silently begging Michael to kiss me again. He lowered his lips back to mine, answering my unspoken request. Fire raged through me as our mouths moved together. Everything about him felt so right, like we were meant to be together. Like it was fate. And wasn't it? I should have died in that crash, but I didn't. I landed safely in the middle of nowhere, no one around for hundreds of miles . . . but him. If that wasn't divine influence, then there truly was no such thing.

My hands came up to dig through his thick hair, and a low, erotic exhale left my lips. Michael's grip on me tightened, and his kiss intensified. Our breaths were quicker now, frantic pants that screamed our rising need for each other. My body was practically vibrating, and I felt like I was flying. All the reasons why we shouldn't do this crumbled into dust as I reveled in the feel of his body against mine.

His beard was tickling my skin, but I was too enraptured to care; every second was bliss. Michael's hands ran up my back, then shifted directions and cupped my backside. A loud moan escaped me, and Michael's lips left my mouth, curving up my cheek to my ear. He started nibbling on a lobe, and I fisted my hands in his hair. "God . . . yes."

I hadn't realized I'd said that out loud until Michael stepped away from me. I gasped as our bodies separated, but when I looked into his eyes, disappointment flooded me. What I saw there was remorse, not acceptance and excitement. "I'm sorry, Mallory. I shouldn't have—"

"It's fine," I told him, stepping forward. "I'm okay with this. I want you to."

Retreating from my advances, he shook his head. "I'm not. It's not fair to you. I'm not going anywhere, and you . . . you're not staying. And my wife, I still . . ." His face scrunched into confusion, like he wasn't sure what he still felt for her.

With a sigh, he quickly turned around, shutting the door on his confliction. My heart fell, but I knew stopping was the smart thing to do, since he was right about me leaving and him staying. I was getting tired of being smart, though.

"Okay, Michael," I said, schlepping to my couch bed.

Michael turned to watch me, and another weary sigh escaped him. "Mallory?"

Wondering if he would apologize again, I looked his way. "Yes?"

We locked eyes for long, silent seconds before he finally pointed at my hard bench. "I'll make you another mattress as soon as I can. I promise."

While it wasn't what I'd been hoping he'd say, it was sweet nonetheless. He was such a good man, and that was what made all of this so difficult. Because I couldn't speak, I merely nodded at him. His eyes were so stricken with guilt that I made myself smile. I didn't want him ending everything because we'd gotten carried away tonight. Stupid as it was, I still wanted his tender touch.

Chapter Nineteen

A pattern began to emerge over the next several weeks, a pattern of pushing forward and pulling away. I was afraid the kissing would end after our heated moment, but to my delight, Michael still wanted our limited intimacy. He just seemed guiltier about it, like he was certain he was hurting me. I tried to make him feel better by being as bright and cheery as I could be, like none of this was bothering me, but in truth, it was wearing me down. I didn't want this to end, but the end was steadily approaching.

But the passion between Michael and me was escalating in a way that was harder and harder to contain. It was like we kept dousing the fire but left the coals smoldering. All it took was the tiniest touch to set off the spark. I wasn't sure what that meant for us; all I knew was I wanted him more and more. I could sense that he wanted the same, but he wouldn't allow it for fear of hurting me, and so the looping cycle of guilt, remorse, and confusion continued. I wished there was a way for us to be together, without the past or the future interfering. If only he didn't hate humanity for his wife's murder . . . then, maybe, I could convince him to give life another chance, convince him to leave with me.

"Do you think your wife would have liked me?" I asked him one night while we warmed ourselves in front of the fire. "I mean . . . if we'd met while you and her were still married, and the two of us weren't . . . doing stuff . . . obviously . . ."

I felt my cheeks heating as my words trailed off. It shouldn't still be awkward to talk about his wife, but it was. It was like she was in the cabin with us. I often pictured her angelic form above us, either frowning at me for wanting her husband in all the ways I shouldn't or smiling at me because I was making him happy.

Michael's eyes shifted from the fire to my face. A small, sad smile crossed his lips. "Yes, I think Kelly would have liked you a lot." His brows creased together, and his smile curved into a frown. "That's the first time I've said her name in . . . a really long time. I'm not sure if that's a good thing . . . or a really bad thing."

He looked up at me like somehow I might have the answer to that very complicated question. I didn't. Not really. "I think it's a . . . normal thing. You're not physically interacting with her every day, so I think it's natural for you to not say her . . ."

Michael had looked away from me while I'd been talking, so I stopped. His expression was darker now, sadder. Only wanting him to feel joy, I put my hand on his knee. "I didn't mean to bring you down. I'm sorry."

He nodded, then sighed. "Is it weird that I still miss her so much I can hardly breathe sometimes?"

Weird, no. Painful, yes.

"I suppose not. You loved her . . . very much."

Michael's eyes flashed to my face, and his expression turned apologetic. "That was insensitive of me. I'm sorry. You're such a good friend—sometimes I forget that you're not just . . . a friend." His gaze drifted to the ground, but I saw the guilt there before he hid his eyes.

Inhaling a big breath, I leaned forward until I caught his eye. "I *am* your friend, first and foremost, and that means you can tell me anything. *Anything.*" And I would find a way to deal with it, because that was what friends did.

He smiled at me, and for the first time since our conversation had begun, only happiness was evident in the grin. "You're pretty amazing—do you know that?"

Leaning back in the chair, I huffed on my nails and rubbed them on my shirt. "Yep, I know."

Michael laughed, and the sound was just as untroubled as his smile. He suddenly disrupted the peace by slapping his hands on his knees and exclaiming, "As nice as this has been, resting time is over. It's time for my bath."

"And your haircut," I quickly added. He'd been putting that off for far too long now. Both of his mops were getting taken care of. Tonight.

He let out a playful groan as he rolled his eyes, but I wasn't caving tonight or letting him distract me from my goal.

Michael prepared the water while I searched for scissors. "They're in that one," he said with a laugh, pointing at one under the counter.

"How long were you going to let me look?" I asked him, mock annoyance on my face.

He shrugged, still grinning with amusement, then went back to his water. When the tub was full, he faced me. "Do you want to step outside for this part . . . or stay?" There was a look in his eyes, a heated expression that told me he'd be okay if I stayed.

A part of me wanted to give him his privacy and leave the cabin for a few minutes. A part of me wanted to blatantly stare at all of his glory being revealed inch by inch. I decided to compromise. I stayed but turned around so my back was to him. I heard Michael laugh; then I heard the sound of rustling clothes. It was extremely difficult to not peek. I curled my hands into fists, then pressed my fists against my legs. Even still, my head wanted to swivel, and it was only by constantly reinforcing my willpower that I kept it in place. It was a relief when I heard clear sounds of Michael entering the water.

Once the sound of rippling water subsided and a long, satisfied exhale left Michael, I risked turning around to look. With his legs hanging off one end, his head leaning back on the other, and his arms resting along the sides, he was the very picture of peace. He looked over at me with a calm smile, and my heart fluttered against my rib cage. God, he was everything I'd ever wanted in a man. If only he'd agree to come back with me, I was sure we'd have an amazing life together. Just as amazing as what he had up here. If he'd only give us a chance . . .

Maybe seeing the sadness sweeping over my face, Michael lifted his head and frowned. "What is it?"

Slapping on my carefree smile, I shook my head. "Nothing. I'm going to . . . read . . . until you're ready for me." *Will you ever be ready for me?*

Grabbing one of the books I'd breezed through at least twice already, I sat on my bed and waited. I tried to read, I really did, but watching Michael bathe was too fascinating. The tub wasn't large enough for all of him, so he had to wash himself in pieces. One leg, then the other, his chest, and then eventually, his head. He used a cup to help rinse off the soap and did a pretty decent job of getting most of the water to stay in the tub. When he was dripping wet, hair and beard soaked, he looked over my way and crooked a finger at me.

I'd been watching him for so long that it took me a moment to realize just what he was telling me. I startled in surprise, then smiled. My turn. Grabbing my scissors and a comb, I headed his way. His eyes followed me the entire time, and my heart started pounding. When I approached the side of the tub, my eyes glanced inside before I could stop them. Michael was covering all of the important bits with his hands. Seeing that he'd been prepared for me to sneak a peek made heat rush over my cheeks, and I instantly glued my eyes to his. He was peacefully smiling at me like he hadn't just caught me looking.

Opening and closing the scissors, I blurted out, "Ready?"

Facing front, he nodded. "Yep. Do your worst."

A small laugh escaped me. "I've never actually done this before, so it just might be my worst."

He laughed too. "If you've never done it before, then it will also be your best. It's all in how you look at it."

That made me feel a little better about possibly making him look like a four-year-old had cut his hair. Maybe next time it would look like an eight-year-old had done it. Assuming there was a next time. Not wanting to think about the end of us—yet again—I smoothed out his hair and made my first cut. He flinched like I'd hurt him, and I smacked his shoulder. He laughed, then relaxed into the tub. I made cut after cut, his hair getting shorter with every pass. I kept getting distracted by his shoulders, his chest, his arms, his abs . . . where his hands were covering. Every exposed part of him that I could see was like a beacon drawing me in.

It wasn't until his hair was as short as I could artfully get it when I noticed something I'd never noticed before. There were very faint markings on his neck, like an old, faded tattoo, one that had been as removed as it could be. And it was in the shape of a cross. I was surprised to see it, and once I figured out what it was, I was stunned. I lightly traced the design with my finger. His belief had been as strong as mine at one point, but grief and despair had ripped it away from him. It broke my heart.

Michael tensed as he felt me tracing the mark he'd tried to remove, then hide. I could tell he was waiting for me to ask about it, waiting for me to bring up a conversation he didn't want to have. Instead of saying anything, I leaned down and kissed the newly exposed skin. A shuddering sigh escaped him, and the tension released from his body. I shifted around so I could see his face. Smiling softly, compassion in my heart and my eyes, I cupped his cheek. *I'm so sorry.*

Like he'd heard my inner condolences, he gave me a tentative smile, one that begged me not to say anything. Respecting his wishes, I turned my attention to his beard. "Now it's time for the food trap."

I started in on it, and he grabbed my hand. "Leave some, okay. It's cold out there."

Frowning, I nodded. "All right, I'll leave you a blanket. It will just be a more aesthetically pleasing one."

He laughed, then smiled up at me. It was harder to cut his facial hair than the rest of him. His eyes glued on me were a thousand times more distracting than his body. I kept stopping and staring, and even though I knew his water was getting colder and colder, he never once said anything when I was lost in his eyes.

Once I was finished and his beard was neatly trimmed, close to his face, my breath caught at the sight of him. "Oh . . . wow . . . ," I murmured.

His brows creased as he felt his new do with one hand. "What? That bad?"

Biting my lip, I shook my head. "No . . . not at all." My eyes roved over his face, taking all of him in. "Don't take this the wrong way, but you are quite possibly the most attractive man I've ever seen." He'd hidden it well behind the crazy hair and life-in-the-woods beard, but now that he was stark naked before me, there was no hiding the truth. He was gorgeous, as attractive on the outside as he was on the inside.

Michael looked away, a small smile on his lips. "Why would I take that the wrong way?" he asked, glancing at me out of the corners of his eyes.

Smiling brightly, I told him, "I don't know . . . all I know is that I'm going to have to kiss you now."

He turned his lips toward me in invitation, and I immediately lowered my mouth to his. The sweetness and warmth enveloped me at once. For the first time, his scraggly beard didn't tickle me, and with the smooth, trim newness, I could feel every aspect of his glorious lips. Heaven. As I moved my hand to his cheek, he ran his through my hair. Desire surged through me, faster than ever before. I'd wanted him for so long now, and I'd tried to satisfy the craving with these mouthwatering kisses, but my body was screaming that it wasn't enough anymore. I needed all of him. But we couldn't go there.

I was just about to pull back, take a breather, when he shifted his position in the tub. Sitting up, he wrapped both arms around me, then pulled me inside with him. A shriek of surprise left me as the nearly lukewarm water saturated my clothes and spilled over the sides. There was barely any room for me on his lap, but it felt completely natural to be there. Michael laughed as I squirmed, then pulled my mouth back to him.

As I grew accustomed to the water, I settled in to the kiss. It felt different kissing him from this angle—more intense. And with him being completely naked beneath me, I could feel, for the first time, just how much he wanted me. "Michael," I murmured, my hand running down his chest to his hip. *God, I want you.*

Michael's breath was fast as he kissed me. The desire running rampant between us was almost enough to make the residual water in the tub start to boil. As my fingers inched down his hip, Michael's drifted up my chest. His hand cupped my breast, and a groan escaped me. *Yes.*

I shifted my mouth so I could kiss along his cheek, heading for his ear. Michael's eyes were closed, and the noises leaving his mouth were pleased and needy. I ground the side of my hip against him, wishing there was more room in this damn tub. As my lips closed around his earlobe, his hand slipped under my wet shirt. Just as I started sucking on his lobe, he pulled aside my bra and swept his thumb over a rigid peak. Another groan escaped me, and I moved my hips just far enough over that my hand could wrap around him.

Michael stiffened beneath me, and he dropped his head back with a groan. While I gently stroked him, he whimpered my name. His eyes were conflicted when I shifted to look at him. Passion and pain were playing across his features. "We should . . . stop," he panted. His fingers squeezed my breast as he said it, though, and I squeezed him in return.

"I don't want to," I said, breathless; then I lowered my mouth to his. Our kiss was frantic, passionate, crazed. His hand worked across my breast while I worked mine over him. I wanted out of this tub. I wanted to lie down and feel every single inch of him. "I want you . . ."

My words made Michael groan. His hand in my hair pulled me tight. "I want you too," he whispered. His words ignited me, and I removed my hand from him so I could get out of this damn tub. His next words froze me in place. "We can't, though."

Pulling back, I stared at him. He swallowed and pulled both of his hands away from my body. "I'm sorry . . . we just can't. You know why."

Like I was stuck in tar, all I could do was stare at him. He was the one who'd amplified this, and now he was pulling back? Now that I was on the edge of not caring about anything—consequences be damned—now he was bringing us back to reality? I supposed one of us had to.

"Yeah," I murmured. Setting my hands on the sides of the tub, I carefully removed myself from the water. I couldn't help but look at him as I got out. He was magnificent, rock hard, pulsing with need . . . for me . . . but still . . . he was right. We had to use our heads here because our hearts would surely lead us in the wrong direction.

Quickly averting my eyes, I walked over to my stuff so I could change into dry clothes. I heard Michael sigh, then heard the water sloshing as he got out. I couldn't look at him again as I dried myself off on one of his towels. I could hear him changing, heard him putting on his boots, but I kept my eyes averted. "I'll go wait outside so you can . . . change," he finally murmured.

My body was still flaring with desire, so I had to imagine his was too. I didn't want him to go outside. I wanted him to grab me, toss me down on his bed, and take me. But he wouldn't, and I had to accept that. "Thank you," I whispered, still not looking at him.

His boots clomped over to the door, and I heard the wood creak open. Michael sighed again, then told me, "I'm so sorry, Mallory," before heading into the darkness.

Tears sprang to my eyes, and silence blanketed me. "I'm sorry too," I whispered to the empty room. I never should have opened my heart to him, never should have agreed to limited intimacies that would both test and strain us. I should have kept my distance from him. But I hadn't, and it was too late to go back now. Because I was fairly certain I was falling in love with him.

Chapter Twenty

As time surged inexorably forward, I began to notice something that made my soul feel heavy with trepidation. Every time I went to the river to fill the five-gallon buckets, there was more water showing and less ice. It was getting warmer; spring was on the way. Spring—and separation.

Just a few short months ago, I'd been heartbroken over how far away spring had seemed. I'd been hurt, stranded, and forced to live with a stranger. I'd been scared for my life and missing my family. But now . . . now, I was kind of at peace here, and Michael was the reason for that.

He'd taken me in, taken care of me, made me feel safe and secure. And loved. We never spoke about our feelings, but every time we kissed, every time we locked eyes, every time we pulled back when things became too heated, we were silently screaming our affection for each other. It was torture, but as much as it hurt, I wasn't ready for it to end.

I felt gloomy and despondent as I trudged back to the cabin with my two buckets of water. Setting them down, I checked that the latch on the door was still securely locked before I unhooked it and stepped inside; I didn't want to run into any more unexpected visitors. After depositing the water in the corner, I decided to follow the trapline and go find Michael; I suddenly felt the need to be with him as much as possible.

The trail was easy to find. It hadn't snowed in a while, and Michael's daily path to work was stomped flat. The mounds of snow around the line were smaller than before; the warmer days were quickly melting them into sodden, soggy heaps. I could even hear water droplets falling from the branches of the tall trees surrounding me, could see the myriad holes in the snow where melted flakes had struck like wet meteorites. Everywhere I turned, I saw signs of winter's demise. It further dampened my mood.

As I trudged along the trail, I came across something that stopped me in my tracks. There was a paw print in the snow just to my right. By its direction, the creature it belonged to was crossing the trail, heading back toward the cabin, and it was huge—grizzly bear huge. Were they already emerging from hibernation? I thought we'd have more time before we had to worry about them again. I felt over my shoulder for my rifle, but it wasn't there. I'd set it down in the cabin when I'd dropped off the water. I'd been so focused on getting to Michael that I'd forgotten to pick it back up. That was a *huge* mistake, one that could cost me my life out here. Going back to get my gun was just as risky as going forward to find Michael—riskier, actually, since that was the direction the bear had headed. I'd just have to continue forward and hope that the bear hadn't circled back to this location.

I was on high alert as I moved up the trail. While I walked, I noticed more tracks, smaller ones, belonging to animals that didn't terrify me. Ignoring them, I swept the trail for signs of creatures higher up on the food chain.

When I finally spotted Michael, I breathed a sigh of relief. He swung around, gun raised when he heard me approaching. Apparently, he was on high alert too; he must have noticed the paw prints. Seeing a gun being pointed at my chest made me involuntarily raise my hands. "It's just me," I quickly told him.

He lowered the weapon, but his eyes never stopped scanning the defrosting landscape. "I didn't know you were coming out today," he told me, a small smile breaking his hard demeanor; he was happy to see me.

I resisted the urge to tell him I'd rushed out here because I'd missed him and instead gave him a nonchalant shrug. "I changed my mind. I take it you saw the grizzly tracks?"

At the mention of the tracks, a look of pride and admiration crossed Michael's face. It was quickly replaced with concern. "Yeah, I spotted a couple of sets. They're out early this year, which means they're probably hungry. We need to be extra careful."

Fear shot up my spine, and I stepped closer to Michael. I knew how I got when I was superhungry; I could only imagine how cranky a hungry bear would be. "Should we go back?" I asked him, watching the trees now too.

Michael pursed his lips as he thought, and for a moment, I was so distracted by him I forgot all about the bear. He'd let me cut his hair and his beard a few times now, keeping it short and neat and oh-so-sexy. I hadn't cut it again while he'd been bathing, though—that had been too tempting for both of us; dreams of that night often woke me up panting and clutching at my blankets. Since that night, I always cut his hair while he was fully dressed and sitting at the kitchen table. While I looked forward to every time he let me take a pair of scissors to him, I couldn't deny that I preferred the nude version . . .

"Yeah, we should go in. All the traps were empty anyway." He indicated the bare basket on his back, and putting my inappropriate fantasy away, I frowned. Michael needed the money he earned from furs, and while he had a decent stack of them back at the cabin, I wouldn't say it was enough to cover the commodities I'd used or the damage the wolf had done. Michael was going to be hurting next winter, and that didn't sit well with me.

We turned to head back the way we'd come. Michael still had his gun out, was still surveying the land, searching for trouble. A forlorn sigh escaped me. I wanted to be somewhere with him that wasn't quite so dangerous all the time. I wanted to hold his hand and go for a walk with him in a park, where nature was still abundant but the predators were kept in check. I wanted . . . a normal life with him.

Michael looked over at hearing my weary exhale. Maybe mistaking why I'd made the sound, he gave me an encouraging smile. "It will be okay, Mallory." He patted the butt of his superpowered rifle. "This thing can take out anything we might come across."

That hadn't been my problem, but I smiled anyway. Michael didn't buy it. "What's wrong?"

Feeling weary to the bone, I kicked at a pile of slush by my feet. "The bears . . . the melting snow . . . the empty traps . . . spring is on its way, and that means we'll be going our separate ways soon."

Michael's face fell, and he looked away from me to check the tree line again. "Yeah, I know. The part I ordered could come any day now . . . and then I'll be able to fix the plane, get you on your way." He looked back at me, confusion on his face. "But that was the plan all along . . . to get you home."

"I know," I said, lowering my gaze to the soggy ground. "I just wish we were heading out together. I feel so close to you . . . I don't want to stop getting to know you right when I feel like I'm finally starting to."

Michael stopped in his tracks and put a gloved hand on my arm, stopping me as well. "I know how you feel, Mallory. I wish . . . this wasn't the end. I wish . . ." He sighed, then shook his head and kept walking. "We knew where this was going when we started, which is why I didn't want to start this." He didn't sound angry, just sad. I understood—I felt the same way.

"I know," I repeated as I followed him. "I just never thought . . . when we started this, I never imagined how much you'd mean to me."

My voice had faded to a near whisper, but Michael heard me. He stopped again, waiting for me. When I caught up to him, he cupped my cheek. His glove was cool against my skin, but the warmth behind the gesture was undeniable. He leaned into me, and I eagerly lifted my lips in anticipation.

Right when his lips were just about to touch mine, I accidentally poured out my heart's wish. "Come back with me."

He froze, then pulled back to look at me. Pain was in his eyes. "Mallory, you know I can't."

Disappointment hit me so hard I nearly stepped back from the recoil. "I know you won't. I know you've given up on people, and for some reason that includes me too. But if you gave it a chance, I think you'd love Cedar Creek. It's quaint, isolated—my parents know every single person who comes into their diner. Crime is virtually nonexistent. It's just about the greatest—"

Michael held up his hand, stopping me from selling him on my hometown. "If it *is* how you say, then it's only that way because it hasn't truly been discovered yet. More people will come, and it will turn into a city . . . just like every other city. You can't change human nature, Mallory. Eventually, your little town will be ruined, and you'll be left with the good ole days. I'm sorry." He looked genuinely apologetic, like he'd looked into a crystal ball and seen his prediction as fact, and he was heartbroken for me.

"Please, Michael. Everyone isn't as bad as you think. There's still hope in the world. Look at you and me."

I smiled, offering him encouragement, but he only frowned. "Our relationship was doomed from the very start. How is that hope?"

His words, laced with razor-sharp truth, cut me to the bone. "Because we *found* each other. Literally, in the middle of nowhere, we found each other, and I refuse to accept that that means nothing. We saved each other . . . that means *everything*. And all over the world, that hope—that salvation—happens every day, every minute, every second. Have faith . . . God's not done with us."

A slow smile brightened his face. "Your optimism is truly remarkable. And inspiring." His smile slipped. "I think I'll miss that most of all."

My eyes burned with forming tears. I still hadn't changed his mind. "Kiss me," I whispered, my heart cracking just as surely as the ice melting on the river.

He stared at me for long, silent seconds, and then ever so slowly, he lowered his lips to mine. When our mouths met, I reveled in the sweet bitterness of our tender touch. Every part of me, down to the very crevices in my soul, ached with joy and pain. How could this be over, when it was only just beginning?

The tears building in my eyes slowly dripped down my cheeks as our heartbreaking connection continued. When Michael finally pulled away, his eyes were as soft as his voice. "We should get going. That bear is still out there, somewhere."

As if the grizzly had heard him say that, a growl cut the silence somewhere in the woods. It raised every hair on my arms and dried the tears still wanting to form. Something was out there, and it was starving. I wanted to clutch Michael's arm, hold him tight, but I knew he needed freedom of movement in case the creature spotted us and charged.

We didn't speak much the rest of the way back, but I dwelled on our conversation. With each step toward the cabin, it felt like we were drifting further apart. It tore at me, made me want to run the other way, foolish as that would be. Looking up at the sky, I prayed for snow, prayed for a storm, prayed for anything that might keep me here—keep me with *him*—longer. I'd always looked forward to spring before, but now I hoped it never arrived.

When we got back to the cabin, Michael did a quick check around it to make sure the bear hadn't found a way in besides the front door. He was smiling when he returned to me. "Everything looks good. Why don't you go inside? I'm going to go check the shed."

Nodding, I watched him leave before I entered the cabin. The first thing I noticed when I stepped inside was my gun, exactly where I'd left it. God. Rookie move. Being unarmed out here wasn't a good idea. Picking the gun up, I was just about to put it where it belonged when I heard a sound that chilled my blood. Shouting, followed by a gunshot. Michael.

Gun clenched firmly in my hand, I scrambled out the door and raced to the shed. I was running so fast I couldn't stop myself when I got there, and I nearly fell on my ass as I slipped and slid on the ice. What I saw in front of the shed door stole my breath. Michael was lying there . . . and the snow around him was splattered in blood; it looked like a crime scene.

"Oh my God, Michael!" He didn't move when I said his name, and for a minute, I was sure he was dead. No . . . he couldn't be gone. As I slid to his side, he turned to look at me, and a shaky exhale of relief left me. Thank God, not dead.

"What happened?" I asked, frantically searching him for the source of the blood. When I found it, Michael inhaled through clenched teeth. Pulling my fingers away from his leg, I stopped to study the torn fabric; the cuts were distinctly claw shaped. "Oh my God," I repeated.

Hissing again, Michael said, "Found the bear. It was trying to open the shed door." He indicated the door, and I marveled at the long cuts down the thick wood. Jesus, that could have been Michael's chest. As I folded back the rips in his pants to examine his skin, Michael flinched. "I nicked it, and it ran off. Lucky for me. Sometimes that just pisses them off."

He laughed like this was funny, but I didn't see anything humorous here. "Can you walk?" I asked him, swiveling my head to take in the bloody tracks leading away from the shed. "We should go inside in case it comes back." He might have scared it off, but that didn't mean it would stay scared. Food was a powerful motivator.

"Yeah." Michael grunted, shifting his weight to stand. I helped him the best I could, but it was a challenge getting him to his feet.

Michael cried out in pain when he put weight on his leg, and I instantly sympathized; it wasn't all that long ago when I'd been the one hobbling around. His pant leg was soaked, saturated with blood, and fear gave me the strength I needed to get him out of there. He had to be okay—he just had to be. He whimpered, holding back the extent of his pain, the entire time we trudged back to the cabin.

I nearly cursed out loud when I saw that the cabin door was swinging wide open. In my haste to get to Michael, I hadn't closed and secured the latch. Well, I dared a wolf to be in there now. What I was afraid of at the moment had nothing to do with wild animals.

Supporting Michael's weight as much as I could, I kicked in the door, yelling loudly in the process. If something was in here, I wanted it to know I was coming. Thankfully, the cabin was as empty as I'd left it. Michael made a pained laugh as we stumbled through the door. "Remind me . . . to not . . . make you mad," he said in strained pants.

Closing the door, I secured the inside latch. "Come on—let's take a look at that leg." I got him over to my couch bed, then made him sit down on it. The bear had clawed him in the thigh. I wasn't an expert or anything, but it looked pretty deep. "You're gonna need to take these off," I said, tugging at his pants.

He tried to smile, but it came out more like a grimace. "This sounds familiar," he mused, undoing the button of his pants.

A nervous laugh escaped me. "Yeah, except I'm the doctor this time."

"You'll do fine, Mallory," he said. "But maybe you could get me some of that pain medicine."

He nodded over to his supplies, and I knew he meant the alcohol. I hoped we had some left. While he took off his boots and pants, I searched for things I'd need to patch him up. Michael called out additional supplies and instructions. "Boil some water to clean the wound.

You'll need gauze pads, tape, scissors, antibacterial ointment. And a needle and thread—this is going to need stitches."

That made me pause. Feeling all the blood drain from my face, I looked over at him. He was lowering his pants over the wound, examining it as he went. It looked bad, looked bloody, but it was what he'd said that terrified me. "I can't . . . sew you."

He gave me a pain-filled expression of encouragement. "Yes, you can, Mallory. You can do it because you *have* to do it. And if there's one thing I know for certain about you, it's that you'll do what has to be done . . . no matter how much you hate doing it." His sentence had an ominous feeling of foreboding about it, and I knew he wasn't just talking about this moment anymore. I had a hard time swallowing the lump in my throat.

I headed over to him once I had all the supplies he'd asked for. I gently placed a gauze pad on the wound and had him apply pressure before I began the process of boiling water. When everything was ready to go, I was fairly certain I was going to throw up. Taking a long gulp of the whiskey, Michael nodded at me. "It's okay, Mallory. You can't hurt me any more than I'm already hurting."

Again, that sentence felt overly full of meaning. My heart couldn't take it. I began with cleaning the wound. In addition to being the first thing I needed to do anyway, it seemed the easiest task. Michael flinched and squirmed the entire time, clenching his jaw so hard all the veins in his neck were bulging. I didn't stop, though. I knew the best way to get through this was quickly.

The seeping blood was nauseating, but even worse was the knowledge that I was inflicting pain on another human being. That made me feel sicker than anything else. By the time the wound was as clean as I could get it, I had tears in my eyes.

Michael let out a relieved sigh when my ministrations stopped and took another swig of alcohol. "You're doing good," he said. "Now for the stitching."

My heart sank, and my stomach roiled. "I don't think I can . . ."

Michael gently put his hand over mine, and I locked eyes with him. "Don't think of it as skin. It's a quilt . . . just a quilt."

Even though his leg was probably radiating with pain, he looked so encouraging, so filled with positivity, like he knew with absolute certainty that I could do this. Like it was no more complicated than learning how to trap animals, collect water, chop wood . . . live his life.

Inhaling a deep breath, I let it out slowly. "Okay," I told him, feeling stronger. "I can do this."

My hands shook a little as I tried to prep the needle. Stopping, I flexed them and tried again. The thread successfully slipped through the eye, and I said a quick thanks. Holding the wound closed with one hand, I hovered the needle near the skin with the other.

Michael had his eyes shut when I looked up at him, his face a mask of concentration. "Michael," I whispered. He popped them open to look at me, and I shook my head. "You know you can't live like this forever, don't you?"

He opened his mouth, and I expected him to tell me he was fine, that he preferred living this way, but instead of speaking, he shut his mouth and looked . . . thoughtful.

While he was distracted with pondering his life choices, I slid the needle into his skin. A pained whimper left him, and I instantly wanted to stop hurting him. I wasn't finished, though, so I choked back the empathy—the guilt and regret—and fixed him to the best of my ability. And that felt full of meaning too.

Chapter Twenty-One

Michael took it easy for the next few days, letting his body heal. I checked his bandages every chance I got, and I had to say, for my first time sewing skin, it looked pretty darn good. That entire scenario was something I'd never imagined myself doing. Ever. Blood and gore, they weren't my favorite things. But even still, the worst part was having to put Michael through that kind of torment. If I could have knocked him out, I would have.

Only three of the bear's claws had pierced his skin, but the ragged marks it had left were deep. Michael would have scars from the encounter. Like most men I'd ever met, he didn't seem too worried about that. It was the whole "chicks dig scars" mentality. While he recovered, I worried. I worried about infection, worried about the injury not healing properly, and worried about the bear returning. That last one was the only one Michael was worried about too. Just a few short hours after I'd cleaned him up, he'd gone out to the shed to remove the blood and fortify the door. I'd helped him as much as I could, and by the time we were finished, I doubted *we* could have gotten through the door, let alone a bear.

Michael relaxed after the shed was protected and spent a lot of time resting in the cabin. When I wasn't doing chores for the two of us, I was with him. Resting. And kissing. And wishing things were different.

"So, how are you feeling today, Mr. Bradley?" I playfully asked him, checking his bandages.

"Like I was mauled by a bear," he answered, a smile on his lips. As he examined my handiwork with me, his smile grew. "Not bad, Mallory. I think you might have a future in health care."

Not ever wanting to cause someone that much pain again, I shook my head. "No thanks. I'll leave that to you." Michael's expression slipped, and I quickly altered my sentence to, "I'll leave that to people like you."

He gave me a half-hearted grin, like he appreciated my attempt to fix my blunder. Then he smiled widely as though all was forgiven. "In all seriousness, you do have talent. Those stitches are excellent . . . and I think it's time they came out."

My blood felt frozen again. I wasn't ready to hurt him again. "What? Already? Wouldn't it be better to wait another week or so?"

Still smiling, Michael shook his head. "That would actually make them harder to remove. Best to do it now, before things get too . . . sticky."

My stomach roiled, but resignation swept over me. "Okay . . ."

Michael reached down to caress my hand. "It will be fine. I'll talk you through it."

"Whiskey," I stated, standing to retrieve the emergency bottle of pain relief.

Michael shook his head. "No, I can take this sober. I'll be fine."

I tossed him a wry smile. "It's not for you." He laughed but said nothing when I grabbed the bottle and took a swig. Or two.

When I felt steady enough, I grabbed a pair of scissors and headed back to where he was waiting on my bed. In his underwear. If there was one thing that I could possibly thank the bear for, it was for giving me an excuse to get Michael half-dressed on numerous occasions. But no . . . that wasn't enough to make up for what he'd gone through. What he *was* going through.

Once I had the scissors and a couple of fresh gauze pads, I squatted down in front of him. "Okay . . . what do I do?"

With a smooth, calm, professional voice, he instructed me on just how I should cut the thread and pull out the pieces. I was very relieved when it didn't seem to bother him as much as I'd feared; he only flinched a few times and let out a pained exhale once, when a stubborn thread near the edge refused to move and I had to yank especially hard. I apologized profusely every time I appeared to cause him the slightest pain, and he told me over and over that it was fine, that he was okay. I truly wished I believed that.

After he was cleaned up and dressed, I headed outside to get us some meat from the shed for lunch. I always took my gun with me now, double- and triple-checking that it was strapped across my back before I headed out.

It was a quiet morning, but even so, I scanned the forest, searching for signs of trouble. All I saw was white snow specked with brown earth, and all I heard was the occasional splish-splashing of water droplets hitting the branches. When I got to the shed, faint remnants of the attack were still visible—places where the snow had been cleaned away, deep gouges in the door. It scared me to the bone to think about what could have happened here.

I was just about to unlatch the shed when I heard something besides the drip-dropping of melting snow. It was an odd, unnatural sound, but a familiar one too. It took me only a couple of moments to figure out what it was, and when I did, my heart started surging in my chest. A plane.

Stepping away from the shed, I started searching the sky for the source of the noise. When the plane appeared, I was surprised by how low it was flying, just above the treetops. If I hadn't been frozen in shock, I could have waved to the pilot, and he easily would have seen me.

The plane flew right over the top of me, heading for the clearing where Michael stored his airplane. I thought it might land, thought we might have a visitor—and an instant way home—but as I watched, a door in the side opened, and a small box was pushed out. The plane continued on while a parachute on the box carried it gently to the ground. Michael's spare parts, what he'd been waiting all winter for.

Sharp pain crashed through me as I thought of what that box meant for us. Separation, finality, the end. I'd go home, and Michael would be left alone. As I watched the box drift below the tree line into the clearing near Michael's plane, I debated not telling him it was here. I could pretend I hadn't seen anything out of the ordinary, pretend nothing had been dropped. But no . . . I couldn't, and I wouldn't do that to Michael. Fixing his plane wasn't only about flying me home. It was also how Michael was going to get the supplies he needed to make it here another lonely year. Avoiding this wasn't a possibility—I had to face it head-on. As hard as that was.

Forgetting about the shed, I headed back to the cabin. When I opened the door, Michael was still resting on my bed. He looked my way when I entered. "Did I hear a plane?" he asked.

Closing the door behind me, I nodded. "Yeah, they air-dropped the part you've been waiting for . . ."

As my voice trailed off, a heavy, ominous feeling settled over the room. Michael stared at me just as unflinchingly as I stared back at him. We both knew what that meant. "Oh," he finally said. "I guess we should go get it before something tries to run off with it."

A part of me wanted that to happen, but again, I couldn't condemn him to complete isolation. I helped him stand, even though I knew he could handle it on his own; I just wanted to be as close to him as I could be, for as long as I could be.

Michael leaned into my side once he was standing, and our eyes locked. There was so much I wanted to tell him, but most of it was along the lines of *Leave with me*—and I already knew his answer. No, no, and hell no. His mind was made up; my mind was made up. We were both impenetrable, unmovable pieces on this game board, and

I think we both hated that we were. In another life, we might have worked.

Clearing my throat, I pointed to the door. "Are you sure you can make it? I can go alone."

Soft words met my ear. "I'll be fine, Mallory. I'm stronger than you think."

When I looked back at him, his eyes were filled with meaning, and I knew without a doubt he was asking me to let him go, to let him stay here and live his life, and to not worry about him once I was gone. Fat chance. He would be on my mind every day. I was sure of it.

We trudged toward his plane in silence. Every step felt heavier than the last. I should have been happy, ecstatic, elated. I'd been waiting for this day for so long, waiting for a chance to leave for so long. Who knew that a warm smile and a set of pale-blue eyes—and a heart cleaved in two—could have so fully and completely changed my outlook? If only I could stay, stay and live out the remainder of my years in social solitude with him. But I already knew I couldn't. When it came down to it, I needed people. I needed my family, my friends, my pets, the security of easily obtainable health care, medicine, and yes, even the convenience of modern technology . . . like running water. And also, I wanted to feel 100 percent certain that I wouldn't be mauled by a wild animal when I opened my front door. Well, 80 percent at least.

There was just so much about my life that I couldn't leave behind for the woods. But in an ironic twist of fate, I couldn't leave the woods behind either. Or at least I couldn't leave Michael behind. He was now one of my life essentials. And that meant that no matter what choice I made going forward, I was going to lose something invaluable. It *killed* me.

When we got to the brown package lying in the snow, I had to wipe away the stray tears that I couldn't keep contained anymore. I didn't want Michael to see them, but of course, his eagle eyes noticed. Holding the much-needed airplane part in the crook of his arm, he removed a glove and cupped my glistening cheek. The tenderness in the gesture made the tears emerge faster. "Mallory," he whispered. "This is a good thing. You need to go home, and I need to . . ." He sighed, his breath frosty in the air. "This entire experience with you has been . . . so good. Better than good, but I don't want it to end with tears. I don't want to cause you pain. I was trying to avoid hurting you."

He sighed again, and I knew what he was thinking: *This is exactly why I wanted to keep my distance.* I wanted to throw on a smile, tell him I was fine, but staring at the box that would eventually rip us apart made it too difficult to be cheery. "You made me happy. So incredibly happy . . . and that's why it hurts. But I'm glad for the tears because they mean it was worth it. They mean my time here mattered. They mean *you* . . . matter." *You're not alone. Even when I leave, you won't be alone.*

Sadness clouded his face, moistened his eyes. He started shaking his head, but then he dropped the box and wrapped me in his arms. "I wish there was a way . . . I wish things could be different. Maybe if I'd met you right after . . ." He paused, and I could feel him shaking his head. "You matter to me, too, Mallory . . . and I'm so sorry." After holding me for a moment, he pulled back to look me in the eye. "On the bright side, we have a little more time together."

I frowned in confusion. "What do you mean? The part is here—how long will it take you to fix the plane?" It was such a small part; surely he could replace it in an hour.

Michael glanced over at the fully winterized plane. Covered in snow, heavy tarps, and thick canvas, it looked like a mechanical sleeping giant, not yet ready to wake. Looking back at me, Michael gave me my favorite boyish grin. "Well, just a few hours, really, but I won't be able to start on it until I'm *fully* healed. Doctor's orders," he added with a wink.

My eyes snapped to the injury hidden under his pants. Did he mean 100 percent healed? Because that could take weeks . . . was he seriously giving me weeks? I was momentarily torn. There were people back home who were hurting because of me, people who were terrified I was dead. Leaving them in limbo for even longer felt cruel. But

Michael . . . once I left him, there was a really good chance I might not see him again—that was torturous. Michael was too important to me to pass on his generous gift of time. Beaming, I pulled him in for another hug. "We better get you back to the cabin then so you can rest up." And so I could hold him, kiss him . . . and pretend that he was mine forever.

Anything to extend the joy and forestall the agony.

I made a big show of making him take it easy when we got back to the cabin, but really, the longer it took him to heal, the happier I would be. Although as I looked around at Michael's dwindling supplies, the items he couldn't make or forage for himself, I saw *need.* Michael *needed* to go into town. Him delaying for me—for us—was sweet, but he could only hold off for so long. Everything I looked at in his cabin, from the pancake mix to the antibacterial ointment, was suddenly a ticking clock, counting down our time together in a steady, unrelenting rhythm. What I wouldn't give to be able to freeze time.

As I fluffed the pillow Michael was lying against as he sat on my bench bed with his legs extended, I suddenly remembered what I'd been doing before the plane changed . . . everything. "I forgot lunch—you must be starving. I'm sorry; I'll go get some meat."

I stood up to leave, and he grabbed my arm. "Mallory . . . I'm not hungry." He patted the space on the bed beside him. "Stay with me."

For a second, I could only stare into his captivating eyes, entranced. Was he asking me to sit . . . or were his words literal? He patted the bed again, and I blinked out of my trance. Michael had never officially asked me to stay because he knew that wasn't what I wanted. And he thought his heart was frozen, incapable of moving forward. I knew the truth there—it wasn't—but Michael hadn't reached that conclusion yet, and I couldn't make him. Like any revelation, he needed to come to it on his own.

But just him asking for my comfort was a step in the right direction. Or maybe it was the wrong direction. I really wasn't sure anymore. I just knew I needed him. My heart was thudding in my chest when I sat in the scant amount of space beside him. I was so nervous, which was ridiculous since we'd done several intimate things before—that night in the tub still haunted my dreams. Sitting next to him now shouldn't make my heart race, but it did.

Smiling at me, Michael tucked a strand of hair behind my ear. "Have I ever told you how beautiful you are?"

I felt my cheeks heating. He was usually the one who got embarrassed after saying something sweet, but now I was the one blushing like a schoolgirl. The tables had turned, and I wasn't sure why. Because we had a definable expiration date now? Was that making him bolder? God, I hoped that wasn't the reason.

"No . . . I don't think so," I told him. "But you probably only think that because I'm the only human female you've seen in months. When squirrels are your only company, anything looks good."

He laughed but shook his head. "No. I have a good memory. I remember what attractiveness looks like . . . and it looks like you."

My breath hitched as I stared at him, and the content feeling of rightness expanded inside me to a nearly painful level. He was so . . . *everything. God . . . why can't I keep him?* Nothing and no one answered me, and I knew there wouldn't be an answer on this. We were destined to find each other, to save each other—and we had—but that didn't necessarily mean we were destined to be together. Happily ever after was never guaranteed.

Needing him, I leaned forward, searching for his mouth. Right before our lips touched, I whispered, "I love you." The sound got lost in our connection, and I was grateful. Proclaiming the growing feeling inside me wouldn't alter our future. It would only increase the pain. And I didn't want to hurt Michael. I wanted to love him. Forever.

Chapter Twenty-Two

I wanted time to move slowly. I wanted it to drip by like a barely leaking faucet. But it didn't. It surged like a river, with each day moving quicker than the last. Every time I saw Michael's leg, I calculated how much longer it would be until he was completely healed, until the searing gashes were merely fading red streaks. I knew his leg was an arbitrary guideline, though, one he'd stated for my benefit only. Survival was the real timeline, and that was something that couldn't be put on the back burner for much longer.

"Michael . . . we're running out of salt."

As the words trickled out of me, dread and sadness filled me. Salt wasn't just a frivolous condiment out here. It was preservation—it was life. And while Michael might not need it right away, since his shed still held a few pounds of stored cured meat, he would need it soon.

Michael sighed as he looked into his large salt container, filled mostly with air now. There was maybe a half cup of salt left. Maybe. "It . . . will be fine. Hunting should be picking up, and then we'll have fresh meat. Plenty of it."

Closing the lid on the salt, I shook my head. "Hunting . . . and that requires bullets. How is your stock of ammunition? Last I saw, there was only one box remaining, and it wasn't entirely full."

He smiled that disarming, untroubled smile. "I guess I better be a good shot then."

A cheerless grin curled my lips. "I know what you're doing, and I appreciate it . . . so much, but it's been weeks. You can't keep avoiding the plane. You need to fix it," I whispered.

Michael swallowed. "I know. I just don't want to."

Warmth filled me, sadness too. "And the fact that you don't want to means a lot to me. But as much as we both don't want you to do this . . . we can't keep putting it off." I reached up to touch his face, and he swallowed again. Then his mouth lowered to mine.

I reveled in the softness of his lips, in the rugged tickle of his beard, in the woodsy scent that constantly surrounded him. This man would have my heart for all eternity . . . I hoped he somehow knew that.

When our tender moment ended, Michael pulled away from me, reluctance on his face. "I guess I better get started. The plane won't fix itself."

"I'll help you," I said, swallowing a thick lump in my throat.

Michael shook his head. "You don't have to. I know . . . how difficult this is."

Did he? Did he truly understand how much I was going to miss him, how much this forced separation was killing me? Did he feel the same? "If this is . . . if the next couple of days is all we have, then I want to spend them with you."

His eyes glazed as he stared at me; then he slowly nodded. "Okay, Mallory."

We dressed for the harsh weather in silence, our hearts heavy with unspoken words. I followed Michael to his shed, where he stored his tools as well as his meat supply. As I glanced over the shelves of meat, I reconsidered my earlier opinion that he had enough to last awhile. Even though he'd hunted more to compensate for having company, his supplies were lower than they should have been for this time of year. Or at least, they seemed that way to me. Maybe that was just because

I was scared to leave him out here all alone, with threats and predators around every corner. Sure, he'd survived five years without me, but all it would take was one bad instance . . . one bear attacking his shed, one wolf lurking in his cabin. *One* wrong move, and I truly would lose him forever.

Michael grabbed his needed part, plus the tools to install it, and stuffed them into his backpack. After he firmly closed up the shed, we were on our way, hiking through the woods to get to the clearing where his plane was resting, waiting, sleeping. I clasped Michael's gloved hand as we walked, needing the contact. He smiled down at me, but there was no joy in the gesture, just melancholy.

When we reached the plane, I felt like sobbing. That one piece of machinery symbolized the end of what we'd been slowly building over the last few months. Maybe we shouldn't have built it in the first place, but we hadn't planned on the connection between us. Hadn't planned on it, hadn't expected it, and hadn't been able to stop it. It had swept us away without our permission. True love had a way of doing that.

After releasing my hand, Michael pulled the tarp off the engine of the plane. He laid it on the melting snow, then set his tools upon it. I watched in silence as he went about his repairs. Occasionally he asked for tools, and heart in my shoes, I handed them to him. A part of me hoped he wouldn't be able to repair the plane, but I knew that was a selfish feeling—he truly would die here if he had no way to leave. We both would. But even still, at the end of the day, when the daylight was fading into blackness and he tested the engine—and it started—I was more crushed than relieved.

Tears were streaming down my cheeks when Michael gathered his tools and put the tarp back over the plane. His heart was in his eyes when he looked at me, and I clearly saw the words *I'm sorry* in his gaze. Since there was nothing to be sorry about, I was glad he didn't voice them.

"It's getting dark . . . we should go back."

I could only nod in response. As we journeyed back to the cabin, disappointment filled me. Why did he have to finish repairing it in one day? Couldn't he have stretched it out for two, maybe three days? A heavy sigh escaped me. No, there was no point stretching it out anymore. It was time.

"You okay?" he asked, his eyes momentarily leaving the path to search my face.

"Yes," I told him. Then I sighed again. "Maybe. I don't know."

The cabin came into view, lightened by the glow of Michael's flashlight. When I glanced up at his face, I saw his lips firmly pressed together and his brows visible under his cap bunched in contemplation or confusion. Not wanting to cause him unnecessary pain, I squeezed his hand. "Yes, I'm fine. Sad . . . but fine."

He nodded. "I know . . . I know how you feel. I feel the same way."

Even as grief crushed my spirit, butterflies flittered through my stomach. It didn't seem possible to feel unparalleled joy and crushing despair all at the same time, but apparently . . . it was.

After putting his tools back in the shed and grabbing some meat for dinner, Michael led us back to the main cabin. He quickly checked the perimeter for animals, then unlocked the door and led me inside with a hand on my lower back. I memorized every touch, every look, every word. This was it. This was the last night we'd be together. It could possibly be the last time we ever saw each other. Life was so uncertain. I'd have to save up for a plane, and by the time I had enough money for one, life could have changed on me again. I could say I'd visit, but only God knew if I'd actually be able to. I didn't want this to end tonight, but regardless of what I wanted, it *was* ending.

Michael and I went through our routine of making dinner. Silence hung in the air as we ate, lacing the room with tension. How could I say goodbye to this man? How could I leave, knowing I might not ever see him again? Knowing we could be together—and be *great* together—if he'd only give humanity another chance and come home with me. Or if

I said goodbye to everything and stayed here with him. The extremes of our choices were so unfair, but then again, most difficult choices were. That was what made them hard in the first place.

After dinner, I put our dishes in the tub, preparing to wash them. When I turned to go get some water, Michael grabbed my hand. "That can wait," he whispered. "This . . . can't." Then he drew me close to him and crashed his lips down to mine.

There was an intensity in his kiss that hadn't been there before, an almost desperate need to connect. My body roared to life as his mouth moved over mine. My breath quickened; my heart raced. Michael pulled me tight against his body, and I knew he was feeling it too—the double-edged sword of passion and pain. Even though I knew it would kill me later, I wanted more. I wanted *all* of him.

He began pulling me toward my bed, and my heart leaped even higher. Was he finally on the same page as me . . . now that we were ending? When his legs hit the back of the bench, he lowered himself onto it, then pulled me with him until we were lying side by side on the moss mattress. Wondering where his head was at, I breathily said, "Michael?"

He broke apart from my lips, his eyes glowing in the flickering candlelight. One of the only good candles he had left. "I just want to hold you," he whispered.

His lips returned to mine, and I ignored the flash of disappointment coursing through my body. He was being smart, still, and I respected that. I respected him. I loved him. With everything inside me, I loved him.

Michael leaned over as he kissed me, half covering me with his body. Sheltering me, protecting me, warming me . . . always warming me. He cupped my cheek, and a strangled whimpering sound escaped him. Pulling back, I searched his face. He looked desolate.

"Michael . . . ?" I knew I didn't need to ask him what was wrong—I already knew—but the words lingered in the air anyway.

He placed a soft kiss on my lips, then my nose. "I just . . . I didn't think I could feel like this again. After Kelly . . . I didn't think I'd ever want to. And now . . . now you're leaving, and I . . . I'm sorry. It's just harder than I thought it would be to let you go."

My heart was thumping so hard in my chest that I was positive he could hear it raging in the silence between us. "You don't have to. You could . . ." I bit my lip, not wanting to ask him, once again, to leave with me. I already knew he wouldn't.

Hope was in his eyes, though. "What if we come back?"

"Come back?" Was he saying we could leave? Together?

Michael cringed like he hated what he was about to say. "What if we fly into town, fill up the plane with supplies . . . then come right back?"

No . . . he wasn't asking to come with me. He was asking me not to leave him *yet*. The hope in my chest faded and flickered. "My family is searching for me. They're scared out of their minds, thinking I'm dead. I can't . . . let them remain terrified." Even just postponing it these last few weeks was selfish. But I hadn't been able to stomach saying goodbye to him, hadn't wanted to feel that pain . . . *this* pain.

"You could call them, tell them you're fine . . . then come back with me?" The pleading in his eyes was almost too much to bear. Was he finally, in a roundabout way, asking me to stay?

"Michael . . . I can't live this isolated life all the time. And you said so yourself: your heart isn't ready for me."

"But maybe it is," he said in a rush. "What if you stayed here, and I stopped . . . resisting. What if we tried . . . to be together?"

God, he was offering me paradise. I only had to give up *everything* to take it. "Michael, I can't."

"Please, just think about it. I don't want to lose you." His lips returned to mine, heavy and urgent. I wanted to think clearly, really toss around what he was saying, but his tongue brushing against mine made coherent thoughts impossible. All I felt was a rising, uncontrollable need, one I desperately wanted to satisfy.

I ran my hands through Michael's hair, pulling him closer to me—I wanted him as close as possible. Our kiss intensified as passion cascaded around us. I felt out of control and yet completely in control at the same time. It was a heady feeling, one that left me delirious with bliss.

My fingers trailed down his chest, darted under his many layered shirts, and wandered up his back. I felt so close to him, but I wanted to feel so much closer. Almost unconsciously, I started pulling on his shirts, wanting them off. Michael pulled away from me to look me in the eye. Here was where our make out sessions usually ended—when one of us crossed the intimacy line. I hoped he didn't pull away now, when so much between us was changing. I needed him.

Maybe sensing my need, maybe feeling it himself, Michael tore off his shirts, depositing them on the floor I could never seem to get clean. As I drank in his bare skin, his eyes drifted to my clothes. My chest felt hot as his pale eyes washed over my shirt. I was scared to move, scared I'd push him away, but I was scared not to move too.

Finally, when I couldn't take the ache of longing anymore, I reached down and started pulling off my top. Michael's hand stopped me, and I nearly groaned in frustration. His eyes were conflicted as he stared at me, and I had no idea which direction his head would send him—toward me or away.

After an eternity, he finally inhaled a deep breath . . . then started removing my shirt.

Realizing just where this might go had me breathing so hard I thought I might pass out. Ordering myself to calm down, I helped him with my shirt. After setting it down on top of his, I began unhooking my bra. I could see Michael's breath increasing as he stared at my chest. When I pulled the bra off, his eyes lingered a moment before lifting to my face. The reverence I saw there stole my breath.

Putting a hand on the center of my back, he pulled me toward him until our bare skin was touching. Our breath and the crackling of the stove were the only sounds, and with the way he was looking at me, cherishing me with his eyes, it was the most romantic experience of my life.

He laid me back on the mattress, then curled his body so he was again half hovering over me. As our kisses became languid, his fingers traveled over my skin, touching everything that had been hidden for so long. When his thumb brushed over my nipple, I couldn't stop a groan from leaving me. I worried he might stop, but he didn't. He made an enticing sound of his own and lowered his lips to my neck. Emboldened that he still hadn't fled, I didn't worry about the next groan. Or the next one.

His breath was fast in my ear as he nibbled on my lobe; then his mouth started traveling down my neck toward my chest. I didn't want to appear too eager, but I desperately wanted him to kiss me there, kiss me everywhere. When his tongue swirled around my nipple, I began to think that maybe I had died in that crash. Maybe *this* was heaven.

He sucked my breast into his mouth, and a long groan left me. Arching my back, I clutched at his hair, never wanting him to leave. But he did. Panting, he looked up at me with heated eyes that were screaming at me that he wanted more. *Yes, don't stop.* "I think . . . I think I could love you."

Pain pierced my heart. "I think I already do," I whispered.

Michael's eyes turned glossy in the flickering candlelight. He swallowed hard, then returned his lips to mine. I kissed him with abandon, pouring all of my emotions—pain and joy—into it. Michael kissed me back just as passionately. We were finally on the same page . . . being torn up by pain while simultaneously falling in love.

After a long moment, I pulled back from Michael to look him over. He was glorious, his body lean and trim from daily hard work, his mind sharp and focused, and his heart . . . his beautiful, broken, fluttering heart slowly on the mend. Because of me, because of *us*. If I left him, how long would it take his soul to shut down again? How long until the light faded from his eyes? How long before he crumbled? But staying here . . . how could I sacrifice my family for love? How could I live out the rest of my life being cut off from the world? Even if it was with the man of my dreams, I didn't think I could do it. *But, God, Michael . . . how can I leave you when you were made for me?*

Feeling lost, I cupped his cheek, then let my fingers trail down his chest to his pants. As I slowly began unbuttoning them, Michael's hand came down to stop me. "Mallory, I don't think . . ."

"I want to be close to you in every way," I said, tears in my eyes. "I don't want to leave here and regret not sharing this moment with you. Especially since it . . . might be all we ever have. Please, Michael, don't push me away. Not tonight. It's our last . . ."

Emotion closed my throat, making speech impossible. Michael brought his lips to mine, attacking me with renewed vigor. His fingers left my hands and sought my pants, unbuttoning them. A few tears escaped me when I realized he wasn't going to push me away. He was going to let me in . . . finally. It broke my heart that this was all we'd ever have . . . but still, I was going to take this moment and cherish it forever.

Once we were both bare, Michael pressed his naked body against mine, and I wrapped my arms and legs around him, pulling him in tight, where he belonged. He sighed in contentment, then leaned over to lower his lips to mine. As we shared soft kisses in the flickering candlelight, my fingers traced every line of his body, and his caressed every curve on mine. He was so strong, so virile, so . . . perfect. It wasn't long before I was aching with need for him. It brought me so much joy and relief to know he wanted me, too, and this time, he wasn't hiding from me, wasn't telling me no for my own benefit. We were going to cross this painful bridge together and figure out how to survive it later.

When I couldn't stand being separated from him a second longer, I urged him on top of me. Our mouths never leaving each other's, he pressed himself against me. I lifted my hips to meet him, silently telling him that I wanted this—wanted us. He pressed inside me, and I gasped. *Oh . . . God.*

Michael's head fell to the crook of my neck. "Mallory . . . ," he murmured, kissing the skin below my ear. "You mean . . . so much to me." I wanted to respond to him, but he rocked his hips against me, moving deeper, and I couldn't speak.

Euphoria flared throughout my body as we began to move together. Every movement was pain and bliss, regret and relief. What would we be after this? What would we be once I was gone? God, could I even leave him now? As our bodies rocked together, heightening the feelings between us, I wasn't sure. Michael's breath in my ear intensified as his slow and steady pace quickened.

"Oh God, Mallory . . . I need you so much . . . I wish you could stay."

I could feel the buildup approaching, stealing my reason, my sanity. "I need you too . . . I wish I could . . . I don't . . . want to lose you . . . but . . ."

The crest hit me, and I cried out as the bliss exploded throughout my body in radiating waves. Michael cried out a second later, and we held each other tight as the sensation amplified, then dwindled.

Michael slowed his pace, then stopped and remained still. Lying on top of me, his head close to my ear, he murmured, "I was wrong before . . . I *do* love you. And I'm going to miss you so damn much."

Chapter Twenty-Three

As I was packing my meager belongings the next morning, images of making love to Michael floated through my mind on an endless loop. We'd done it. We'd crossed that last intimate line . . . and now I was leaving.

I couldn't help but watch my rugged mountain man as I stuffed my bag. He'd allowed all his walls to come down last night, told me he loved me and how much he was going to miss me. I'd never felt anything quite so painful as hearing those words. They'd etched themselves across my heart, forever leaving a scar, and I felt no joy over the fact that I was on my way home. I was going home and leaving home, all at the same time.

Michael was sitting on my hard bed, watching me as I subtly watched him. There was conflict in his pale eyes, heartache on his sleeve. If he could have postponed this another day, another month, another year, I was sure he would have. *I* could postpone it if I called home, assured them I was alive and well, and then flew back to the cabin with Michael. I'd been gone so long, though . . . and I truly did miss my family, missed my dogs. I wanted to see everyone, hug them, take comfort in their presence after a long, hard winter. And honestly, postponing this a couple of weeks, a couple of months . . . it wouldn't change how hard leaving Michael was going to be. It might even make it harder to let him go. But I had to let him go . . . I couldn't live like he did. Not forever.

Grieved by the pain I saw on his face, I quietly asked, "Are you okay?"

His sad eyes locked with mine. "No. Not really. Are you okay?"

I sighed as I zipped up my bag. "No. Not really."

Michael stood, then looked down at the bed where we'd physically said goodbye to each other. Pain tore through my chest, and I grabbed his hand, needing to be near him, right up until the very end. He looked back at me while his thumb caressed mine. "We should go. We're wasting daylight."

I wanted to tell him that it was impossible to waste anything when I was around him, but I knew he was right—we couldn't fly at night, and Michael had to make a return trip today . . . without me. Nodding, I grabbed my bag and started for the door.

The air was warmer than I expected it to be when I stepped outside. A reminder that spring was here, and it was time for me to leave. Michael grabbed the stack of furs he was planning on selling—the lifeblood that would allow him to buy essential commodities—then we headed for the plane.

It took quite a few minutes to load and prep the plane, but it felt like mere seconds had passed before Michael was spinning the propeller, starting the engine. I wanted to cry when it burst to life, but I'd shed enough tears. Now was the time to be strong. I'd fall apart later, once Michael was . . . gone.

When the plane reached cruising altitude, I was surprised I wasn't scared. I had thought that remnants of my terrifying crash might have made flying difficult for me, but I felt completely at ease by Michael's side. Probably because I *was* by Michael's side, and he had a way of making me feel safe, even in the midst of terrible danger. That, and what was a plane crash compared to losing him? Nothing this mechanical beast did to me could make me hurt worse than I already was.

We arrived in Fairbanks much too soon, and as the plane finally stopped on the small runway just outside the city, I felt the beginnings of a panic attack clawing at my insides. *Not yet. I'm not ready.* Taking off his headset, Michael looked over at me. "Do you want to call your family now? Or maybe . . . help me buy supplies?"

Relief gushed into me, extinguishing the attack. Any second I could delay moving away from him was a second I would cherish. "I'll help . . . if you don't mind."

He smiled, his expression brightening for the first time this morning. "I'd love that." *I love you.*

His remembered words rang through the small space between us. My heart skipped a beat. *I love you too. And I don't want to go . . . but I have to.* Fighting back tears, I leaned forward to give him a heartfelt kiss. He returned it warmly, softly kissing me back. When we pulled apart, he swallowed. "There's still time. We don't have to do this right now."

I nodded, fighting back my own rising pain.

Once our emotions . . . settled, we hopped out of the plane and unloaded Michael's furs. Selling those was our top priority. Once we were loaded up, Michael found a small car rental place and arranged for a van to use for the day. Seeing him behind the wheel of anything other than a plane was . . . odd. He seemed so natural in the woods that I often forgot he'd had a life before his self-imposed isolation.

Once we got into town, Michael drove us to the fur trader. When I stepped out of the van, I was assaulted by noise—car engines, horns, whining power tools in the distance, yelling, boisterous laughter, radios blaring, dogs barking, and cats mewling. Combined with the unnatural lighting everywhere and the constant bustle of people ceaselessly moving, it was almost sensory overload after my months of quiet living. It made me long for the forest.

Michael noticed me cringing. "Takes getting used to again, doesn't it?"

Nodding, I told him, "Yeah." My voice was loud to me, like I was overcompensating for the noise. And what made it even worse . . . this wasn't even a big city. Not really. It was relatively small in the grand scheme of things, but it felt massive after how we'd been living.

We stepped inside the fur trader's shop, loaded up with our bundles, and a small bell above the door announced our arrival. A weathered old man looked up from behind the counter at hearing the familiar sound. "Well, I'll be . . . Michael Bradley. I was beginning to worry about you. You're typically here earlier than this."

Michael gave him a sheepish smile while I stared at him in surprise. He was known. And expected. For some reason, I imagined him not saying two words to people when he came into town. Hiding in plain sight. "Yeah . . . I had some plane trouble. Took longer than expected to fix."

The man nodded. "Yeah, Gary said that was probably it. Told me he couldn't get your part to you before the weather hit. Hope you stock up on parts earlier this year instead of putting it off to the last minute."

Michael laughed. "Well, that all depends on how much you give me for these."

As I watched, stupefied by the exchange, Michael laid out his furs for inspection. Once prices were negotiated and Michael had been paid, the old man pointed a stern finger at me. "So, Michael, are you going to introduce me to your lovely lady or not?"

Michael's cheeks under his neatly trimmed beard flushed with color. "She's not . . . we're not . . ." Scratching his head, he turned to me and said, "Oh, uh . . . this is Mallory. Mallory, this is Billy. Or Grumpy Old Man, whichever you prefer."

With a laugh, I extended a hand to Billy. "It's nice to meet you."

Billy grunted as he clasped my palm. "You don't listen to him . . . I'm not old. I'm just experienced." He smiled at me. "It's nice to see someone taking care of Michael. The missus and I worry about him out there in the woods all alone."

Michael cleared his throat, uncomfortable. "Yes, well, anyway . . . it's good to see you again, Billy. Tell Judith I said hello."

Billy waved. "Will do. You take care, Michael . . . Mallory." He winked at me after he said my name, and I gave him a broad smile as I waved goodbye.

Oh my God . . . people cared about Michael, and he cared in return. He wasn't completely shut off. He hadn't given up. There was still *hope*.

The next stop was the general store, where Michael stocked up on all the commodities he couldn't make for himself. Much like Billy, the clerk behind the counter knew Michael, had been expecting him. They chitchatted for several minutes while he rang up Michael's purchases, and I watched the exchange in awe.

I was seeing a completely different side of Michael. I was seeing society Michael . . . Dr. Michael. I'd only known the hurt and broken recluse. It was strange and exhilarating to see him how he must have been . . . before. And it made me realize that he *could* do this, could reintegrate into civilization. He was already doing it, if only on a smaller scale and for a shorter amount of time. Michael just didn't realize that he was doing it.

The last stop on our list was Gary's—the mechanic where Michael got parts for his plane. Gary looked to be around Michael's age, maybe a few years older, and had grease in every nook and cranny. Like everywhere else we'd been today, Gary was happy to see Michael and surprised he hadn't seen him sooner. "Michael, so good to see you up here. I was worried when you didn't show up a few days after your delivery. I thought maybe the part didn't work out for you."

Michael waved off his concern with a smile. "I was having . . . other problems."

He flashed a glance over at me, and Gary's smile widened. "Ah, I see. Name's Gary. Nice to meet you."

"Mallory," I said with a smile.

Gary shook his head as he looked back at Michael. "I don't know where you found a woman in the woods, but I'm happy for you, man."

"I didn't . . . she's not . . ." With a sigh, Michael stopped trying to explain what we were. Or weren't. "I need to stock up on spark plugs, belts, oil . . . the usual. Hopefully nothing else major will go out. Getting here without a plane was brutal."

My gaze snapped to him as my jaw dropped. "How did you get here without a . . . ? Wait, did you walk here? From the cabin?" I couldn't even imagine how long that had taken him.

Michael shrugged. "Like I said before, I don't have a phone. My plane wouldn't start, so I did what I had to do."

Gary cringed. "I'm sorry we had to order it in for you. I hate not having every part on hand, but you know how it goes."

With a friendly smile, Michael told him, "I'm just glad I was right about what part it needed. Making that trip twice . . . probably would have killed me."

He laughed after he said it, but I didn't laugh with him. His comment had too much truth to it. God . . . what if his plane broke again? And he had to make that hike again? What if he failed next time . . . ? He'd die alone in the woods . . . and I'd never know.

As we were leaving Gary's, my mood turned even more melancholy than this morning. Not only was I leaving him, but it suddenly felt like I was leaving him to die.

"What's wrong?" he asked, studying me as we loaded the van.

Pausing, I told him, "You walked . . . over a hundred miles, over mountain passes, through wilderness teeming with wildlife. You could have been . . ."

Michael smiled at me. "It was early fall and still relatively warm. It wasn't as bad as you're thinking it was."

"And the next time your plane won't start?" I asked, raising an eyebrow.

His lips curled into a frown. "Then I'll do it again. It's part of my life out here, and I've accepted that."

"I don't think I have," I whispered.

His voice was soft when he answered me. "I know. That's why you're going home."

A tremor of hope fluttered through me as I remembered the many people Michael had connected with here. If he could do it here, couldn't he do it anywhere? "Michael . . . you know . . . you know you're not as much of a recluse as you think you are, right?"

He tilted his head at me like he didn't understand. "I've never really thought of myself as a recluse, but what do you mean?"

I swung my arm out to indicate the town. "Here, these people . . . you like them, and they like you. You have community here."

Michael's face hardened, and he shook his head. "I know what you're thinking, but this is different. People here . . . they look out for each other."

"It's not just here," I said, clutching his arm. "Back home, people are just like this. Almost to the point of being busybodies, but still . . . they care. There are pockets of goodness everywhere; you just have to look for them."

A small smile cracked his hard facade. "Forever the optimist."

"One of us has to be." Relaxing my grip on his arm, I slowly said, "So what do you think . . . about coming home with me? If my home is like this, do you think you could . . ." *Stay with me?*

Michael let out a long sigh and grabbed my fingers, removing them from his arm. "Mallory . . . I've never led you on about this. I know you think I can do it . . . and maybe I can, but the point you're missing is that . . . I don't want to."

"Not even for me?" I whispered, my quiet voice shaking with emotion. "Not even for us?"

His eyes were anguished as he relentlessly stared at me; I felt like he could see all the way through my soul. "No. I'm sorry . . . I truly am, but my answer is still no."

My heart cracked wide open—again—pouring hope and faith all over the frozen sidewalk. I'd so thought he could . . . but no . . . he couldn't. Or he wouldn't, at any rate. "Oh . . . okay . . . well . . . I should . . . I should call home, see if my parents will buy me a ticket since I don't have much on me."

I felt dazed, broken. I never should have asked when I already knew the answer. I never should have hoped . . . because it was the hope that was killing me, not Michael. He'd told me from the beginning that he didn't want to leave his little cabin in the woods. I was a fool to think love would change his mind.

"Mallory," he said, stepping forward to engulf me in his arms. "I don't want to hurt you. I never wanted to hurt you. I'm sorry I fell for you . . . I'm sorry you fell for me." Pulling back, he studied me with watery eyes. "I'm sorry this is ending."

Feeling tears dropping to my cheeks, I shook my head. "Don't be sorry for loving me—don't be sorry that I love you. Love is the most precious commodity we have, and . . . even if it's temporary . . . it should be cherished."

A small smile curved his lips. "I *am* going to miss you."

Nodding, I sniffled. "I'm going to miss you too. So much."

His lips lowered to mine, and I forced myself to put the past and future aside—to completely stay in the moment with him. Because our moment was quickly running out.

After our tender kiss ended, Michael wiped my tears dry, then grabbed my hand. "There's a working pay phone on the corner," he told me. He began leading me there, and with every step, I found it harder and harder to not think about . . . anything. Staying present was difficult when a tidal wave of emotions was rapidly approaching.

Michael lifted the handset and handed it to me. He plopped in some quarters; then I entered the number to my mom's diner. It was the middle of the day, so if she was anywhere, it was there. I looped my finger around the cord as it rang. Nerves mixed with excitement—I couldn't wait to hear her voice again.

When the phone finally picked up, my heart was thundering in my chest. "Nana's Diner, this is Nana."

"Mom?" My voice cracked, and I could feel the tears building already.

"Mallory, oh my God, is that you? Is that really you? Are you okay? Where are you? You were gone for so long—we thought, oh my God, we thought . . ."

I could hear her begin to sob; my own tears were instantly flowing down my cheeks. "I'm fine, Mom. I'm fine, and I want to come home." Now I was sobbing, racked by pain. Pain for hurting my parents, pain from hearing my mom's voice again, pain for the sentence that had just left my lips. *I want to come home . . . and leave Michael behind.*

When we could both breathe again, I had Mom book a flight back home for me. "I'll call you at the airport so you can let me know the details."

"Okay, honey. I love you so much. I'm so glad you're coming home." Her voice broke again.

"I love you, too, Mom. I'll see you soon." Afraid that I would lose it again, I hung up as quickly as I could.

Michael rubbed my back. He was smiling softly when I looked up at him. "I don't want to say this, but . . . if I'm going to make it back to the cabin tonight, I need to leave soon."

My heart was instantly in my throat. Leave. Soon. Wiping away a tear I hadn't felt fall, he said, "I'll take you to the airport first."

My insides were screaming—*No! This is wrong!*—but I nodded and let him lead me back to the van. The airport we were going to was different than the small one we'd arrived at. It was the largest in town, for commercial flights. Michael and I were silent for some time; then I broke the quiet between us.

"Would you like me to . . . contact your father when I get home? Let him know you're okay?"

Michael instantly shook his head. "No."

"Michael, he would want to know that—"

Michael's eyes flashed to mine before returning to the road. "No, Mallory. He doesn't need to know anything about me."

"Why?" I quietly asked.

Michael sighed, and I thought for sure he wouldn't tell me. Then he softly said, "He gave up on her . . . Kelly."

Bunching my brows, I tried to understand what that meant. "I don't . . ."

Michael briefly closed his eyes. "He's a cop . . . in New York. A captain, actually. He's the one who closed Kelly's case when it turned cold. He shut the door on my wife and let her murderer get away free and clear. He might as well have helped the asshole do it."

"Michael, I'm sure he wanted to keep looking. It couldn't have been an easy decision for him."

Michael's hands on the wheel tightened. "Don't. Don't defend him. He gave up . . . and he told me I should give up too. 'Move on, son. That's what Kelly would want.' And maybe that is what she would have wanted . . . but I wanted justice. He should have kept trying."

Just like you should keep trying. You've given up . . . on society, on people . . . on life. Don't you see that?

I couldn't tell him that, not without starting a fight, so instead I told him, "Okay, Michael . . . okay."

His entire posture relaxed like a weight had been removed from him. "Thank you . . . for understanding," he told me. I didn't. Not entirely, but I hadn't been there. For me, it was just a story. For Michael, it was pain incarnate.

When we finally arrived at the airport, I felt the weight of change crushing me. This was it. Our last moment. Maintaining an even breath was a challenge, especially when I stepped outside and Michael handed me my bag. It felt heavier than I ever remembered it being.

As we stood there on the sidewalk, people coming and going around us, words escaped me. What could I say to fully encapsulate what he meant to me? He'd saved me, patched me up, cared for me, fallen for me . . . made love to me. There was no simple phrase to thank him for all that, no easy way to tell him I'd never get over him. He was forever a part of me now. Maybe one day I'd move forward, love someone else . . . but I'd never move on. I was stuck. Right here. With him. For eternity.

"Mallory . . . I . . ." Michael seemed lost too. The English language just didn't have enough words.

"I know," I told him. He smiled, glad I understood. Setting my bag down, I laced my arms around his neck and pulled him to me for one final kiss. It was soft and sweet . . . and hurt like hell. My insides were acid, burning every single part of me.

When we broke apart, I felt like I couldn't breathe. Would I ever be able to fully inhale again? Michael's eyes darted between mine like he was memorizing me. "I will . . . always love you," he whispered, his voice intense.

A wail stuck in my throat, but I choked it back. "Me . . . too." It was all I could spit out through the grief tearing me in two.

Michael grabbed my face, kissing me again. There was a voracity to this kiss that sent me reeling. Every movement, every exhale, every sound was a goodbye. Michael pulled away from me without warning. Eyes closed, he turned around and woodenly stormed over to the van like he was forcing every step. I wanted to reach out for him, beg him to stay, but I couldn't. He had to leave, and I had to let him. It was the ultimate mutual torture.

I watched in a panic as he started the van, backed up, and squealed away, making people nearby shout curse words at him. A part of my heart stretched away from my body as his van began disappearing from sight, and the second it was completely gone . . . it snapped. Broke. Shattered.

The tears were falling now, and nothing I did could hold them back. He was gone. We were done. Dropping my head into my hands, I let the grief pour through me uninhibited.

Goodbye, Michael. I love you. Always.

Chapter Twenty-Four

I cried almost the entire flight home. The man in the seat beside me must have thought I was mental. He kept scooting farther and farther away from me and never once asked me what was wrong. Maybe Michael had a point about society. Still, I needed to be a part of it just as much as he needed to be away from it. In the end, we just weren't as compatible as I'd thought.

When the plane finally touched down in Boise, my eyes were dry, but my soul felt drained . . . empty. I couldn't even feel happy to be home yet. I knew that would come, eventually, but I had a feeling it would take a few days. Or months.

I didn't know what to expect when I trudged down to baggage claim to get my bag. Mom had said she'd pick me up; Dad had probably agreed to go with her. What I saw when my foot stepped off the escalator stole my breath—it looked like half the town was here. Mom, Dad, my sister, all of my friends and extended family, most of my neighbors, and my ex-husband, Shawn. They'd all driven over ninety minutes to watch me get off a plane?

I felt the tears resurface as I took in the sea of friendly faces. *See, Michael, this is what you've forgotten about. Society isn't just hate, fear, intolerance, and indifference. There's love too. And loyalty and family, brotherhood, sisterhood, comradery . . . if only you had come with me, then you'd see for yourself.*

Wiping away the tears I didn't even think could form, I rushed over to my parents. They wrapped their arms around me, holding me tight. "Mallory, thank God . . . we were so scared."

Having felt that fear myself, I nodded as I pulled back to look at them. "I was too. There were so many times I thought I wouldn't make it . . ."

"How *did* you make it?" my father asked. "How did you survive for so long all alone?"

"I wasn't alone. A man . . . saved me."

A lump tightened my throat. My parents exchanged a look, but before they could ask me anything, I was assaulted by my sister. "Mallory! Don't you ever almost die on me again."

"I'll try not to, Patricia." I laughed, squeezing her tight.

The tiny woman in my arms pulled back to look at me with a stern expression. "No more trips into the wilderness. I've always said it's too dangerous, and this disaster only proves my point. You only get one life, Mallory."

Her dark-as-midnight eyes were pleading with me to believe her *and* listen to her. I didn't want to let one bad incident shape my entire future . . . but for now, I didn't have a choice. "My plane is gone, my camera is gone, and most of my equipment is gone. I'm not going anywhere for a long, long time."

Patricia shook her head of dark curls, then pulled me tight again. "Good. I'm glad to hear it." I wasn't. It meant I had absolutely no way of seeing Michael again for a long, long time, but I understood where my sister was coming from, so I didn't mention my heartache.

After my sister, I was welcomed and hugged by everyone who'd come out to see me. The outpouring of love was overwhelming, and I was exhausted long before I got to the last person . . . Shawn. My ex was almost the opposite of me, with sandy hair, pale eyes, and an almost constant smile on his face. He wasn't smiling now, though. He looked like he'd been torn apart piece by piece, then raggedly sewn back together.

"Jesus, Mallory . . . I thought you died." He pulled me into him, wrapping his arms around me so tight I could barely breathe. "I thought you died," he repeated.

Feeling erratic waves of desolation and grief radiating from him, I rubbed tiny circles into his back. "I'm fine, Shawn. I'm completely fine."

He ran a hand down my hair, holding my head against him. "Don't ever scare me like that again, Mallory. I can't . . . I can't lose you."

His voice warbled as he spoke, and I knew he was barely holding on. Shawn had always been emotional—some of our fights were legendary in town. He wore his heart on his sleeve, though, and I never had any doubts about how he felt. The nakedness was refreshing after dealing with Michael's walls. God, Michael . . . he was home by now, alone in his little cabin. Was he thinking of me? Probably. There wasn't much else to do there but think.

Burying that pain deep inside, I told Shawn, "I'm so sorry. If I could have let you know I was okay—let everyone know I was okay—I would have. There just wasn't a way."

Pulling back, Shawn's glossy eyes studied my face. "What the hell happened to you?"

A tired smile on my face, I told him, "Can I tell you in the car? I want to go home."

Shawn immediately nodded, then scooped me up like he was sure my fatigue had suddenly made me an invalid. "I can walk, Shawn," I told him.

Giving me a half smile, he said, "Just because you can doesn't mean you should." I'd heard that argument a time or two before. In our marriage, Shawn often thought I should just sit and relax while he did *everything*. It drove me crazy.

But just this once, I caved to his chivalrous nature . . . because I really was tired. In fact, I fell asleep on the way home. Or I'm assuming I did. When I woke up, I was in my own comfortable, spacious, pillow-top bed, surrounded by my three little pugs: Frodo, Pippin, and Samwise. Soft morning light was streaming through my windows, and the smell of bacon was thick in the air. God, it was good to be home.

Like they could sense I was awake, my dogs began licking every part of me they could reach, grunting and snorting like little excited pigs. Their curled tails were furiously beating back and forth, almost fast enough to create a current in the room. Wrapping my arms around all three of them, I pulled them in to me for a hug. "I missed you guys so much!"

Little barks met my ears, little tongues flicked my cheeks . . . all was right in the world. Sort of.

Feeling melancholy beginning to weigh down my heart, I pushed my pups away and climbed out of bed. That was when I noticed I was in my pajamas. When had that happened? Wow, I must have really been out of it. As I wondered just who had dressed me, I shuffled off to the kitchen; my dogs followed me, trailing so close to my feet they tripped me a few times. "Mom, did you . . . ?" My voice trailed off as I stared speechless at Shawn, standing in my kitchen making breakfast.

"Oh good, you're awake. How many eggs would you like?"

"Shawn? What are you doing here? And did you undress me?" I reflexively crossed my arms over my chest, even though it was too late. He'd already seen everything. Several times.

Shawn rolled his eyes at my question. "Was I supposed to put you to bed in those filthy clothes? And besides, you thanked me as I was doing it. Although you called me Michael . . ." He frowned, and my cheeks suddenly felt red hot. I didn't remember any of that. God . . . I'd called him Michael. Michael . . . he'd be well into his day by now. Sunlight was precious up north. Was he hunting? Gathering water? Splitting wood? Was he okay?

"Why are you still here?" I asked, changing the subject and redirecting my thoughts. "You could have gone home. I'm fine."

Shawn suddenly looked very sheepish. "Well, actually . . . I've been living here."

My jaw dropped at that news. Seeing my surprised expression, Shawn shrugged. "I knew you'd want someone to take care of your house and stuff." He pointed a spatula at Frodo, Pippin, and Samwise. "And them. I knew you'd want them to have constant companionship, not just your sister's daily drop-ins, so after it was clear something went wrong, I moved in . . . to take care of them. To take care of everything."

I was stunned that he'd done all that for me . . . basically put his own life on hold for me. "Oh, wow . . . thank you, Shawn. That means a lot to me." I'd hoped someone had taken care of my life while I'd been gone—taken care of my dogs, my home—and my heart surged with relief to hear that someone had. That Shawn had.

Setting down his spatula, Shawn walked over to me. Rubbing my arm, he said, "I'd do anything for you, Mal—you know that. But . . . if you want me to, I can move my stuff out this afternoon. Unless . . . do you want me to stay for a while? You must be pretty shaken up."

After everything he'd done for me, it seemed cruel to immediately kick him out, but I knew it would be misleading if I let him stay. "No, I'm fine. You can go home."

I started heading for the slider so I could let the dogs out, but Shawn stopped me. "Mallory . . . wait. I don't . . . I don't think we should . . . I mean, I think we should . . ."

"Shawn?" I said with a smile. "Are you going to start making sense soon?"

Shawn let out a nervous laugh, then ran a hand through his shaggy hair. After exhaling a deep breath, he said, "I love you, Mallory. I've always loved you, and thinking you were dead . . . well, that put things in perspective for me. I think we divorced too soon. I think we should get remarried." He nodded like his thoughts were suddenly completely clear; then he dropped down on one knee. "Will you marry me? Again?"

Staring at my ex-husband, on his knees, proposing . . . again . . . suddenly made me exhausted. "Shawn, come on . . . get up." Not letting him argue, I reached down and helped him to his feet.

Before I could tell him that I wasn't going down that path again, he held his hands up. "I know you've just gone through a huge ordeal, and I know it's going to take you time to adjust. I'm not trying to pressure you or rush anything, just . . . think about it, okay?"

With a soft, compassionate smile on my face, I shook my head. "I don't need to think about. I already know my answer." *It's the same as every other time you've asked me.*

He put his fingers against my lips, silencing me. "No . . . I don't want to hear it yet. I'm going to ask you again later, and you can tell me your answer then. Once you've had time to think about it."

Annoyance began to eat away at my gratitude—he did this to me *all* the time. "Shawn," I said, my voice firm even with his finger over my mouth.

He shook his head. "Nuh-uh. Tell me later. Now, how many eggs do you want?"

I could only gape at him. He was so bullheaded sometimes. And I knew from experience he wouldn't listen to a single thing I said right now. Even if I told him there was no way I'd ever marry him again, he'd ignore me and ask me again in a few days. Persistence was Shawn's specialty . . . it was how he'd gotten me to marry him the first time—a fact that continually bit me in the ass, since now he believed that as long as he didn't give up, I'd eventually say yes.

Throwing up my hands, I told him, "Fine. Three. Over—"

"Over easy, I know. I remember." His smile was huge as he got to work. Huge and hopeful.

After breakfast, I politely asked Shawn to move his stuff out. Shocking the hell out of me, he actually did. I think the only reason he did was because he was confident he'd be moving back in a few days when I said yes to his proposal. *I'm sorry, Shawn, but that's not ever going to happen.* My heart was utterly and completely tied to another man. A man I could never have.

I thought about Michael all day long. I couldn't help but wonder what he was doing, what he was thinking, and what he was feeling. Was he as torn open as me? Scoured from the inside out? Whenever I pictured his scruffy beard, ice-blue eyes . . . warm smile, I felt like sobbing. I cried so often and so quickly that I was genuinely concerned I wouldn't be able to stop. It was like I was mourning him. I supposed I was. He'd made his choice to stay; I'd made my choice to leave. I was mourning *us*. What we could have been and what we would never be now.

My parents and my sister came over at dinnertime, hands full of food from the diner. Good thing, since I was still in my pajamas and hadn't felt up to the task of making dinner. Kind of strange, since making dinner now would be so much easier than it had been all those months. Did I actually miss the hundred thousand steps it took to make a meal? Was it . . . too easy now?

"Hi," I said, throwing on a smile as I opened the door wide.

Mom didn't buy my fake cheeriness. Or maybe my outfit had tipped her off. "Are you okay?" She tilted her head as she examined me. Mom was letting her hair gray naturally, and there were long streaks of silver mixed with the brown; the way she put it up in a loose bun emphasized the coloring. She had a few extra pounds on her and rarely wore makeup anymore. She said it was to look the part—her restaurant being called Nana's Diner implied that she was older than she actually was—but I think she just liked not having to worry about her looks.

I nodded at her question, then shook my head, then nodded again. Finally, I shrugged. "I'm not sure what I am, Mom," I said with a sigh. "Glad to be home, but . . ." *Missing Michael with every breath.*

"But what?" Patricia asked. Her piercing eyes turned analyzing, like I was suddenly a patient, not a sibling.

"But hungry," I told her, not entirely lying. I hadn't had anything since Shawn's breakfast.

I ushered them into the house, then shut the door behind them. I'd been fielding phone calls all day from concerned friends and neighbors. I'd told everyone I was fine—when I was anything but—and it had zapped me of my strength; I collapsed onto the couch with a huff.

Mom looked at me, then gave Dad all the containers of food. "Why don't you go set the table, dear. I think we need a girl talk." Patricia nodded in agreement while I let out a groan.

"We don't have to do this," I told her. "I'll be fine. It's just . . . been a long winter."

"One you haven't told us much about," Mom countered. "You fell asleep five minutes into the ride home last night."

Dad gave me a warm smile; oddly enough, it reminded me of Michael. "Talk to your mom, Mallory. You know it will help. It always does." Dad also had speckles of gray in his dark hair. In made him seem older, too, and wiser.

He left the room, and Mom and Patricia sat down on either side of me. Patricia grabbed my hand. "I have to imagine that after the extreme survival experience you went through, you must be experiencing some sort of posttraumatic stress. I can help you through it, Mallory, but you have to talk to me."

I didn't want to be rude, since she was only trying to help, but I couldn't stop myself from rolling my eyes at her. "I'm not going through PTSD. I'm fine."

"You don't look fine, and you don't seem fine," she said. "You seem . . . sad. Are you sad you made it? Survivor's guilt?"

Compressing my lips, I firmly told her, "I can't have survivor's guilt when no one died, Patricia. That's not it at all."

Patricia opened her mouth to ask more questions, but Mom put a hand on her knee, silencing her. "Instead of trying to guess what you're going through . . . why don't you tell us? From the beginning, what happened to you?"

Looking between the two of them, I could feel my eyes watering. I didn't want to talk about it . . . which meant I probably should talk about it. I'd never truly heal until I verbally released my burden. "Everything was fine until I hit a storm. My plane stalled; I couldn't get it restarted. I thought I was dead . . . but somehow, I wasn't. But I was hurt. And scared."

I looked over to see that my dad had quietly reentered the room. His warm brown eyes were full of sympathy, and he nodded at me to continue. "I managed to make a shelter, but I didn't have a lot of supplies. I knew it was just a matter of time before . . ." I paused to swallow a rough lump in my throat. "And then . . . *he* appeared. He came out of nowhere and saved my life. He took me to his home, patched me up. He shared his food, his supplies . . . his life. He kept me alive." *And then he made me feel alive.*

Mom shared a look with Dad. "Who, honey? Who saved your life?"

A single tear dropped to my cheek as Michael's smile floated through my brain. "Michael. He lives all alone in the woods near where I crashed. He gave me everything he had; then, when he could, he brought me home."

My voice cracked, and my tears grew thicker. Mom looked confused. "Isn't that a good thing?" she asked, rubbing my back. "Why are you so . . . upset?"

"She's in love with him," Patricia whispered.

As I looked over at her, a sob escaped me. "And I'm never going to see him again. He wouldn't come home with me. He said he loved me . . . but he wouldn't leave."

I completely fell apart after admitting that to her. She pulled me into her arms. "I'm so sorry, Mallory," she whispered. "I'm so, so sorry."

"I love him so much. It hurts . . . so much."

"I know," she said, rocking me back and forth in a soothing pattern. "But it will fade with time. I promise. Once you're done grieving, the feelings will fade."

I knew she meant her words to give me hope, but they didn't. They only filled me with more despair. I didn't want my feelings to dim with time . . . and I didn't believe they would. Michael had touched me too deeply. If only I'd been able to touch him half as much, then maybe he would have picked me over solitude.

Chapter Twenty-Five

Days passed. Then weeks. I tried to get into my old routine, but I'd become so adapted to life in the woods that I'd forgotten what my "normal" routine was. I didn't need to get water, didn't need to chop wood, didn't need to do much to prepare my food. My days were so wide open they felt empty. And my nights . . . those were pure torture. Because my sister was wrong. My feelings weren't dwindling—they were growing. Every day apart from Michael was worse than the last, not better.

Since I didn't have enough money to buy another camera, and I couldn't do my job without one, I was working for my parents at the diner. I didn't mind being there; it was like a second home to me, but it wasn't where my heart was. Of course, that was true on several levels, so it didn't bother me as much as it should have.

I was just dressing for my shift when I heard my doorbell ring. All three dogs started barking. They were great at letting me know people were here . . . once I was already aware of that fact. "Shush! Quiet down, you three. Don't make me get Gandalf." That was what I affectionately called my disciplinary water bottle. The tactic didn't work as well on dogs as it did cats, but it had its moments.

As I stumbled toward the door, I shouted, "Coming! Hold on."

Breathless, I swung the door open . . . and saw Shawn standing there, holding a dozen roses. "Okay . . . it's been three weeks. You can answer me now."

Wishing I could rewind time and *not* open the door, I let out a weary sigh. "I really don't have time for this right now, Shawn. Mom wants me to make some pies, and baking isn't my strong point . . . as you know."

Shawn laughed as he stepped into the house. "Yeah, I remember. But an answer only takes a few seconds. Surely you have a few seconds to spare?" He paused to dramatically get down on one knee. "Mallory Reynolds . . . will you be my bride, for the second time?"

Inhaling a deep breath, I let it out slowly. "I'm sorry, Shawn, but my answer is no. I just want to be friends. Now can I please finish getting ready for work?"

Frowning, Shawn stood up. "You need more time. I understand."

Digging my nails into my palms, I calmly told him, "I really don't need any more time to think about it. I'm one hundred percent certain I don't want to be married to you. That's why I divorced you in the first place. We don't work as a couple." *Mainly because you never listen to me.*

Setting down the flowers, Shawn took a step forward. "Come on, Mallory—don't be hasty about this. Just think about it; think about us; think about . . . this." Before I could stop him, he bent down and attached his lips to mine. Even though Shawn and I had been very intimate before, it was odd to have him kiss me now . . . like I was kissing my brother or something.

I instantly shoved him back. "Damn it, Shawn. Now you're starting to annoy me. As I've told you several times before, I don't want to be with you like that. You and I are just friends, but if you keep pushing me, you're going to lose—"

Shawn finally looked upset as he cut me off. "Is this because of that Michael guy? The one who saved you?"

Shock made me suck in a quick breath. Hearing his name hurt. "How do you know about Michael?"

Shawn rolled his eyes. "Your mom. She let it slip to Suzy, Suzy told Judy, Judy told Beth, and Beth told my mom. You know how small towns work."

I blinked in surprise. "Yeah, I do . . . I'm sorry. I should have told you, but . . . I didn't want to hurt you."

He nodded like he understood. Then he said, "You're going through a breakup. I understand how much that sucks. I'll give you space, Mallory." Leaning in, he kissed my cheek. "You can keep the flowers."

He was gone before I could object, and I knew with absolute certainty he'd ask for my hand again. Once he felt I'd had enough time to get over my loss. Like I ever would . . .

Spring transitioned into summer so slowly it was almost like someone kept pressing the pause button on time. Michael was on my mind every day. Nothing I did seemed to shake him for long. His eyes haunted me during the day; his lips haunted me at night. I couldn't stand not knowing what he was doing. Was he getting enough to eat? Was he sleeping okay? Was he missing me every second too?

Being around my family eased my pain some. Mom was helping me master my baking skills—it was a painstaking process. Dad was giving me odd jobs around the house, helping me stay busy. Patricia stopped by the diner almost every day for lunch. She said it was to support the family business, but I knew she was also checking up on me . . . cataloging my mental state. Shawn proposed to me every single day. And no matter how many times I told him no, he was never deterred enough to stop.

Today he'd decided to do it in the middle of the diner. Down on both knees this time, he held his hands wide open. "Mallory Reynolds . . . I can't live without you. Please be my wife."

The patrons in the diner were both amused and touched by his romantic display. I was just annoyed. "Shawn, please . . . I'm serious. Stop asking me to marry you. My answer from here on out will always be no."

Shawn dropped his hands but stayed on his knees. Some of the customers frowned and shook their heads at me. Mom was watching me with a concerned expression on her face, and my sister, here for lunch, was alternating between watching the exchange and writing stuff down in her journal.

"Mallory, why are you killing me? You know you and I are destined to be together."

Reaching down, I pulled him to his feet. "Yes, Shawn, as friends. Although if you keep this up, I can't guarantee that we'll have that for much longer. And besides, don't you remember how we were together? We were a disaster."

He crossed his arms over his chest. Some customers went back to their lunches, but most were still watching the show. "We were young; maybe it would be different this time."

Turning him around, I started pushing him toward the door. "Or maybe it would be exactly the same. But regardless . . . my heart is somewhere else, Shawn."

Irritated, Shawn stopped letting me manhandle him. "With a man you'll never see again? A man you've put on a superhigh pedestal, leaving zero chance for anyone else? That's really not fair, Mallory."

Tears burned my eyes as I stared at him. "Do you think I want to be in love with someone I can't be with? Do you think this is fun for me, Shawn?"

His shoulders slumped, and his expression—for once—looked sympathetic. "No . . . I'm sorry, Mallory. If you really want me to stop asking . . . I will."

"Yes, please stop. I don't want to lose your friendship, but that's what you're killing each time you ask me something you already know the answer to."

Shawn stared at me for long seconds, then turned around and left the diner without another word. A soft sigh escaped me as I watched him leave. I could tell I'd hurt him, but honestly . . . how many times did I have to tell him no before he believed me?

Patricia came up behind me, putting a hand on my shoulder. "He'll be fine, Mallory. He knows it's over. He just doesn't want to accept it."

I nodded as I put my hand over hers. "Yeah, it figures, though—the guy I want to be with is completely unobtainable, and the one I'm not interested in won't leave me alone."

"I think he got the message this time," she said, giving me an encouraging smile.

I wanted to believe her, but I knew how tenacious Shawn could be. A fact that was proven to me when I got home and found another dozen roses on my doorstep with a note that said, "I'll give you more time."

"Shawn . . ." I groaned, opening my door. Maybe if I tattooed *No* on my forehead, he'd finally believe that I meant it.

My dogs attacked me with yips and kisses when I walked inside. I reached down to pet them, but it didn't boost my mood. I walked to my bedroom and flopped down on my bed. They hopped up with me, comforting me with their presence, since they could tell I was down. "Thanks, guys," I murmured, scratching Pippin's belly.

Somehow, I needed to find joy again. I was sure Michael would want me to be happy. It was so hard, though. I felt so . . . incomplete. I'd purchased a new camera last week, but it was still in the box, unopened and untouched. There was something about opening it that felt like I was letting Michael go, moving forward with my life. Ridiculous, but that was how I felt.

Shifting my gaze, I looked over to my nightstand. A cordless phone was resting there next to my lamp and alarm clock. If only I could talk to Michael. Call him, find out if he was okay. I desperately wanted to know if he was all right. Sitting up, I was struck with a sudden conversation I'd had with Michael.

"Would you like me to . . . contact your father when I get home? Let him know you're okay?"

"No."

"Michael, he would want to know—"

My pain of the unknown was so brief compared to Michael's father's. And yes, I understood why Michael didn't want to talk to him, but leaving him in the dark because he'd acted with his head, not his heart . . . well, it seemed cruel. And I knew deep down, past the hurt, Michael wasn't cruel. Just in pain.

Picking up the phone, I wondered how I could possibly find his father. New York City was huge. But I didn't have anything else to do . . . besides miss Michael. My mind made up, I headed to my computer and started finding phone numbers for every police station I could.

Early the next morning, I started making phone calls. Since I didn't have much information—just his rank and his last name—I felt like I was about to undertake an impossible mission. Clutching my cross, a necklace that painfully reminded me of Michael now, I prayed for luck.

Fate was with me, and on my third attempt, I was met with an unexpected response.

"I'm looking for a Captain Bradley?"

"This is he. How can I help you?"

My heart started pounding in my throat. "Mr. Bradley? Father of Michael Bradley?"

The line was silent for a moment. "Yes . . . Michael is my son." The pain in his voice was crystal clear. "Who is this? And what do you know of my son?"

Relief coursed through me in waves. "Hi. My name is Mallory Reynolds . . . your son saved my life."

"Ah . . . at the hospital? If you're looking to get it touch with him, I'm sorry . . . he left the city some time ago."

"No . . . this was last winter. My plane crashed, and he saved my life."

His voice brightened with hope and eagerness. "You've seen him? You've seen Michael? Is he . . . okay?"

A slow smile spread over my lips. "He's fine. He's living in the mountains, in Alaska. He's . . . alone . . . but he's fine."

A long exhale met my ear. "Thank God. I was so . . . he's been gone for so long, and nobody's heard from him. I was beginning to think the worst."

"I know—that's why I wanted to call you. To let you know he's fine."

"You said he's living alone in the woods?"

"Yes, it's very . . . remote. But he does occasionally go into Fairbanks. In fact . . . if you were to leave a message at one of these three places, I'm sure he'd get it." I then proceeded to give him the name of the fur trader, the mechanic's shop, and the general store. If Michael's father wanted to contact him, one of those three guys would surely pass along his message. And . . . my message . . .

"Thank you, Mallory. You have no idea how much this means to me."

I smiled into the phone. "I know how it feels to be worried . . . about a loved one."

"Does he know that you love him?" he asked, his voice soft.

My mind flashed back to our tearful goodbye. "Yeah, he knows."

"Don't give up on him, Mallory. He'll . . . he'll come back."

By the crack in his voice, I could tell that he'd repeated that line in his head millions of times. "It was nice to sort of meet you, Mr. Bradley. I hope we can meet in person one day."

"Please, call me Noah. I look forward to meeting you one day, Mallory."

We said our goodbyes after that, and I had to admit—I felt a hundred times better. Alleviating someone's grief had momentarily lifted mine. But realizing that there was something else I could do made me feel even better. Opening my nightstand, I reached inside and grabbed some paper and a pen. Using a thick book for a writing surface, I began pouring my heart out to the man I loved.

Dear Michael,

First things first . . . I miss you. And I love you . . .

Chapter Twenty-Six

Months. That was how long Michael and I had been separated. We'd been apart longer than we'd been together, but my heart still ached for him with the same intensity. I wrote him a letter almost every day now. I wasn't sure when he'd be going back to Fairbanks for supplies, and I didn't know if any of the shops I'd addressed letters to would pass them on to him. They could just be throwing them away, cursing my name for sending them so much junk mail. I refused to believe that, though. They cared about Michael; they would want to make sure he knew he was missed.

But even if Michael didn't get my letters, it didn't matter anymore. I was done sitting here, waiting around, missing him. It was time for my annual trip, and I was going to take it. I was going to see him again. I'd once thought marrying Shawn was the biggest mistake I'd ever made, but I was wrong. Leaving Michael . . . that was my biggest mistake, one I was going to fix. I'd come home and made peace with my family. Now I needed to make peace with my heart.

"Mallory, you can't do this. You don't have a plane."

I looked over my shoulder at my mother, father, and sister. All of them looked upset; Patricia looked scared. Throwing clothes into a bag, I told them, "I know you don't understand, but I *have* to do this. I have to go to him. And as for a plane . . . I'll hire a bush pilot to take me to him. I'll be fine."

Patricia put a hand on my shoulder and turned me around. Her eyes were wide and glossy. "That's what you said last year—*I'll be fine.* And your plane crashed. It *crashed*, Mallory. You shouldn't have survived, but you did . . . and now you want to tempt fate by going out there again?"

Shaking my head, I put my hands on her shoulders. "I'm not tempting fate . . . I'm answering fate's call. I was led to Michael. We're supposed to be together."

"In the middle of nowhere? You're really going to live like . . . like a caveman?"

A small laugh escaped me. "It's not quite that old school, but yes . . . to be with Michael, I'll live like a caveman. I have to . . . I can't live without him. Not fully." Dropping my hands, I looked between her and my parents. "I feel like a part of me is missing. And nothing I'm doing here has changed that. I'm surrounded by people, by love and family, but I still feel . . . alone. I *need* him."

Shawn stepped into the room, yet another bouquet of roses in his hand. "The door was open, so I . . . what are you doing?"

Patricia sniffed. "She's leaving. She's leaving us for that . . . mountain man."

I frowned at her comment. "I'm not leaving you . . . I'm going where I'm supposed to be. And I'll come back. Maybe I'll spend summers here, winters there . . . I don't know yet. I just know I'm supposed to be with him."

"But what about us?" Shawn whispered. "You and me?"

With a sigh, I looked around the room. "Could you give us a minute?"

Mom and Dad turned and left the room. Patricia firmed her lips in a hard line. "We're not done discussing this," she said before following our parents.

Another sigh escaped me as I twisted to face Shawn. He still looked shocked and sad. "I'm sorry, Shawn, but there is no us. I'm in love with Michael. I want to be with him . . . I'm *going* to be with him."

He shook his head. "He doesn't want you, Mallory. He *let* you leave. He chose deer and bears over you. Don't you see . . . you didn't mean that much to him."

Every word he said jabbed a knife right through me, especially since, during dark and insecure times, I'd had that same thought. But Shawn didn't know the whole story. Michael *did* want to be with me. It was everyone else he didn't want to be around. "It's . . . complicated, Shawn, but it's real . . . we love each other."

Setting down the flowers, Shawn took a step toward me. "We love each other too."

Shaking my head, I grabbed his hands. "We *loved* each other. Past tense. Now we care for each other, and that's great . . . but it's not enough. Sometimes I wish we'd worked out, Shawn. But *every* moment, I know Michael and I *will* work." Squeezing his hands, I told him, "You'll find your person, I promise, but . . . it's not me."

"Yes, it is . . . you're my Michael." Frowning, he shook his head. "You know what I mean."

A sad laugh escaped me, and I tossed my arms around him. "You just think it's me because you haven't experienced anyone else. Let yourself let go, Shawn. Let yourself love someone else."

Shaking his head, he pushed me away. "It's not that easy, Mallory. You're all I've wanted since the first grade." I reached out for him, but he held his hand up. "I can't . . . I can't do this right now."

Turning around, he practically fled from me. Guilt roiled in my stomach, but I pushed it back. I'd been as forthcoming with Shawn as I could be, telling him no time after time. He just hadn't wanted to listen, and unfortunately, now he didn't have a choice . . . I *was* leaving. Sometimes actions did speak louder than words.

Once Shawn was gone, my parents and my sister trudged back into my room and continued telling me what a horrible mistake I was making. It was hard to pack when I knew I didn't have their support. It was hard to leave that way, too, but . . . it was time. I couldn't stay here anymore. As much as I loved Cedar Creek, my heart was way up north, under the northern lights.

"Look, guys . . . I know you mean well, but I've made up my mind, and this is happening. My friend Ann is going to be renting my house while I'm gone. She's going to take care of the dogs and the bills, so you guys don't have to worry about anything this time." It hurt my heart to leave my pups behind, but they wouldn't fare well in the cold. It was in *their* best interest to stay here. Shaking off that small misery, I told my family, "I'll do my best to keep in contact, but during the winter months, I won't have a good way to communicate. You'll just have to trust that I'm okay."

Mom wiped beneath her eyes, then muttered to Dad, "We should get back to the diner." She started to leave, then stopped, turned around, and wrapped me in a hug. "I love you, Mallory. Please be careful."

Her voice was shaking so hard it made my eyes water. I wasn't trying to hurt them . . . I was just trying to live. Fully and completely. Dad hugged me next. "Chase your dreams. You're the only one who can."

Sniffling, I sputtered, "Thank you, Dad."

He released me, then shepherded Mom out the door. Once they were gone, I turned to my sister. "I don't want to leave with you mad at me."

She was furiously tapping her foot, her arms crossed over her chest. She looked about ready to explode. Then she sighed and threw her arms around me. "I'm not mad—I'm just redirecting my fear into anger so I can deal with you being gone and in danger and gone."

"You said *gone* twice," I said, holding her tight.

"I know. I'm struggling with that part the most." Pulling back, she cupped my cheeks. "I just got you back."

Grabbing her hands, I told her, "I'm not disappearing without a trace this time. I'm following my heart. This is a good thing."

She nodded. "Maybe in a few months I'll be able to accept that."

I gave her another quick hug, then sheepishly asked, "Can you give me a ride to the airport? And give me a hand with all my stuff?"

A dramatic sigh escaped her. "God . . . maybe I won't miss you after all." She paused to wink at me. "Of course."

She took a couple of bags, while I took one bag and my favorite item—a chainsaw for Michael. He needed one. Badly. My heart was in my throat as we headed outside to her car. As much as I wanted to see Michael again—couldn't wait to see him again—Shawn's comments were on my mind. I hadn't heard anything from Michael since we'd parted ways at the airport. He hadn't written me, hadn't called. I'd given him every possible way to get ahold of me in all my letters . . . but then again, if he hadn't gone into town, if he hadn't received my letters, well . . . then it was perfectly reasonable that I hadn't heard from him.

But still . . . what if he didn't miss me like I missed him? What if he didn't want me to show up unexpectedly? *If, if, if* . . . I was really sick of that word.

Patricia carried my bags to her car, then unceremoniously dropped them on the ground. "Hey," I told her. "My camera is in there." Still in a box, still unopened, but packed and ready for Michael.

She smirked at me as she unlocked her car. "Sorry, I guess I . . ."

Her voice trailed off as we both stopped to watch a bright-yellow taxi driving down my long gravel driveway. What the hell? I hadn't called for a taxi to the airport. Nor would I. That trip was pricey. Confused, I watched the car stop right in front of me. The rear door opened, and I sucked in a breath, positive I was dreaming. Michael . . . was here.

Everything I was holding fell to the ground with a heavy thud. He was here. I could only watch in stunned silence as Michael grabbed a duffel bag from the driver, then paid him a thick wad of cash. The cab began turning around to leave, and I was still gaping.

"Mal? Who is that?" I heard my sister ask. I couldn't respond. Michael's clear blue eyes were locked on mine. His dark-brown hair was longer, scragglier, and his beard was in desperate need of another trim. He hadn't been keeping up on his grooming with me gone. Of course, he lived alone, his only companion the occasional animal wandering through the forest, so why would he? What was he doing here?

He took a tentative step toward me, then stopped. "Mallory? You're probably wondering why I'm . . ." He glanced to my sister, swallowed, then returned his eyes to mine.

Taking him in . . . the lean, chiseled body; the rough, rugged exterior; the carefully hidden scars, both outer and inner . . . our time together hit me like a tidal wave, nearly knocking me over. All the fear, all the comfort, all the confusion, heartache, and disappointment. All the love.

Shaking my head in disbelief, I flung myself into his arms, wrapped myself around his body, and quickly found his mouth. My lips worked furiously over his like I was drowning and he was air. He kissed me back just as desperately, clearly conveying his loneliness without a single word.

In the background, I vaguely heard my sister say, "I'm assuming this is Michael?" When we didn't pause to acknowledge her, she chuckled, then said, "I'll just let you two get . . . reacquainted. It was nice to kind of meet you, Michael." I felt him raise a hand in greeting, but his lips never left mine.

My heart was swelling with love and happiness as I heard my sister's car pull away. He was here. He chose me. Was he staying? *God, please let him stay . . .*

Finally, knowing we'd need to talk at some point, I pulled back to search his face. "You're here? Why are you . . . ? How are you . . . ?" I shook my head. "I can't believe you're here."

"I . . ." His eyes drifted from my face to the bags littering the ground. "Are you leaving?" When his eyes returned to mine, they were laced with concern.

My smile was uncontainable. "I was going to you. I was done being without you, so I was going to hire a plane and show up at your door."

Michael's face broke into my favorite grin. "I guess I beat you to it."

Biting my lip, I hesitantly asked him what this meant for me, for us. "Does that mean . . . ? Are you . . . staying . . . with me?"

His eyes lowered; then he peeked up at me through his lashes. "If you'll have me . . . yes, I'd like to stay with you."

I was floored, stunned, shocked with happiness. "I thought . . . what about living among people again? I thought you were done with that?"

He sighed, then tucked a strand of hair behind my ear. "I thought I was, too, until I tried living without you. I think I'd rather live in the center of a bustling city than spend one more day without you in my life." He cupped my cheek as his voice intensified. "I can't spend another day apart from you, Mallory. I love you."

My eyes watered, and my chest swelled. "I love you too."

Michael's eyes were a swirling mixture of emotion—joy, fatigue, relief. He seemed like a man who'd finally had a tremendous weight lifted from his shoulders, and he almost didn't know how to handle the lightness. "Let's get all this stuff inside . . . since neither one of us is going anywhere."

I was giddy as I began grabbing bags. Michael helped me, then stopped when he reached down for a case that was suspiciously shaped like a chainsaw. "What is this?" he asked, looking up at me.

"A gift . . . for you," I demurely said.

His eyes returned to the tool. "You were bringing me a chainsaw?" he asked, his voice still sounding stupefied.

"Yes . . . I wasn't spending another winter out there without one. In fact, I was trying to figure out how to get a snowmobile to your place, too, because you spend entirely too much time walking back and forth to your traps."

Michael's eyes were filled to the brim with love and affection when he looked over at me. "What did I do to deserve you?" he asked.

"I asked myself that a lot after you found me." I touched my fingers to my necklace, saying a quick thank-you to the heavens for returning him to me.

Michael tracked the movement, then smiled . . . and nodded, like he completely understood my gesture and *agreed.* It made my heart thump even faster, and I practically scurried to get our things inside my house.

Once we were in my living room, and Michael had been briefly introduced to my three barking beasts, I tossed my arms around his neck and kissed him. I never wanted to stop now, and from the way Michael kissed me back, I could tell he felt the same. Pulling on his neck, I led him to my bedroom, then closed the door behind us. My dogs instantly complained. They could complain all they wanted, though—I wanted to be alone with my man, a man I never thought I'd have in my home, a man I'd been about to give up *everything* for. Because what was it without him?

Without another word, Michael and I began undressing each other. Once we were bare, we fell onto my bed. Michael kissed every inch of me, cherishing me. He stopped at the scar on my leg, the lingering reminder of the crash that had brought us together. Leaning down, he placed a reverent kiss there, then placed his cheek upon it and closed his eyes. He almost looked like he was saying a quick prayer, and a smile erupted over me.

"I love you," I said, running a hand down his exposed cheek.

Opening his eyes, he looked up at me. "I love you too. So much. And I'm so grateful . . . to be able to feel that way again. I didn't realize how empty I was until you . . . crashed into me." Lifting his body, he settled over me, then lowered his lips to mine. "I don't ever want to feel that empty again."

He slid into me then, and I closed my eyes as the euphoria of the moment filled me. Clasping our hands tight, we began to slowly move together, intensifying everything we felt for each other. Love washed over me in waves, escalating with each pass, and as I was filled to the brim with emotion, I began to wonder if I'd been empty too. All my life I'd been searching for truth, for meaning, for a deeper connection to the world around me. And I'd found it in the middle of nowhere, with a man who hadn't wanted any sort of connection to anything. He'd completed me, and I'd opened him.

The buildup grew to something intense and profound, and an explosion of life and beauty coursed through me, vibrating every nerve ending. I'd never felt so alive, so connected, so much a part of something vastly bigger than this mortal coil I was bound to. I squeezed Michael tight as the ecstasy flooded me. He reached his apex, holding me just as tightly, and together we transcended time and space . . . a brief moment of endless, perfect bliss.

We clutched each other for long moments before we separated, and joyful tears were in my eyes when we did. Michael brushed them away with his thumb, then kissed my eyelids. His beard tickled my face, and I giggled as I tugged on it. "We're going to have to cut this soon."

Michael laughed and ran a hand through it. "Yeah, I figured I'd just shave it off, since I don't need it here."

A lump suddenly appeared in my throat. "Does that mean you're not going back?" *You're not going to run away on me?*

Smiling softly, Michael ran his fingers along my cheek. "I might go up there to hunt on occasion, but only if you come with me. I don't want to be somewhere you're not."

Grinning, I leaned up to kiss him. "Good. I was kind of hoping you'd keep the cabin as a getaway. I'd love to pick up photography again, and it's the perfect spot for my annual trip. Or maybe it could be a semiannual trip now."

Michael's face was serene as he looked at me. "However often you like, Mallory."

He pulled me over so my head was lying on his chest, and I reveled in the steady thump of his heart under my ear. "For a long time when I got back . . . I never thought I'd get to feel this again. Feel you again."

Propping myself up on my elbows, I looked up at his face. "So are you really going to be okay living here most of the year? Are you really ready to give humanity another chance?"

His lips pursed in thought. "I might have been . . . too unforgiving." He briefly closed his eyes, and when he reopened them, they were filled with regret. "Do you remember the story I told you? About the way my wife died?"

Confused, I bunched my brows. "Yes."

"Well, I realized . . . when I let you walk away, I was doing the same thing as all those people who'd refused to help my wife . . . refused to get involved. I'd walked away, leaving a woman to bleed out alone. Only in this case, I was the one who'd made the lethal cut too." He sighed, then shook his head. "I hurt you, then refused to change out of pride, stubbornness . . . fear. I've decided to give the world another chance . . . for you."

I was touched by his willingness to change, but a little scared too. "It won't be perfect. And if you expect it to be, you'll be let down. Because people are just what you said they were—crazy."

He gave me a carefree smile. "I know, but I have faith it will turn out okay in the end."

I blinked in surprise. "Really? *You* have faith?"

Michael laughed, then nodded. "You crash-landed in my backyard. And survived. And cared for me, a loner in the woods. You pulled me back to civilization . . . restored my *hope* in humanity. What else could I have but faith?"

His finger traced my necklace, a peaceful smile on his lips. I leaned over to kiss him, happy that he finally felt that peace—that he was finally healing from the senseless tragedy that had ripped his life apart.

Our tender kiss lingered for long seconds; then a thought popped into my mind. Pulling back, I asked, "Did you get any of my letters?"

Biting his lip, he nodded. "On my way out of town."

I tilted my head. "On your way . . . *out* . . . of town?"

His grin grew. "Yeah, I was already on my way to you. I was already done missing you. I read them all on the plane, Mallory, and every word . . . meant so much to me. It helped me . . . get through the chaos of so many people suddenly around me. Thank you for that."

"You're welcome. It took me far too long to think of that way to contact you." Thinking of something else, I sheepishly asked, "Did you . . . get anything else?"

He raised an eyebrow. "You mean a letter from my dad? Yeah, several of them. And a package containing a lot of cash, along with a note telling me that I'd regret it for the rest of my life if I let you get away. I guess you made quite an impression on him."

I couldn't help but cringe. "I'm sorry. I know you didn't want me to contact him, but I had to let him know you were okay. I knew how hard it was . . . to not know."

He stroked my cheek, alleviating my guilt. "It's all right, Mallory. I'm glad you called him. And his letters . . . they touched me too. In fact, second thing tomorrow, I think I'll give him a call. Let him know . . . I'm home."

My cheeks flushed at hearing him call Cedar Creek home, but something he'd said was tugging at my curiosity. "The *second* thing you're going to do tomorrow? What's the first thing?"

Pulling me all the way on top of him, he crooked a smile. "For the first thing . . . I'd really like to do that again with you."

Giggling, I kissed him. "I think that can be arranged." All day, every day . . . wherever Michael was, that was where I wanted to be too.

We were meant to be, destiny. My prayers had been answered: I'd not only survived a seemingly hopeless situation, but I'd saved someone else from his own hopeless situation. I'd met my soul mate—then I'd been allowed to keep him. In this crazy, messed-up, beautiful world, Michael and I were being given our happily ever after, and we would never take that miracle for granted.

ACKNOWLEDGMENTS

First off, I want to thank everyone who took a chance and picked up this book. I am so in love with this story! My heart bleeds for these characters, and I'm sure yours will too. Thank you so much for being a part of their journey.

A huge thank-you to my superagent, Kristyn Keene of ICM Partners, who has always been so patient, supportive, and encouraging. I would be lost in this publishing world without you! Hugs all around to everyone at Montlake Romance / Amazon Publishing. Touring your offices and getting to meet all of you in person was so much fun! And a special thank-you to Lauren Plude and Lindsey Faber for all your help and support on this book. It has been a pleasure working with you, and I can't wait to collaborate again!

To all the blogs, readers, and authors who have supported me over the years—from the bottom of my heart, thank you so much! Your continued love and support blow me away. Special thank-yous to T. Gephart, Monica James, Sunniva Dee, K. A. Linde, Nicky Charles, R. K. Lilley, J. Sterling, Rebecca Donovan, A. M. Madden, Katie Ashley, Michelle Mankin, Lori, Becky, Julie, Madison, Lysa, Hang, Aim, Charleen, Nicky, Emilie, KP, Amy, Tina, Nicole, Jenny, Diksha, Kristina, Ellie, Karen, Mindy, and *so* many more that I don't have room to mention you! Thank you for the help—thank you for the love!

And lastly, to my family, thank you so much for loving me unconditionally—quirks and all. I know I am forever loved, and that is the best feeling in the world.

ABOUT THE AUTHOR

Photo © Tarra Ellis Photography

S.C. Stephens is a bestselling author who enjoys spending every free moment creating stories that are packed with emotion and heavy on romance. Her debut novel, *Thoughtless*, an angst-filled love story featuring insurmountable passion and the unforgettable Kellan Kyle, took the world of romance by storm in 2009. Stephens has been writing nonstop ever since.

In addition to writing, Stephens enjoys spending lazy afternoons in the sun reading fabulous novels, loading up her iPod with writer's block–reducing music, heading out to the movies, and spending quality time with her friends and family. She currently resides in the beautiful Pacific Northwest with her two equally beautiful children.